S0-CFG-236

FIRE DJINN

Published in 2007 by **JERBOA BOOKS**
PO BOX 333838 Dubai UAE
www.jerboabooks.com
ISBN 978-9948-435-11-2

Approved by the National Information Council UAE:
No 5053 12 October 2008

Text © LINDA DAVIES
Cover Design: WILL HILL

All rights reserved. No part of this publication may be reproduced, stored
in or introduced into a retrieval system, or transmitted, in any form, or by
any means (electronic, mechanical, photocopying, recording or otherwise)
without the prior written permission of the copyright owners. Any person
who does any unauthorised act in relation to this publication may be liable
to criminal prosecution and civil claims for damages.

This book is for

Tommy, my Firecracker,

radiant and brilliant as fire,

with all my love,

beyond the universes,

forever.

Novels in the Djinn Quartet by Linda Davies:

SEA DJINN

Look out for Storm Djinn, coming in 2009

Adult novels by Linds Davies

NEST OF VIPERS

WILDERNESS OF MIRRORS

INTO THE FIRE

SOMETHING WILD

FINAL SETTLEMENT

These books are for adults,
and your parents might enjoy them!

You can read more about Linda Davies on her website:

www.ex.ac.uk/~RDavies/arian/linda.html
or simply type in Lindadavies.com

Praise for Sea Djinn by Linda Davies

Media Comments

'Dubai's Harry Potter' Emirates Today

'A joyful fantasy.. steeped in the heritage of the region. Wonderful.' Time Out Dubai

Time out Dubai chose Sea Djinn as the only children's book in its Books of the Year 2007

'A fine piece of prose.' Friday Magazine

'A fast-paced, beautifully descriptive adventure with just the right mixture of compelling characters, well-obserevd humour and page-turning excitement. The Arabian flavour is perfectly balanced so that the book will appeal to children in Dubai, Arabia and far beyond.'

'The author has an amazing feel for words and puts it to effective use.' Khaleej Times

Reader comments

'This exciting and innovative story opens the door to a new world. I loved it and look forward to reading Fire Djinn.' Pauline, 14, English College

'Sea Djinn is the best book ever! The characters are hysterical and it was fun reading about the same sea that we swim in. Can't wait for Fire Djinn.' Jay, 8, Dubai American Academy

'This book is extremely creative and uses a lot of description so you can actually picture the setting in your head as well as what is happening. It made me want to read more and more of it because of the action. I can't wait for Fire Djinn!' Jack, 11, Repton

'I think Sea Dijnn is a fantastic book with lots of action and adventure. My Mum and I read this together and we couldn't put it down! I loved the way it was set in Dubai and even knew the road Finn lived on so I sort of felt part of the whole story!' Simon, 11, JESS Arabian Ranches

'I was hooked from the first few pages.' Dale, 11, Jumeirah Primary School

'A book that unleashes the dangers of the undiscovered world' Muhammad, 15, English College

'Sea Djinn makes you feel as though you are on a long, exciting journey,' Sophie 9, Jumeirah Primary School

'It is a very exciting book. I think it as good as Harry Potter - very nearly better. We couldn't wait to get to the next chapter because it's so good and Linda stops at really exciting places.' James, 8, Fulham Prep, London

'My son and I both loved Sea Djinn. It became a part of our lives when we read it together. We can't wait for Fire Djinn.' Clare Slater, forty something, London

FIRE DJINN

by

LINDA DAVIES

Fear one thing in all that is....

Fear the Djinn.

The Wishmaster. 1993

CHAPTER ONE

∽ The Vision ∽

FINN, GEORGIE AND FRED sat by the camp-fire, staring into the flickering golden flames. Around them, the deserts of Dubai stretched out for hundreds of miles, a kingdom of sand, apparently empty. The sickle moon cut a crescent into a night as dark as sin. Cold stars burned in the heavens, gazing down upon the earth like a million watchful eyes. The wind that had screamed through the dunes earlier, whipping sand into their faces had died. Save for the whisperings and cracklings of the fire, the night was eerily quiet. The silence of the listener not the sleeper.

Fred's parents were camping in the next *Wadi*, so the children felt quite alone, which is just how they wanted it.

Finn stared intently into the flames. It was funny how the flickering fingers seemed to form images; a hand, which then became a nose, lips and eyes. The burning branches framed the outline of the face. Finn stared into those eyes. It almost seemed as if they were staring right back at him. Finn froze suddenly.

'What?' asked Georgie, instantly alert.

'Thought I heard something. A voice,' answered Finn.

'Hallucinating,' pronounced Fred, reclining in the sand, polishing off his fourth brownie. ' 'S what happens in the desert,' he added sleepily.

Finn stared into the fire, unconvinced. The silence and the darkness seemed to deepen around him. His head suddenly felt as if it were vibrating. Threat. Threat all around. Finn's fighter's senses were screaming. Something was there. Veiled by darkness. Finn leapt to his feet, reached towards the fire to grab a burning branch as a weapon, but before he or Fred or Georgie could raise an arm to fight, they were hurled backwards. They were unconscious before they even hit the sand.

The words came first, cutting through the night, sliding into their heads:

'Help me. Free me. DarkFighters have me. Imprisoned…end …. earth…people…dead….LightFighters …. Free me. Stop them…..'

Then the images: a palace, glittering with lights….a hole in the ground….. the palace blowing apart….a hurricane of flames erupting from the earth….the heat on their faces, the scorching shamal of the desert in August, only a million, billion times worse…. heat, awful liquifying heat…. bones melting, blood vapourising….. the inferno roaring on…. over sand, over sea, over mountains… nothing and no-one left, just ashes and smoke as the planet burned.

Chapter Two

∽ Contagion ∽

FINN WOKE SCREAMING, EYES careening; camp fire, not inferno. Tent intact, glowing in the firelight. Normal. So far. Bodies on the sand.

He leapt to his feet and ran to them.

Fred and Georgie lay motionless on the sand, legs and arms askew as if they had been flung by an overwhelming force.

'George! Fred! Wake up, please.' He shook Georgie's shoulder, pulled at Fred's arm. Nothing. Heart pounding with fear, he lowered his ear to Georgie's chest and listened. A heartbeat. Thank God. Fred had one too, but they both lay immobile, trapped in unconsciousness.

He ran for his backpack, pulled out his mobile, began to dial Fred's parents. The phone refused to work. Refused to even turn on, though Finn had left it on. It was dead, and no amount of pushing buttons and thumping it against his thigh would bring it back to life.

He took out the walkie-talkie and tried that. Dead too. A great scream rent the air. He wheeled round, dropping the walkie-talkie.

Georgie was sitting up, screaming. Finn rushed over.

'It's all right, George. It's all right.' He grabbed his

cousin, then recoiled in horror. Her eyes had rolled back in her head. All that showed was the whites.

Then, to her side, Fred woke with a blood-curdling scream. His eyes too had rolled back in his head.

There was hysteria in the night. Madness too. Finn could feel its fingers creeping over him like a contagion.

CHAPTER THREE

ᴏ The Presence ᴏ

FINN FOUGHT TO CALM himself. Ruthlessly, he stilled his breathing. He stood silent and motionless in the desert, probing the night with his eyes, with all his senses. He could feel a presence, a presence of great power. It was all around. It was in their heads. It was roiling behind Georgie and Fred's sightless eyes. He would have to get it out.

He screwed shut his eyes and called upon his powers; all the powers acknowledged, and all those not yet known. He felt them build from his feet, slowly at first, then in a great rush that surged through his body like electricity. When he felt he would explode, he stretched out his hands towards Fred and Georgie.

'Go!' he yelled. 'Leave them.' He imagined the power shooting out from his hands like a magnetic force, repulsing the other thing that had entered so violently. He saw it in his mind. He used his mind to move it back. Inch by inch. Foot by foot. He felt it. He pushed it. His brain was hammering. The sweat coursed down his face, but still he pushed. Suddenly he fell forward onto the sand as the resistance ebbed and died and the presence yielded.

Fred fell silent. Georgie fell silent. Then in turn their

eyes rolled back into their proper position. Four eyes flickering with horror and terror stared at Finn.

'Did you see?' asked Finn, voice faltering. 'Fire? Burning?'

They nodded. Both of them.

'Words too,' croaked Georgie, in an appalled whisper. 'Then the fire. Thought I was dead. Thought everyone was dead.'

'Felt it too,' rasped Fred. 'The heat. The wind. Like it was real.'

'What the heck was it?' asked Georgie, rubbing her eyes in disbelief. 'A simultaneous nightmare?'

Finn shook his head.

'A vision,' he said. 'Someone's playing with us. Someone incredibly powerful, so powerful that he knocked us all out, just with his thoughts.'

'Is he still out there?' asked Georgie.

Finn nodded, 'I reckon so.' He could still feel it, hovering in the darkness.

'My parents,' gasped Fred. 'Maybe they got hit too.'

'They might still be out cold,' said Finn, or worse, he thought. Fred and Georgie had appeared quite dead to him.

'Let's go and check on them. Now,' urged Fred.

They headed for the quad bikes, mounted them and fired up.

'It's just round that dune, over there, isn't it?' asked Fred, pointing.

Finn stared at the dune. It looked different somehow. But then they had left Fred's parents in daylight and things often looked quite different at night.

'Er, yeah, yeah. I guess so,' said Finn, unnerved by the failure of his normally rock-solid sense of direction. Seeking reassurance, he reached for the hand-held GPS inside his backpack. With a feeling of dread, he tried to turn it on. Dead, like his mobile, like the walkie-talkie. The presence, whatever it was, had wiped out their electronics.

He dropped the useless GPS into his backpack. They wouldn't need it, he told himself. Fred's parents were less than half a mile away, just round that dune. It'd be easy to find them, wouldn't it?

Chapter Four

∞ The Palace ∞

FRED ROARED OFF LIKE a boy possessed, rending the silence of the night. Quad bike bucking and bouncing, he accelerated through the shallow valley of sand where they had pitched their tent towards the distant dune. Finn swore under his breath and followed, praying that Fred wouldn't roll the quad.

Fred quickly reached the large dune. The powerful beams of his headlamps banked up its steep walls. Fred slowed and aimed his bike at the dune wall. Up it roared, engines revving wildly. Finn and Georgie eased their machines up more slowly. At the top of the dune, Fred's bike flew through the air for a few moments before bumping back down onto the sand and racing down the other side.

At the bottom of the dune, he stopped. There was no sign of his parents or their tent. Panic welling in his chest, he turned off his quad and waited for Finn and Georgie.

They pulled up beside him and cut their engines.

'That was the right dune, wasn't it?' queried Fred. 'I mean if it is, then they should be here, my parents. They have to be here.'

'I'm not sure it is the right dune Fred,' replied Finn. 'It should have been. I mean, I reckoned it was in the right direction, but I thought before we set off that the dune looked different. This dune is sharper than the other one, almost like a pyramid.'

'GPS,' said Fred. 'Let's go back and get it. Their position's marked.'

'Um, no it's not,' said Finn, and he told them about the dead GPS and the dead mobile and the dead walkie talkie.

Fred and Georgie tried their phones. Both dead.

'What's going on?' asked Georgie in a hushed voice.

'It felt like a person, or something living that sent the signal,' said Finn, face grim.

'God. I really want to get out of here,' urged Georgie. 'Find your parents Fred and put as much distance between all of us and that thing as possible. I think that dune looks more like it,' she said, pointing to one to the north east. 'Don't you think?'

'I think we should go back,' said Finn. 'Retrace our steps. Set out from our base.'

'No, Georgie's right,' countered Fred. ''I'm sure that's the right one. I have a feeling.'

'Fred, mate, we really don't want to get lost,' cautioned Finn, as mildly as he could manage.

'They're my parents. I have to make sure they're all right,' shouted Fred. He paused for a moment to glare at Finn. 'I'm sure that's the right dune,' he added in a tone of conciliation. 'Let's go to it from here. It'll be quicker,' he added determinedly.

Finn had heard all the stories of how easy it was to get lost in the desert, how under the blistering sun and endless dunes death was only a slow blink away.

Against all his best instincts, Finn followed Fred.

Fred accelerated so fast he felt the air roar past his ears. He aimed his quad along the valley between two dunes before veering right up onto the dune he felt sure shielded his parents and their tent from view. It was enormous, steep too. The quad climbed laboriously, engine screaming with effort. The image flashed through Fred's mind of tipping the quad and having it tumble over him. He banished it quickly. Concentrate, he chided himself, and you will all be fine.

As the quad passed the half way point, Fred felt sure he was going in the right direction. He felt a strange sensation pulling at him, guiding him almost, but it came and went.

He stopped atop the dune which was truly towering. Finn and Georgie, both mightily relieved at having reached the top of the dune without rolling, stopped beside him. They gazed down onto a plain below. No tent. No parents. Instead, perhaps a mile away, surrounded by nothing but sand, stood a palace all lit up.

They gasped, speechless.

Finally, Finn found his voice. 'The palace. From the vision.'

'And the hole in the ground where the fire erupts,' whispered Georgie, pointing at a gaping maw in the earth.

CHAPTER FIVE

Pledge of the LightFighters

'WHY DID WE FIND this place?' Georgie asked, horrified. 'And why did we see the vision?'

'Someone put it into our heads. Deliberately,' answered Finn, 'as a warning. As a plea for help.'

'Maybe not our heads,' suggested Georgie. 'Perhaps we just tuned into something that we weren't supposed to.'

Finn shook his head. 'The Voice, before the vision, he called out to LightFighters, remember?'

In the mania of the vision and the pain of its aftermath, Georgie had forgotten. Fred too.

Finn reached for the sea glass pendant hanging at his neck. He, Fred and Georgie each had one, their gifts from Triton in recognition of the battle they had fought against Hydrus, and, against all the odds, won. The gift that hailed them as LightFighters.

'So what do we do?' asked Georgie. 'Whoever sent us this vision, he's dangerous. He hurt us. Left us unconscious. Fried all our electrical equipment, fried our brains making us lose our way so we'd come here and see the palace.'

'I know,' said Finn, 'but I don't think he meant to hurt us. I got the feeling of immense power, but not evil.'

'What d'you mean, got the feeling?' asked Georgie.

Finn hesitated for a second before he spoke. 'You were both unconscious, then you woke up eyes rolled back, screaming. I couldn't get you to stop. I didn't know what to do. I was panicking, so I forced myself to calm down and then I sensed him, this force, inside your heads, and I knew I had to get him out.'

'So how the heck did you get him out of our heads?' asked Fred, horrified.

'I sort of pushed him out,' replied Finn. 'I gathered my powers and I used them to push him back. It was hard at first but then he suddenly just yielded. It was as if he had made his point and now he could go. Then your eyes rolled back, and you were sort of normal again.'

Fred, despite himself, gave a chuckle. 'Who's normal?'

'Well, none of us, that's for sure,' answered Georgie with a smile. 'But that doesn't answer the question, does it? What do we do?'

Finn blew out a long breath. 'We go and find the Voice. We help him. We stop the fire.'

Fred stared down at the glittering palace. He studied it for a good minute before he spoke.

'I think we have no choice. Much as I wished we did. It's no co-incidence we've found this palace. I think we were guided here. If what we saw in the vision really is going to happen, then my parents and yours and us and everyone else will be dead. We've seen the vision, so we have to do something.'

'Find the Voice. Stop the fire,' said Georgie desolately. She wished desperately that they had not heard the voice, had not seen the vision. After everything the three of them had lived and nearly died through three months earlier they knew better than most how fine was the line between

life and death. But Georgie knew too that the moment the Voice had spoken to them, the moment they had seen the vision, the line had already been crossed. The Voice had pulled them across it and now there was no going back.

'I really don't want to do this,' said Georgie.

'I don't either,' replied Finn.

'Nor do I,' agreed Fred.

All three fell silent for a while.

'We've done madder things,' said Finn at last, 'or just as mad.'

'Sailed beyond the Known Sea,' said Fred.

'Capsized in a storm conjured up by Hydrus and survived,' said Finn.

'Been captured and escaped,' said Georgie.

'Passed through into the Dark Kingdom,' said Finn.

'Trapped a Dark Djinn in a bottle,' added Georgie.

'Killed many DarkFighters,' said Finn.

'Who are we fighting this time?' asked Fred.

'Dunno,' said Finn, 'more DarkFighters. Human ones.'

'We can do it again,' said Fred.

Georgie, her face a picture of conflicting emotions, blew out a sigh. 'We can.'

Finn gave a grim smile and raised his fists to touch Georgie's and Fred's. 'We will!'

Back at their camp the fire flared around invisible kindling. In the neighbouring *wadi*, Fred's parents slept, oblivious. Fred, Georgie and Finn headed towards the light. Their green sea-glass pendants swinging against their chests, turned dark.

Chapter Six

∽ Road to Hell ∽

FINN HEARD SOMETHING APPROACHING, from the far distance. He turned his head, straining to hear. His eyes scanned the night, searching.

'Helicopters!' he announced. 'Sounds like lots of them, getting nearer.'

Fred looked puzzled. 'I can't hear a thing.'

'Nor can I,' added Georgie.

'They'll be here in a few minutes if they stay on the same bearing.' Finn gazed round at the bare dune, wishing there were some branches, dead wood, anything with which to disguise the outline of the quads.

They stared into the night, waiting. After a minute and a half, Fred and Georgie sighted what Finn had seen for a while; distant lights probing the dark sky like eyes.

'Helicopters,' mouthed Fred. Then he picked up their distant roar.

'Now I hear them,' said Georgie, looking at Finn incredulously. 'How on earth could you have heard them so far off?'

Finn shook his head. 'Dunno, but I did.'

Georgie and Fred exchanged a glance. 'Your powers, Finn. They're increasing.'

Finn looked awkward. He had noticed for a while that he could hear and see things that other people couldn't. It was a wonderful gift, true, but it was also yet another reminder that for him, life would never be normal, and normality, at least for a while, was what he craved.

The huge, marble house stood on a plain with sand dunes protecting its back. Fountains glittered in the lights that blazed from the windows like glaring eyes. Armed guards dressed head to toe in black, patrolled back and forth between the house and the great chasm in the ground. Close up, Finn could see that it was the entrance to an enormous tunnel that led underground.

The phalanx of approaching helicopters landed near the house, whipping up a dust storm that veiled their passengers as they stepped out and hurried into a fleet of waiting Hummers, which whisked them off into the mouth of the tunnel. Car upon car disappeared into the bowels of the earth.

Fred, Finn and Georgie crouched watching from behind a clump of thorn bushes a few hundred yards from the house and just twenty metres from the patrolling guards.

'What're they all up to?' whispered Finn.

'I don't know,' said Georgie softly, 'but I don't like it.'

'I reckon the Voice is here,' said Fred. 'Down there somewhere.' He pointed to the cars heading underground.

'Reckon you're right,' agreed Finn. 'But how're we going to get down there? Place is crawling with guards.'

Fred gazed around thoughtfully. 'See that lorry, the one with the tarpaulin on the back?'

'The one the guards are checking?' asked Finn.

'We can crawl over, climb up into the back and hide under the tarpaulin.'

'Are you mad?' demanded Georgie. 'We'd be seen.'

Fred shook his head. 'Look. Loads more helicopters coming in to land. They'll whip up more sand. The guards'll move on. We'll go then.'

Georgie fingered her pendant and it gave her courage. 'All right. You say when.'

The helicopters, as Fred had predicted, whipped up the perfect sandstorm. The guards moved off and disappeared in the whirling sand. The noise from the scything rotor blades was almost overwhelming. 'Now,' mouthed Fred.

They crawled as fast as they could. Even under cover of the swirling sand, they felt horribly exposed. The guards with their machine guns were so close. Georgie could hear their shouts even above the roar of the helicopters.

It seemed to take ages to cover the twenty metres of desert that separated them from the truck, but they made it. They quickly climbed up the back and squeezed under the tarpaulin.

Whatever it was covering was hard and painful and had lots of bits sticking out. They all bruised themselves trying to get comfortable under and around the cargo.

They felt the rumble as the great engine started up, then the truck moved forward and soon they had the sense of descending. Round and round went the truck in a sickening downward spiral. After a few minutes, Georgie, desperate for air, lifted the side of the tarpaulin and gazed out.

They were in a massive underground cavern, lit by flaming torches protruding from sulphuric-yellow walls. In front of them and behind, a cavalcade of cars wove its way down the spiral road which clung to the sides of the cavern. The road to hell; the words popped unbidden into Georgie's head. In the centre of the cavern, was a void.

Georgie tried to look down into it, but all she saw was a kind of unearthly red-tinged darkness.

Finally they came to the bottom of the cavern. Georgie gasped. Stretching out all around her was what appeared to be a complete, underground city.

Finn and Fred had each lifted the tarpaulin enough to see out. They too stared open mouthed at road markings, traffic lights, shops selling food, clothes, DVDs and CDs, Oxygen cylinders, water. There was a doctor's surgery, a small hospital, a vet, pet food shops. There were apartment buildings, swimming pools, children's play areas with swings and slides. The only thing missing was the people. Nobody crossed the streets, pushed prams along the pavements, shopped in the stores or swung on the swings. It was like a ghost town.

The lorry rumbled on for another five minutes, Finn timed it, before pulling up before a huge building that looked like a grand office complex. Finn tucked himself back under the tarpaulin.

The driver's door slammed shut.

'Got a ton of chairs to unload,' he said to someone.

Finn tensed. They would be exposed any minute.

'Go round the back,' called another voice. 'Park up by the big doors. I'll meet you there and show you where to take them.'

The door slammed, the lorry rumbled back into life and Finn breathed again.

The lorry took some sharp corners then parked up again. Finn heard the driver get out and walk away. He risked a peek.

There were in a gloomy service area, ill-lit, with rubbish bins stacked up around them, and not a soul in sight.

'Quick,' he whispered to Fred and Georgie. 'Let's get out now.'

They hurried down off the back of the lorry.

'Where to?' asked Georgie

Finn swept his eyes over the building.

'Look, there's a door over there, behind the bins. Let's try that.'

They ran quickly across the open ground. Finn tried the handle just as they suddenly heard voices. The driver returning. Finn said a quick prayer. The door opened, they all ducked inside, closed the door quietly behind them.

It was dark and it stank. They listened.

No Voice drifted through the rank air, but Finn felt a great agitation, as if he himself were trapped. He felt sure that this was the place, that the LightFighter who had called to them was near.

Chapter Seven

∽ The Phoenix ∾

GRADUALLY, THEIR EYES GREW accustomed to the darkness and they began to make out the contours of the walls and the floor and huge, looming shapes - massive bins, Finn realised, standing around them like stinking sentries. At the far end of the room, stood a second door.

Finn weaved round the bins, tried the handle, inched open the door. A sliver of light cut in. The door opened onto a brightly lit, empty corridor. On tiptoeing feet the three of them crept out, listening hard for any signs of life, trying to sense the Voice, to feel where he may be.

The walls were painted a deep terracotta, like fired earth, and the tiled floors were the same colour. The corridor was lit by gashes of wall-mounted fluorescent lights and by the occasional flaming torch. As they passed by, one of the flaming torches seemed to flare and hiss.

The first corridor led to another, leading left and right. Finn, following instinct, turned right, then right again at the next fork. Then he slowed, and Georgie could see his shoulders tense.

Finn could sense it. The Voice was near. He could feel power, monumental power. He paused before a door, heart quickening. He cracked it open an inch.

A grand, and empty auditorium lit by flaming torches stood before him. Just off to the side was a stage. In the distance he could hear the chatter of voices, the drumming of footsteps approaching.

He turned to Fred and Georgie.

'Quick, people coming. Follow me.'

He ran into the room, sprinted up the stairs to the stage and ducked behind a curtain at the side of the stage. Fred and Georgie followed as fast as they could. The chatter got louder, closer. Fred was on the stage, heading for the curtain. Georgie tripped on the stairs, fell, swore under her breath, scrambled up again. The voices were so close. Georgie sprinted across the stage and ducked behind the curtain Fred was holding open for her just as the door at the far end of the auditorium was flung open and crashed into the wall with a bang.

Georgie and the boys could see nothing, but all the hairs on the back of Georgie's neck stood up. She had an overwhelming sense of an animal, a predator, some-where close, sniffing the air. There was a chaos of sound; a hubbub of voices, the clatter of feet on marble and the teeth-grinding scraping of chairs.

Silence fell. Someone walked up the stairs on to the stage and paced impatiently just yards from them. The smell of aftershave wafted across, so pungent it made Finn's nose twitch. He grabbed it, held it tightly closed, willed himself not to sneeze.

A voice began to speak; a low, smooth voice, a voice used to being listened to, a voice of power.

'Thank you all for coming, although I know that many of you have paid handsomely for the privilege. Half a billion dollars. A lot of money, but building this facility, and the sister facilities has been rather expensive. And, let's face it, half a billion dollars is a small price to pay for life, a life so different from the lives we all lead now. Life on this over-crowded planet is not even a half life.

'A planet screaming at the seams, a planet we are polluting, raiding, desecrating and killing year by year in our ignorance, our selfishness, our abject avarice and stupidity. But I offer you another way. I offer you a planet cleansed of all but the few. Cleansed of disease, cleansed of criminals, cleansed of the stupid, the ignorant, cleansed of all but us and a few others we will pick up to provide the gaps in the perfect gene pool.' The Voice rose.

'We shall have a new earth, cleansed by fire. You and I. The Chosen Ones.'

There was a roar from the invisible audience. Fred, Georgie and Finn looked at each other in horror. 'The vision,' mouthed Fred. Finn nodded.

The voice went on. Supremely confident, seductive, the words were like snakes slithering into their minds. They almost wanted to believe this man. They almost wanted to agree with him until their brains, their minds, their hearts rejected the words with a silent scream of horror.

'Natural disasters used to do the job for us,' continued the voice. 'The great plagues were a service to mankind, culling the weak, leaving the strong, but medical science has degraded the gene pool and this is what we are left with: the good, the bad and the dross, and the survivors. That, Ladies and Gentlemen, is who we are. By reason of our attainments, financial and otherwise, we will be the survivors.'

The voice dropped. 'We will take cover here, in my Fire Ark, and then I will unleash the fires of hell. Every kind of fire; bush fires, house fires, street fires, city fires, and the greatest fires of all: Nuclear fires.'

There was a gasp, from Georgie, Finn and Fred and from the audience.

'The fires of destruction will cleanse. While the inferno rages we shall live here, half a mile below ground, with plentiful oxygen, food and water. We have enough to last two years, but it is my belief that our planet will be re-habitable after just eighteen months. Our planet, to be shared between The Chosen Ones. All the others, every last remaining member of mankind from above ground, will perish. And we, the mighty, shall inherit the earth. I give you, Ladies and Gentlemen, Operation Phoenix.'

Again came the thunderous applause. Georgie could stand it no longer. She had to see who this madman was, who planned to murder the world, and who were the followers applauding his plan. As she drew back the curtain a fraction, Finn and Fred looked out too. They saw a man, tall and slender, pacing, his back to them. He had luxuriant black hair that fell to his collar. He wore an immaculate dark suit and white shirt.

At right angles to them stood a huge television screen which showed the man prowling back and forth in close up. Now they could see his face; white skin with a choleric tinge; aristocratic long, straight nose; thin, hard lips lit by a secret smile as if he alone knew the answer to life's mysteries. Eyes bright with mania, framed by wings of dark hair. He brushed the hair from his eyes and Georgie saw large, golden cufflinks glittering at his wrists. They were in the shape of a phoenix. She also saw, vivid red against the white of his skin, a savage burn mark covering the back of his left hand. This was the animal presence she had sensed, the predator sniffing the air.

Facing the man, in the rows of seats, was an avid audience of men and women. Some of the faces looked familiar. Georgie recognised some from television and newspapers; the despots and dictators of the world who lined their Swiss bank accounts with billions of dollars while their countries starved; the war criminals. She felt sick.

The man suddenly ceased his prowling and turned in their direction, almost as if he had sensed them. Georgie dropped the curtain, shielding them. She prayed she had done it in time.

'Let's get out of here. Now!' she urged.

Chapter Eight

∽ The Getaway ∽

UNDER COVER OF THE tumultuous applause, they hurried round the back of the stage, all the time, hidden by the curtain.

They kept going till they found a door. Georgie cranked it open an inch. A dimly lit corridor. All three plunged into it.

'Which way?' urged Fred, desperate to get away.

'Left,' guessed Finn, praying that his normally feral sense of direction had returned. He set off at a run.

They cut through a labyrinth of corridors.

Finn paused, getting his bearings. 'It's near here, the way out. I know it is,' he said.

Just then they heard voices coming towards them. They quickly ducked into a side room. The lights were off. The room was pitch dark but it stank.

'The bin room,' whispered Georgie.

'Get into the bins,' said Finn. 'Cover yourself with rubbish.'

'You must be joking,' said Fred.

'I think they're coming this way, those voices. And you don't want to get handed over to the Phoenix man, do you?' whispered Finn heatedly. He knew enough about evil to know what would happen to them if they were caught.

'No,' agreed Fred and Georgie in chorus. They each leapt into a bin, and liberally spread papers and what seemed to be leftover sandwiches over their heads.

It was hard to breathe. They could just suck in small wisps of air.

Seconds later the door swung open and the lights were switched on. Two sets of heavy footsteps approached.

'Right, let's get rid of this,' grunted a deep voice.

' 'S wat I'm doin', innit?' replied a strangled-sounding voice testily.

Georgie held her breath. Her heart pounded with terror. She felt a sickening tilt as her bin was angled. She could imagine the hands reaching down, removing the rubbish, exposing her. But no hands appeared. Instead the bin was wheeled through the room. She heard another one of the bins being moved and wondered if it was Fred or Finn.

A door opened and her bin was pushed down a ramp. Moments later a lorry engine started up. Then her bin was hoisted through the air, upturned and Georgie and all the rubbish tumbled into the back of the lorry.

Georgie landed on her back. Pain ripped through her shoulder but she stifled her shout.

Moments later another bin was mechanically hoisted and she saw Finn tumbling through the air. She rolled out of his way.

Finn flipped in the air and landed, cat-like on his feet. He grinned at Georgie. Georgie stifled a laugh. He had a sandwich sticking out from behind his ear and crisps stuck in his hair.

Fred waited, alone in his stinking bin. Stay calm, he told himself. They'll come back for you, the two men. You have not been left here alone.

Just as he was beginning to panic, footsteps approached and stopped by his bin. Fred said a silent thank you as the man tilted the bin and marched out of the room and down the ramp. Seconds later Fred was tumbling through the air and into the lorry.

He wiped a sandwich from his face and grinned at his friends, lying almost totally concealed in a bed of rubbish. Finn and Georgie grinned back. More rubbish loads came, showering them with cans and papers and Styrofoam coffee cups and then finally the lorry rumbled off.

The road from hell, Georgie thought as the lorry spiralled up and up away from madness and megalomania.

Finally the lorry drove up the ramp and out into the desert night. The three of them sucked in lungfuls of fresh air, but they stayed lying in their bed of rubbish, papers and food strewn over them in case any of the guards with machine guns checked the cargo. Moments later the lorry stopped and they heard voices. The guards.

'What you got in there then?' asked a voice.

'Rubbish, innit,' came the answer. 'Can't you smell it?'

'I can smell something that stinks,' answered the guard, 'but I reckon that would be you.'

Raucous male laughter burst out, cut with a curse from the driver.

'Go on, rubbish man. Take your smell away with you,' said the guard and they were on their way again.

Finn fought free of the rubbish and crawled to the side of the truck. There was a crack in the metal and he could just see out, enough to confirm that they were on what looked like a reasonably well-used desert track. He lay down again on the rubbish, eyes gazing at the stars, trying to block out the stink.

He looked fierce, unafraid. His powers gave him an air of wildness, of danger. Finn, often to his own disquiet, never blended in. He was medium height, lean, tanned and muscled from all his swimming and surfing. His hair was collar length, sun-bleached, honey coloured like his skin. There was something about him which seemed almost to shimmer. His eyes were the green of a stormy sea. They were quick eyes that looked deep, eyes that had seen wonders and horrors. Now they were hard with resolve.

Georgie too looked fierce. She was kind, deeply loyal, quick witted and quick tempered. She had an elfin face framed by masses of wavy chestnut hair. She had suffered and triumphed in the months gone by, rescuing her father from certain death when everyone else had given up on him. The iron will and the strength that had saved him now burned in her eyes.

Fred stared determinedly into space, his ferociously bright mind seeking to conjure answers from the universe. His skin glowed white against his dark hair. He was thin, the result of an equally ferocious metabolism, and he wasn't sporty, but the school bullies never bothered him anymore. Fred had taken on and beaten the worst of them in a battle to the death off Bone Island and a new steeliness showed in his eyes and kept the bullies at bay. His life before meeting the cousins Finn and Georgie had been black and white; work, work, home, home all the time trying to be the perfect son his parents demanded. Since meeting his new friends, since sharing their battles, his life had become a rainbow.

The lorry rumbled on through the darkness. Finn glanced at his watch; four a.m. Dawn was an hour and a bit away. He was wondering whether they should attempt to jump from the moving lorry when suddenly they slowed. He peeked through the cracked metal. They were approaching a giant landfill.

'Get ready,' he whispered to Fred and Georgie. 'I think we're about to be dumped.'

The lorry turned round then reversed. The reversing alarm pinged loudly in their ears.

'Any second now,' said Finn. 'Curl into a ball and pray we don't get seen.'

The back of the lorry was opened.

'Tip,' shouted a voice.

The back of the lorry canted up, then the rubbish and the children rolled down, hit a slope and carried on rolling. Plastic bottles, cans, sandwiches, cartons and paper rolled along in a flurry of arms and legs. Finally they came to rest.

'OK?' whispered Finn.

'OK,' whispered back Fred and Georgie. For a while they lay motionless in the stinking tip. Then, far above them, they heard the sound of the lorry moving off.

Slowly, they emerged from the rubbish, scraps sticking to their hair and clothes. On all fours, they crawled up the steep slope towards the rim of the tip, a few hundred yards above them. Close to the rim the slope steepened. Finn, in the lead, suddenly fell as the rubbish below him gave way and avalanched down the pit. Then Georgie fell, then Fred.

With shaking limbs they tried again, and again, each time falling down in a tumble of rubbish.

Exhausted, they sat for a while, regaining their breath. No-one spoke. The same unspoken thought hovered between them; what if we can't get out of here?

Finn gazed around, eyes picking out details in the seemingly impenetrable darkness. 'The slope looks a bit gentler over that way,' he said, pointing. 'We'll get up there. I'm sure.'

Wordlessly they hiked and clambered around the side of the pit until they got to the slope about four hundred yards away. It did look less steep. Marginally.

Finn went first. Rubbish threatened to give way underfoot but he moved on so fast that it stayed put. The rim beckoned him, just another twenty feet above him.

Go on he urged himself. You will do it. He could feel the rubbish trembling beneath his feet, ready to avalanche at any second. His muscles burned as he climbed up. Just feet to go. Five more steps, four, three, two, one. He got there! He hauled his leg over the side and called out to Fred and Georgie. 'Come on. Much easier. Go fast and you'll make it.'

They did, both of them. Then collapsed gasping at the top.

'Thank God for that,' said Fred, breathlessly.

'Phew,' agreed Georgie.

Finn peered around. All clear. They got their breath back.

'Let's get back to the quads sharpish. It'll be light in about an hour.'

They set off at a fast walk, sticking to the rough road used by the lorries. They reckoned they would hear anything coming from far enough away to sprint off to the side and take cover in the bushes dotted around, but Finn felt horribly exposed.

The desert rang with silence, but Finn was not reassured. The man with the burnt hand, the Phoenix as he called him, was out there, just miles away, possibly searching for them at that very moment.

The night was hot and humid and sweat slicked down their faces into their eyes. They needed water badly but still they kept up their pace.

Suddenly, Finn veered off the road.

'We need to be able to take cover in the dunes,' he said. 'It's nearly dawn.'

'Are we close?' asked Georgie, covering her tiredness with a smile.

'Getting there,' replied Finn.

The terrain was rough. As they scaled and descended the dunes it felt as if they were wading in treacle. Georgie and Fred's legs trembled as if they were about to buckle but they both refused to slow down.

Finn spotted the first ribbon of dawn lightening the distant horizon. They pushed on. Finn prayed that his sense of direction had returned, that he wasn't leading them away rather than towards the quads.

Finally, cresting a dune, they saw the faintest outline of their quad bikes at the bottom. About a quarter of a mile beyond, over a couple more dunes, loomed the Phoenix's palace, still blazing with lights. Three helicopters gleamed white on the tarmac to the side of the house. Four black-clad guards patrolled the periphery.

Finn, Fred and Georgie slid quickly down the dune, out of sight, and collapsed by their bikes, breathing hard.

'Phew,' said Georgie, wiping sweat from her face.

'We need noise,' whispered Finn. 'The guards are too close. They'd come hunting the minute we fired up our engines, and with helicopters, they'd find us in minutes.'

'We can't just wait here,' said Fred, sitting up in alarm.

'D'you want to get caught by the guards?' asked Georgie.

'Of course not,' replied Fred. 'But I don't want to hang around he -'

The sudden roar of helicopter engines starting up stole his words. Light peeled across the horizon. They were losing their cover of darkness second by second. They and their bikes were horribly visible.

A helicopter rose into the sky, hovered, and accelerated away.

'Now,' cried Finn, praying that whoever was in the helicopter would not look down. 'Let's go. No lights'

CHAPTER NINE

Death of Operation Perfect Son

THE HELICOPTER DID NOT spot them. It sped past and disappeared in the direction of the city.

They, meanwhile, got back to their camp unscathed. Mouths cracked with thirst, they attacked their water supply, draining six bottles between them in quick succession.

'Thank God,' said Georgie, slumping down on the sand. 'It feels like we've escaped from hell.'

Finn and Fred, mouths full of water, nodded their agreement.

They peeled off their stinking clothes, washed hands and faces and were just pulling on clean clothes when they heard the roar of a car engine. They looked at one another in terror. There was nowhere to hide.

'It'll be my parents,' said Fred, fervently. 'I hope. Please let it be them.'

A white Range Rover bumped its way round a dune and into sight.

'It is them!' yelled Fred. 'It's my parents and they're all right!' He turned to Finn and Georgie.

'Not a word. They think I'm delusional already.'

'Not a word,' agreed Georgie.

'Not to your parents either George,' said Finn. 'They'd stop us, they'd lock us in the house if necessary.'

Georgie nodded her assent.

'Fred! Freddie!' trilled Fred's mother who was leaning out of the car window and waving delightedly at the sight of her son.

Fred grinned and waved back. Since his running away episode as his mother called it, his parents were changed people. They actually showed him love, and kindness. They treated him as if he were a normal boy.

They no longer pressured him into Go-On maths, or piano performances at their important dinner parties. Fred still played the piano, because he enjoyed it, but he played for himself, not for an audience of adults. Operation Perfect Son seemed to be over. Now they listened to Fred, they accepted that he needed some excitement in his life, some legitimate danger that didn't involve stealing the family boat and running away to sea with Finn and Georgie.

Hence the quad bike. Fred's parents had bought him one first, then after serious pleading, so had Georgie's and so had Finn's. All three sets of parents were so grateful that their children had returned alive and relatively unscathed that they indulged them. But not without rules and regulations; speed and boundary limits, all of which had been roundly broken last night and this morning.

'Morning Mum, Dad,' said Fred, giving them a hug as they stepped from the car.

'How are you, Freddie?' asked his father, grabbing Fred in a hug. He turned to Finn and Georgie. 'Did you all have a great time last night?'

'Great,' replied Fred.

'Absolutely,' agreed Finn.

'Wicked,' confirmed Georgie.

'You look a bit tired,' said Fred's mother, staring into Fred's eyes. 'I bet you stayed up too late.'

More like didn't go to bed at all, thought Fred. He just shrugged.

'Oh well, that's what camp outs are for,' said his mother, with her new understanding. 'No harm done.'

'You two OK?' asked Fred.

His parents exchanged a puzzled glance. 'Of course, Fred. Why wouldn't we be?' asked his father.

'Er, no reason,' replied Fred hurriedly.

Two hours later they were home. Fred's parents had dropped off Finn and Georgie at Georgie's house, where Finn still lived. His parents were sailing back to the UK with his sister Bess, after three months all together in Dubai. They'd only been gone for a week, and now this. But not even they could help. Only Triton, with his enormous powers, stood any chance.

Georgie's parents welcomed them back extravagantly, even though they'd just been gone one night. Georgie yelped when her parents hugged her. Her mother ministered to her with consternation and ice packs and Calpol.

'Bed for you,' said her mother.

'I'm not tired,' insisted Georgie. 'I've just got a bruised shoulder.'

'What from?' asked her mother. 'Did you fall off your quad bike?'

Georgie thought it was easier to say yes to this than explain being tipped from a rubbish bin into a rubbish lorry.

'Er, yes,' she muttered.

Her mother shook her head in exasperation.

'I'll be fine,' pleaded Georgie.

'Quiet day for you, whatever you say,' decreed her mother.

Finn burned with impatience until sun-down. As the *Muezzin* call echoed through the streets, he turned to his Uncle and Aunt.

'Uncle Johnny, Aunt C. I'm just off to the beach for a walk. Won't be too long.' He tried to sound casual, to betray none of his desperation.

'How long's too long?' asked Johnny, putting down his book and peering up at Finn.

'Coupla' hours. I just want to walk and sit. Be by the sea.'

Johnny contemplated his nephew. He knew how Finn needed to be by the sea, how passionately he loved it.

'All right, but no longer,' said Johnny.

'Great, thanks,' said Finn, glancing at Georgie.

'Oh, Finn, can I tag along?' asked Georgie as if it were just a spontaneous idea.

'With a torn shoulder muscle?' asked her mother. 'I don't think so.'

'Ple-' started Georgie.

'Sorry, love,' said her father. 'Your mother's right. You need to rest. You look exhausted too.'

Georgie spun on her heel and stalked off to her room. Finn followed her.

'Bad luck, George.'

'Flipping shoulder. Triton would've cured it too,' she said.

'If I get to see him,' said Finn.

'Go now,' said Georgie, grabbing his hand and squeezing. 'Go and tell him. Get him to help.'

CHAPTER TEN

⨳ Triton ⨳

FINN JOGGED THROUGH THE hot streets towards the sea. Everything looked deceptively normal. The call of the *Muezzin* drifted across the rooftops, summoning the faithful to prayer. The towers and minarets of the mosque stood silhouetted against the setting sun, black against gold. Men in their *kandoorahs* glided towards the mosque in quiet conversation.

Finn hurried past them, only pausing to wait for a lull in the traffic that roared along Beach Road.

He sprinted the last fifty metres. He could smell the sea, the tang of salt, the seaweed hint of the deep. His heart quickened when he crossed 2B street and saw before him the ribbon of beach and the darkening slate green of the sea.

Too many people, he thought with dismay. The kite surfers were packing up their kites, but they would stay to picnic. Families were gathering their wet towels and beach toys to go, but still there were too many people. And he only had two hours. He couldn't afford to wait until most of the people had gone.

He stepped out of his sandals and headed left, up towards the fishermen's village. He thought of the bomb that had been intended to blow it up, just three months ago. On Ivan Drax's orders. So many maniacs, he thought. So much evil. He shuddered. He felt strangely uneasy, as if hidden eyes were watching him.

He climbed up on to the rocks, jumping nimbly from rock to rock until he was sitting on the furthest point of the promontory. The sea ebbed and flowed before him, washing his toes.

If anyone saw him, and a few people had glanced his way as he passed, all they would have seen was a boy who looked like a surfer dude. They had no idea what else he was, no conception of who he was hoping to meet.

The sun turned a burnished red and fell into the sea with a dying blaze. Night fell quickly and the beach began to empty, but not enough.

Finn held onto his sea-glass pendant and thought of Triton. *Triton, I need you. Please come.* He saw the raging inferno laying waste to the world and he knew the only hope to stop it was Triton.

Over and over, he repeated his plea, summoning Triton with all his will.

The night deepened and the sickle moon rose. A whole hour had passed and still there was no sign of Triton. Finn stared at the moon and wished. He glanced around from time to time, still unable to shake off the sensation that he was being watched. His shoulderblades prickled as if some hidden watcher were taking aim at him, but he could see no-one.

There was a splash out to sea. He strained his eyes but could see nothing. There was another splash.

Finn eased his body into the sea, took a quick breath and swam down under the water. He surfaced where he had heard the splash. There, in the rippling water before him, was Triton, the Sea Djinn.

Finn gasped. He'd never get over the sheer, fantastical shock of seeing the Djinn. Triton was half-man, half enormous dolphin, although that part was hidden by the sea. He had thick silver hair, swept back by the sea. His face was burnished, the planes of his features noble and smooth like a bronze sculpture from antiquity. His lips were caught in a smile. Behind his ears fluttered the gills of a fish. His shoulders were enormous, his arms and chest hugely muscled. Power and a feeling of profound goodness radiated from him.

His eyes, green like Finn's, seemed to look into Finn's soul for they darkened as they saw the turmoil there. Finn felt relief wash over him. With Triton, anything was possible.

'Finn, my friend,' said Triton in his deep, mellifluous voice.

'Hello Triton.'

'You are well, but you are troubled.'

Finn nodded.

'Climb on my back. There are too many people here.'

'Where are we going?' Finn asked.

'To the Cave of Light.'

CHAPTER ELEVEN

∽ Cave of Light ∽

FINN CLOSED HIS EYES and held on tight as they sped along under the surface. The water sluiced off Finn's body and he felt as though he were flying. He felt a wild exhilaration and would have whooped with delight if he could have opened his mouth. On they sped, Djinn and boy, slicing through the salty darkness.

Triton stayed under a long time. When he felt Finn tapping his chest with one hand he surfaced. He smiled to himself. The boy was growing stronger. They had never stayed under for so long before.

Finn, lungs burning, sucked in air voraciously. He recovered quickly.

'I'm ready,' he told Triton. The Sea Djinn dived under the water again and took Finn far out to sea. A few more stops for breath and they suddenly slowed. Finn felt Triton descend and then stop. Then the Sea Djinn passed a rock into his hand; the meteoric rock. Finn recognised its contours, its sheer weight. Finn slipped from Triton's back and, weighed down by the super-density of the rock, his feet found the floor of the Cave of Light. Triton passed him a shell, and he put the shell inside his mouth like a snorkel and he breathed.

He'd never tasted air like it anywhere else. It seemed like pure oxygen, and for a moment, his head spun with the richness of it.

He kept his eyes tightly shut until he felt Triton gently waving his hands back and forth across his face. When he opened his eyes, they did not stream from the salt water and he could see clearly in the rapidly lightening gloom.

Golden light poured from Triton and from his own body too, until the Cave of Light was almost dazzling.

'Your powers have increased, Finn,' said Triton. His deep voice of above sea had been replaced by the high, bell-like voice of below sea.

Finn nodded, gazing in amazement at the light flooding from his body.

'Now, tell me everything,' commanded Triton gravely.

Finn tried to still his thoughts so that Triton could read his mind, but his head flickered with images of the Phoenix and his inferno, the Vision and the Voice.

'Fire,' said Triton. 'Where?'

'Everywhere,' thought Finn.

'Start at the beginning, Finn,' said Triton, his voice slow with the patience of the deep.

Calmed by him, Finn tried again. When he had finished conveying his thoughts, Triton stayed silent. The silence stretched until Finn felt it would snap.

'Did you get any idea from this Phoenix as you call him, when he's planning to unleash Armageddon?' asked Triton.

'That's the problem. We didn't manage to find out.'

'Can you go back?'

This was the question Finn had feared.

'I can,' he nodded.

'And Georgie and Fred?'

'Fred will. He seems even wilder about this than I am. I think Georgie is torn.'

'And who can blame her? But the three of you together have a power far greater than individually. If you can…'

'I could go alone,' thought Finn. 'I could travel…,' he added.

'Even more dangerous, if you get it wrong,' said Triton. 'Have you been practising lately?'

Finn shook his head. 'I wanted to be normal for a while.'

Triton gave him a smile both sweet and sad.

'Your powers make you extraordinary, Finn, not abnormal. Life can be a battle, you know that better than anyone, but you are choosing to live your life unarmed and untrained, all because you do not want to stand out from the crowd.'

'And what's wrong with that?' thought Finn.

'Finn, you will never be part of the crowd. Anyone who ever looks into your eyes can see that.'

'What's in my eyes? What do you see?' thought Finn.

'I see fires burning. Oceans raging. Voices talking. An unquiet earth and an unquiet mind. Arm yourself Finn. Practise, but try not to go in alone. You need your friends. You know that by now.'

'I know I do. But they can't travel, and I don't want to expose them to danger again. I wish I had some kind of weapon,' thought Finn, 'so that I can protect them.'

'You have the best weapon of all. Yourself.'

'I can't point my finger and shoot the Phoenix.'

'You'll think of something better. Trust me, Finn, and more importantly, trust yourself. Ask for your powers to come to you. Seek them out.'

'How?'

'Think the impossible.'

Finn gave a start. 'That's what Mr Violet said.'

Triton nodded. 'He was a good pupil. And a great teacher.'

'I have no teacher now,' thought Finn sadly.

'Would the Prince of Atlantis allow the King of the Sea to offer some tips?'

Finn beamed at Triton. 'Would you? Would you really?'

Triton bowed to Finn. 'It would be an honour.'

Finn glowed inside.

'We'll start now,' said Triton.

'Great,' thought Finn. 'What are you going to show me?'

'Nothing.'

Finn faltered. 'Er, sorry. I don't understand.'

'What are you going to show me?' asked Triton.

'Nothing,' thought Finn. 'I mean I can swim well, I can travel, I can read minds, a little bit. You know all that.'

Triton smiled. 'You can do a lot more than that, Finn.'

'Like what?'

'What do you want to be able to do?'

Finn thought for a moment. What would be useful in a battle?

'Do it,' said Triton, reading his mind.

Finn swept his gaze around the Cave of Light until his eyes picked out the large conch shell at Triton's feet. He locked his eyes upon it, focused all his will on it. Seconds passed. Nothing happened.

Finn blew out a breath of frustration.

'You want to do this?' asked Triton, turning his gaze upon the conch, which then levitated gently up off the floor of the cave into his outstretched palm. He moved it on towards Finn, who took hold of it with wonder.

'Yes,' he thought. 'That is exactly what I want to be able to do.'

He gazed down at the conch, which seemed to be almost pulsating slightly in his hands. 'Your summoning Conch!'

Triton nodded. 'It is. I can summon all the Light-Fighters in my world with this conch.'

'It seems almost alive,' thought Finn.

'It is alive. In its own way. It has its powers too. That's what you are feeling.'

Finn nodded. He stretched out his hands, holding the conch aloft. He tried to move it but it stayed stubbornly pulsing in his palms. Triton levitated it back to himself.

'Practise,' said Triton, 'until you can do this.'

'You think I'll be able to do it?'

'If you think so, yes. Equally, if you think you cannot, then no.'

Finn nodded.

'In the meantime, I will send out my spies to investigate, and I will do everything in my power to stop this. But from you, my friend, I must know when. And it would help if I knew who this Phoenix is. His name.'

Finn nodded. 'I'll go as soon as I can,' he thought. 'I'll try to rescue this LightFighter too.'

'Good,' said Triton, 'but be careful, Finn. Be patient. Be wise. You are powerful and growing in power, but we know nothing of this Phoenix. We don't yet know what you are up against.'

Finn saw a flash of something in the Djinn's eyes that made his stomach clench with fear.

'Who might we be up against? Do you know?'

'Not yet, Finn. Not yet. But we know there's power and there's madness and there's evil. That's enough, isn't it?'

Finn nodded. 'I'll be careful. I promise.'

'Thank you. Now, I'll take you back to shore, and then I would like you to travel back to your room. If you think you can.'

'I'll give it a go,' thought Finn, goaded by Triton's gentle taunt. 'Before we go,' communicated Finn, 'how's Hydrus?' Finn thought of the Dark Sea Djinn, his and Triton's sworn enemy, writhing away in the bottle inside which Finn had trapped him, just three months ago.

'Trapped. Contained. Hidden far from here.'

'Good,' thought Finn. 'And Mr Violet? How is he? Is he-?' Finn thought of his friend, who had taught him so many things, who had revealed to Finn so many of his own powers, before becoming corrupted and terminally tainted by Hydrus.

Triton looked away into the distant sea. 'Another time, Finn, my friend. Now climb on my back. You've been holding your breath for eight minutes and even you have your limits.'

Finn took one last look around at the glittering cave, at the stalactites descending from the ceiling like dripping daggers, at the mother of pearl roof glowing opalescent thirty feet above them. He wondered if he would ever come here again. He put down the meteoric stone and climbed onto Triton's back.

The Sea Djinn pushed out into open water, lashed his enormous tail and within moments they surfaced. Finn gasped in air and gazed around. The ocean and sky were ink black after the brilliance of the cave and Finn could see nothing save the stars glittering high above and the sliver of new moon. They were alone in the sea, miles from shore.

Finn felt the enormity of what lay ahead. He would have to steel himself against pain, exhaustion, terror. Again. He would start now.

'I'll travel from here,' he said determinedly.

Triton's eyes darkened. 'Are you sure?'

Finn nodded. He didn't need Triton to tell him; get it wrong and he could land in the middle of the ocean, truly alone. For a moment he thought of Bone Island, of the Dark Kingdom, and then he banished the thoughts from his head. Once in any lifetime was more than enough. He NEVER wanted to go back there and if he filled his head with images of it he just might.

Triton turned and gave Finn his hand. Finn shook it and felt the surge of electricity jolt through him. He let go of Triton's hand and summoned his own powers. He thought of Mr Violet, he heard his voice in his mind;

You have to believe. See where you want to land. Use all your focus. CCR, he'd called it; confidence, concentration and relaxation.

Finn tried to concentrate, to believe, to relax. He filled his mind with images of the beanbag in his bedroom.

Then he disappeared.

CHAPTER TWELVE

↶ Necessary Deception ↷

GEORGIE LAY ON HER back in her bed wide awake and silently blazing. She should have been with Finn. Her cursed shoulder. She'd taken a pain-killer and still it throbbed. She glanced at her watch. Finn had been gone for nearly two and a half hours. Her parents were downstairs laughing and watching a movie but soon they'd remember that Finn was due back.

Another twenty minutes passed and still no Finn. Georgie got up and paced around her room. Any minute now her mother would be on the warpath and her normally mild father soon would be too. The last thing they could afford was to be grounded.

She eased from her bedroom and into Finn's. She took some towels from his bathroom and clothes from his cupboard and padded out his bed. She wrestled the duvet, thumped the pillow, and as a final touch, crumpled up a clean pair of shorts, a clean pair of underpants and a clean t shirt and strew them across the floor in the direction of the bed. Then she ducked behind Finn's blinds and unlatched his window. Satisfied, she nipped back to her own room, climbed into bed and waited.

Moments later, she heard footsteps on the stairs

and then her door opened gently and her mother's face appeared.

Georgie smiled. Her mother crossed the room to her.

'You all right Georgie?' she asked. 'How's the shoulder?'

'All right,' lied Georgie.

Her mother gave her a sceptical look. 'Mmm. Finn back?'

Georgie nodded. 'Yep, half an hour ago, slunk off to his bedroom, didn't want to talk. I think he's got a headache,' she added.

'I'm not surprised. Lack of sleep and all the excitement of your camping trip.'

Oh, if only you knew, thought Georgie. 'Well, he's sleeping it off, I expect,' she said.

'I'll just take a peak. Night night, love,' said her mother, stooping down to kiss her.

'Night night, Mum,' said Georgie. She listened as her mother closed her door and opened Finn's. She imagined her standing in the doorway, the light from the hallway illuminating Finn's room. She crossed her fingers under the duvet and prayed.

Seconds passed. Georgie held her breath, but there was no explosion of sound, just a quiet click as her mother closed Finn's door and then the soft tread of her slippers down the marble hall. Georgie exhaled. Now all she had to do was wait for Finn.

Chapter Thirteen

∽ The Dark Shark ∽

FINN FELT THE FAMILIAR rushing sensation. His whole body felt as if it were being compressed, and then he landed with a great splash, in water. He floundered, took in a mouthful of sea, gagged and began to panic. He kicked hard, willing his mind and body to calm. Seconds later he reached the surface, coughing and gagging and gasping in air. He looked around him and his heart slammed with fear. Sea, black, undulating, endless, all around him. He'd got it wrong. Horribly wrong. Instead of landing in his bedroom he had landed somewhere in the middle of the ocean. He'd feared this, just for a second before he launched himself and this image must have been the more powerful.

'Idiot!' he yelled. To think he could do this with no practise. He was like a toddler with a Ferarri. That's what Mr Violet had called him when his first attempt at Astral Travel landed him in an ice cream shop at Park and Shop, and he'd laughed, thought it was funny. Well now he'd crashed and there was no-one to rescue him.

He trod water, turning a full circle. He could see nothing, no coastline, just the endless sea. Time to try again.

He stilled his panicked breathing, conjured the image of his beanbag. See Believe Launch. He cast his mind. And nothing happened. He tried again. And again. He remained in the sea, treading water, despair rising like a fog in his soul.

I can't do it. Why can't I do it? He shouted.

His efforts had tired him. His limbs, normally so lithe in the sea, felt like lead. Then the worst thought of all entered his head. Perhaps, like on the voyage three months ago, he had left the Known Sea and was beyond, in the Dark Kingdom, in the Sea of Tranquillity or in the Bay of Honour. Perhaps he had gone beyond the Ocean of Storms, the Sea of Crises and was in the Serpent Sea. He whirled around, panic gripping his heart.

'TRITON,' he yelled with all his breath. 'I'm lost. I'm nowhere, anywhere. Please come and help.' But there was no answering cry. The minutes passed and no figure appeared in the water. Ten minutes passed. Finn made up his mind. He consulted his watch. Flickering on the dial was a compass. He would assume he was somewhere in the Gulf.

He would swim south and very slightly east and he would keep going until he found land, or died trying.

He started with breast-stroke so that he could see more easily where he was going. He swam for half an hour, checking his compass at intervals, then he stopped to rest. He strained his eyes, staring into the distance. Dark sea all around. No sign of land. He flipped onto his back, floated there, gazing up at the stars. What an idiot, he thought again, over and over until despair set in.

'Stop it!' he yelled. 'This will get you nowhere.' He gave himself five minutes, checked his compass, then he set off again, front crawling this time.

Below him, thirty feet down, the briny water swirled with energy as fish scattered and fled. Behind them, lazily cutting through the sea was a shark. The shark had no interest in the fish. They were distractions, easily tuned out. His interest was in the boy. He'd felt the jolt of electricity five miles away and had set himself on course for its source, like a heat-seeking missile. Now, so close, he could feel the electricity pumping from above. No ordinary electricity. No ordinary human. If he were right, and he rarely made mistakes, then this was the Boy of the Prophecy. The Prince of Atlantis. He'd seen him, just three months ago, in the Dark Kingdom. The Boy who had captured Hydrus in a bottle. Hydrus, his master. The boy who had poisoned most of the Commanders of the Dark Army. He, the shark, had been one of the few survivors.

He had vowed revenge. And now, like a gift from the Djinn, here was the boy. He swam closer. The pulse of energy was unmistakable. And who else could it be, swimming alone at midnight in the middle of the ocean. No ordinary boy, that was for sure.

The shark flicked his tail and descended. There, below the boy, he swam circles, calculating his angle. Then, like a torpedo, he gathered his strength and exploded up through the water.

CHAPTER FOURTEEN

Blood in the Water

TRITON KNEW IMMEDIATELY THAT Finn had failed. When he tuned in he could always sense where the boy was, and when Finn summoned him, or screamed his name into the ether he could place him exactly.

Triton knew that even if Finn had tried and repeatedly failed to Travel, he should be able to swim home, even though he was still many miles from shore. The sea was Finn's second home and he was an exceptional swimmer, but Triton also knew that Finn could swim in the wrong direction. He could encounter enemies.

Seconds later, as if alerted by the thought, Triton's senses picked up the presence of a DarkFighter, a powerful one. Closing in on Finn.

Triton calculated speed and distance. He was too far away, however fast he swam. He lashed his great tail into the water, leapt from it, and summoning all his powers, he became the wind.

He flew through the air, just above the ocean, hurtling towards Finn.

Finn swam on, stroke after relentless stroke. He tried to still his mind by counting the strokes but failed. His body tingled with apprehension. He hated swimming in this black water. He imagined all sorts of terrors lurking below. He could not shake off the sensation of evil. Perhaps he really was in the Serpent Sea and soon Bone Island would hove into view.

Suddenly he heard a great howling. Around him the waves steepened and banked as a strange wind roared in. He stopped swimming and whirled around. A storm was on him, but the sky remained clear. Terror gripped him. He battled with the waves, trying to keep his head above water, but it wasn't the waves that terrified him.

The last time a storm had come at him from a cloudless sky it had been Hydrus. Surely it could not be. He was contained, far away. Triton had just said so.

Suddenly, just as abruptly as it had blown in, the wind died. The waves calmed and the air grew still.

Triton hit the water like a whirlwind. As soon as he was covered, he metamorphosed back into the man-dolphin. His eyes scanned the water. He saw Finn above him, legs treading water and he saw a force erupting from the deep, a shark, great mouth agape, heading for Finn.

With a roar, Triton powered through the water. He caught the shark by its tail and dragged it down. The shark jack-knifed round. Triton released its body, caught its neck and ripped off its head.

Blood spurted through the water. It rose to the surface just after Finn had started to swim again. It missed him by inches. He smelled something strange but discounted it. It was his sixth sense he was pre-occupied with. It screamed danger. It screamed death. Finn knew both. And he knew they were near. Just get away, he told himself, get far away from here.

He carved his way through the water, stroke after stroke. He used all his strength, all his power. Only when he had been swimming for over an hour did he stop, flip onto his back and gaze exhaustedly at the stars. The moon was dipping down. It was two a.m. Every part of his body ached and still there was no sign of land.

He gave himself five minutes to rest, checked his compass bearing, then started to swim again, this time on his back.

He gazed at the stars as he swam, at Sirius the Dog Star, Orion the Hunter and Venus, glowing in the heavens. Beautiful, he thought, quite beautiful. He distracted himself with them for another hour. He would not think of his parched throat, or of his lips, cracking with dehydration, or of his arms and shoulders and neck, burning with effort. Most of all, he would not think of the possibility that, rather than swimming towards land, towards Dubai, he was swimming further out into the open sea. Towards Iran. Just look at the stars, he told himself, over and over, and keep swimming.

This time, when he flipped onto his front and surveyed the sea before him, he saw land. He saw the skyscrapers of Dubai, twinkling with lights, more beautiful at that moment than the whole galaxy of stars.

Chapter Fifteen

∞ The Nightmare ∞

EORGIE THRASHED AGAINST HER duvet, caught in the grip of a nightmare. She had intended to wait up for Finn until he returned, but at midnight she had finally fallen asleep. Suddenly she sat bolt upright in bed. A noise had woken her. It had come from Finn's room.

She slipped from her bed, knuckling the hair from her face. She cracked open her door and peeked down the hall. No sign of life from the other bedrooms. She crept along to Finn's room and gingerly opened the door. Finn wheeled round to her. He was in the act of pulling on his pyjamas. Georgie could see that his arms were shaking and he could barely stand.

She rushed over to help him.

'Finn, my God. What happened to you?' she whispered. Finn was too exhausted to reply.

'Here let me help you into bed,' said Georgie. Finn draped his arm over Georgie's shoulders. Pain fired out of her injured muscle but she took Finn's weight and hauled him across the room and into bed.

'C and Johnny?' croaked Finn.

'I stuffed your bed. Told Mum you weren't feeling well, gone to bed with a headache after you got in from the beach. She fell for it.'

Finn blew out a big sigh of relief.

'Can I get you some food? Some water?' Georgie asked quickly.

'Water,' croaked Finn. 'Marmite sandwich.'

'Coming up,' said Georgie.

Three minutes later she was back. Finn was fast asleep, but Georgie reckoned he had to eat and drink something. She finally managed to wake him up, then watched him down a litre bottle of water and devour four marmite sandwiches.

Finn reached up and patted Georgie's shoulder.

'Thanks George,' he mumbled.

Georgie felt a glow spreading through the injured muscles of her shoulder. She took Finn's hand and gazed at it.

'You've got phosphorescence on your palm, look,' she said.

'Triton. Shook my hand. Sleep now. Need to,' said Finn. His eyes closed and he tumbled into oblivion.

Georgie watched him for a moment to make sure he was still breathing, then she returned to her own bed. She felt the warmth healing her shoulder; the phosphorescence from the Sea Djinn; the shimmering dust of his power, healing her.

Georgie's alarm went off one and a quarter hours later. It was followed by her mother's gentle knock.

'Morning Georgie,' she called.

'Morning Mum.'

Georgie dressed quickly. As she did so, she noticed that her shoulder felt much less painful and that there was still the slightest tinge of phosphorescence on her white night-dress. She hid it in her cupboard so her mother wouldn't chuck it into the washing machine, then she rushed through to check on Finn.

Her mother was standing by his bed, a worried look on her face.

'He won't get up,' she said to Georgie. 'He wakes for a moment, then just goes straight back to sleep. I think I should get the doctor. You said he had a headache last night.'

Finn suddenly thrashed in his bed. 'No!' he shouted. 'Leave me alone!' His eyes opened and he sat bolt upright in bed. His pupils were dilated, lit with terror at some inner vision. He seemed oblivious to both Georgie and her mother as they gripped his arms and smoothed his forehead.

'Finn, it's all right, it's just a nightmare,' they both crooned, voices soothing, faces taut with alarm.

Finn, gripped in the nightmare, wanted to tell them that it wasn't all right, but he couldn't speak, couldn't pull himself free. He tried to frame words but all his mind conjured was the sound of a hiss.

Finn thrashed, fighting wildly, then the hissing abruptly stopped, Finn's eyes closed and he slumped back onto his pillow.

'I'm going to call the doctor,' said Aunt C, her face creased with worry.

She ushered Georgie out of the room. Once in the hallway, her look sharpened.

'What's going on Georgie? Something is, I can practically smell it.'

Before Georgie could answer, Cressida came running from her room.

'Muuuum! Muuuummy! Cordelia's vomiting. She's in the loo, and it's everywhere.'

Georgie and her mother rushed in to Cordy, who, having comprehensively emptied her stomach, was looking pale and shaky.

'Oh, you poor thing. Come here,' said Camelia stripping Cordy and putting her in the shower. 'Well that explains what's wrong with Finn, then,' she said over her shoulder to Georgie. 'His turn next, I suppose. Johnny,' she called above the torrent of the shower. 'Can you give Georgie and Cressie breakfast and take them to school? I'm going to get the doctor to come and check out Cordy and Finn.'

When her mother nipped from the room to ring the doctor, Georgie rushed back to her room to grab her nightdress.

'Cordy, come here for a hug,' said Georgie. Cordelia stepped into her arms, and Georgie gently dabbed at her face and throat with her nightie which still bore a trace of phosphorescence. Cordy didn't say a word, just allowed herself to be cosseted. Georgie finished dabbing her then led her back to her bed. With a slight smile, Cordelia closed her eyes and fell fast asleep.

The Doctor came one hour later. He pronounced that Cordelia was probably suffering from a twenty four hour vomiting virus, which, from the look of her, had already passed since she appeared to him quite rosy cheeked if a bit tired. As for Finn, the Doctor poked, prodded, and asked him to say Aaah , then pronounced him fighting off a virus, dehydrated and over-tired. After his examination, Finn drank another litre of water, ate four Shredded Wheat with half a litre of camel's milk, then slept the entire day.

When Georgie arrived home from school at two forty five, she was delighted to see Cordelia looking quite recovered. Finn, however, was still asleep. Georgie decided extreme measures were called for.

'Mummy,' she called. 'Can I make some lasagne for tea? I really feel like it today.'

'Lovely, darling,' replied her mother, who knew how much Georgie enjoyed cooking. 'Make a big one, would you, then Daddy and I can have some for our dinner too.'

'Sure, Mummy,' said Georgie, getting to work with a grin. At five thirty she opened Finn's door, then went back down to the kitchen and removed the lasagne from the oven with a flourish. Pain flared in her shoulder, but half a minute later, she had her reward. She heard movements from Finn's room, stretching-yawning sounds, then the patter of feet. She was serving up the lasagne when Finn appeared, rubbing his eyes.

'I could eat a horse,' he said, yawning extravagantly.

Georgie smiled. 'Double portion of lasagne instead?'

'Make it a triple and I'm in your debt forever,' said Finn.

'You can pay off all your debts by just telling me what the heck went on last night,' whispered Georgie.

'Just as soon as I've eaten this and drunk a bottle of lemonade,' said Finn, as Cordy and Cressie joined them at the table, lured from their own room by the smell.

Finn finished his heroic portion then headed up to his room to collapse on his beanbag. Georgie followed him, closing the door firmly behind her.

'So spill,' she commanded.

Chapter Sixteen

The Excellence Academy

FINN SLEPT DEEPLY THAT night. The sleep of the exhausted, or of the enchanted. Nightmares assailed him again. He heard voices, hissing voices talking at him. He seemed almost to be talking back to them, though he didn't want to. He thrashed and moaned, resisting them until finally they fell silent, leaving him to sleep in peace.

The next morning, he woke with the memory of the nightmares swirling around him. He banished them. He was fine, he told himself forcibly.

'Fully recovered,' he confirmed to his Aunt C as she came into his bedroom to check on him.

'Excellent!' she announced. 'Cordy is too. Let's have pancakes to celebrate.'

They all wolfed down their pancakes dripping in maple syrup in record time. On the way to school, every traffic light was green, so they arrived five minutes earlier than normal.

Their school was grandly titled the Jumeirah Academy of Music, otherwise known as JAM. It wasn't really much more musical than any of the other schools, but the name gave it a cultural superiority that was visible in the strut of the headmaster, Mr Strummer. Georgie often said he'd got the job by virtue of his name alone.

Georgie's mother parked between a red Ferrari so highly polished it hurt to look at it and a sand-encrusted Land Cruiser with a battered spare petrol tank fixed to the rear doors. No more *wadi* bashing for you, thought Finn, watching a tanned, long haired father emerge from the Landcruiser with a tribe of tanned children. On his other side a pale, pinstriped, bald man emerged with a nervous-looking girl from the Ferrari. No more mega-deals for you, thought Finn. No more anything. For anyone, save the Chosen Ones. Unless he and Georgie and Fred and Triton could stop Operation Phoenix. He felt a hard fist of anger close around his heart and with it, a ruthless resolve.

Aunt C kissed Georgie and Finn goodbye.

'Look after yourselves,' she said, eyes grave. Finn knew she still hated to let them out of her sight. He could hardly blame her.

'Bye Aunt C,' he said, giving her a kiss on the cheek in return.

Her eyes opened wide in surprise. Finn wasn't normally so openly affectionate. She gave a smile of pleasure, then headed off with the twins to drop them at their classroom.

Finn and Georgie headed straight to the acacia tree, where Fred was already waiting.

'What happened to you?' asked Fred, jumping up and peering worriedly at Finn. 'Are you all right now? Did you s-?'

'Ah. Finn Kennedy and Fred Adams!' Boomed a voice with an strong Slovakian accent. 'Just dur boys I've been looking for.'

The three of them looked up at the towering, hat-topped figure of Mr Slavel, the head of Achievement.

Mr Slavel was six foot seven without his hat, six foot ten with it. He wore a different hat each day. Today's was a blue trilby. He was slim, wiry and slightly stooped from constantly having to come down to other people's level. Rumour was he had played tennis for Slovakia years ago before a knee injury had cut short his career. He was also reputed to be a member of Mensa, having an IQ of 150. Whenever anyone quizzed him about either rumour, he merely smiled and modestly suggested people shouldn't believe everything they heard. He spent half of his time as a sort of roving teacher. He would appear suddenly, banishing the numeracy or literacy teacher and proceed to entertain and enthral the class with a wide range of subjects from star constellations and navigation to parallel universes and quantum physics. Whatever subject he talked about, his passion and knowledge made it fascinating. He'd only been at JAM for one term, but already the pupils loved him. The less enthralling of the teachers hated him.

'Hi Mr Slavel,' said Finn with a smile.

'Hi sir,' chimed in Fred, his annoyance at not being able to hear Finn's story muted by the feeling of good cheer that seemed to emanate from Mr Slavel.

'Like your hat,' said Georgie, 'very dashing.'

'Dank you Georgina. Kind as always.' He tipped his hat to her like a Victorian gentleman.

'Now boys, ve have an interesting situation cooking up. One of dur parents vishes to sponsor an Academy of Excellence and he is gathering together a group of dur most able students. Dere will be a meeting today directly after school to discuss it. I am going to telephone your parents to ask permission for you to attend.' He nodded enthusiastically.

For once, Fred and Finn failed to look enthralled by Mr Slavel.

'Vat is it?' he asked perplexed. 'You don't vant to go?'

Finn gave a hapless shrug. How could he explain that they had rather more pressing things on their minds, like a maniac planning to burn down the world.

'Er, well, it's just, well, for a start, I'm not that excellent at anything. My literacy's OK but my maths stinks.'

Mr Slavel shook his head. 'Dosn't stink, Finn. No, just dosn't smell of roses yet, but dat's another matter. You vud be dere in your capacity as a swimmer. Physical brilliance vill be rewarded as vell as mental.'

'Rewarded how?' asked Fred.

Mr Slavel glanced around then stooped down to Fred.

'Dere's a rumour of scholarships. Of school fees being paid, but don't tell anyone or I shall be stampeded by parents demanding dat deir child be excellent and have his or her fees paid and I shall be squashed flat as a beetle by dur end of dur week.'

Fred grinned, but a steely glint had entered his eye.

'So, I shall ring your parents and if dey give permission, Miss Roose shall send you up to the Achievement Centre for dur meeting, straight after school.'

'Great,' said Georgie, knowing her parents and Fred's would be delighted by the idea and definitely send Finn and Fred to the meeting. 'And what are the ordinary citizens, the non-brilliant ones meant to do while the brilliant ones are being feted?' she asked Mr Slavel acidly.

'Georgie, you must not say dat. You are a rounded, happy individual, brilliant at life.'

Georgie beamed. So there! she mouthed at Finn and Fred.

The school bell rang, drowning out their replies

'See you later,' announced Mr Slavel with a bow before striding purposefully across the Astroturf.

'Great,' repeated Georgie, setting off with Fred and Finn towards their classroom. 'Some boring meeting for you. My mother will definitely say you can go Finn.'

Finn nodded glumly. 'My parents could really do without having to pay my school fees. I overheard them before they left, worrying about how they'd shot up again.'

'Well, at least you don't have that worry Fred,' said Georgie.

Fred cleared his throat and looked awkward. 'Well, actually, I might. My father's been acting quite strangely recently, I mean apart from being nice to me. I've overheard him talking to my mother. He's been saying things like: I can't see the point in it anymore, day in day out, grinding away, not seeing much of you or Fred, and he's complaining of the stress. He's even suggested that he and Mum and I take a year or two out and go sailing round the world.'

'What!' exclaimed Georgie, stopping to stare at Fred open-mouthed. 'Your mother leave Jumeirah for the open sea?'

'You'd be surprised, Georgie,' Fred answered rather curtly. 'She's changed too. She's economising, giving things up. She's even stopped having Botox.'

'I wondered why she smiled at me the other day,' said Georgie. 'Sorry,' she added quickly, seeing Fred's glare. 'I know she's changed, it's just a bit of a shock how much. So you'll be signed up for this Genius Academy for sure then.'

Fred nodded glumly.

CHAPTER SEVENTEEN

All and not Quite All

AT BREAK TIME THE three of them re-convened under the acacia tree.

'So,' said Fred, sitting down cross-legged and fixing Finn with an urgent stare. 'Did you see Triton?'

'I did,' replied Finn. He sat down and told not quite all.

'So we have to go back,' said Fred, eyes staring off into the distance.

Finn nodded. He paused for a while before saying: 'I could go back on my own. I could travel.'

'I don't think so,' said Georgie vehemently. 'Look what happened to you last time you tried.'

'What happened?' asked Fred, eyes narrowing.

'He skipped that bit,' answered Georgie. 'Go on Finn, tell him yourself.'

Finn gave a weary sigh. 'I tried to travel back from the middle of the sea, from Triton's back, but I got it wrong. I think I had a fear of getting it wrong and landing far out at sea, and that's what I did. For some reason, I couldn't make it work, couldn't travel home, though I tried time and time again. Had to swim in the end. Miles.'

'God, Finn. You could have died!' exclaimed Fred.

Finn looked down, shamed.

Fred grabbed his arm. 'Finn, you just need to practise, you know that. You were brilliant at it before. Remember the ice cream shop?'

Finn did and laughed.

'But Georgie's right,' Fred went on. 'You're not going alone. We'll all go, won't we George?'

'Bet on it,' said Georgie.

'Question is, how'll we do it?' mused Fred, rubbing his hands together in fierce concentration. 'I don't think I can persuade my parents to do another camping trip so soon, and I'm not sure we can afford to wait for the weekend either.'

'I might be able to persuade my parents to take us this weekend,' said Georgie, 'but I agree with you. It's too long to wait. By then this could all be....' she waved her arm in an arc encompassing the school and all the pupils in it.

'A raging inferno,' said Finn grimly.

Chapter Eighteen

Vlad, the Skinhead

THE SCHOOL BELL EXUBERANTLY rang out the end of the day, but not for Fred and Finn.

Miss Roose approached them wearing her special smile.

'Finn, Fred, there is going to be a special meeting taking place in five minutes. Quite an honour and-'

'Mr Slavel told us,' said Finn slightly sullenly. He was feeling claustrophobic, desperate to get out of school and try to figure out what to do about the Phoenix.

'Oh, shirty, shirty Finn Kennedy,' teased Miss Roose, turning to Georgie. 'Your mother has asked if you could spend the next forty minutes in the library as the twins are going on a play date, then she'll pick you and Finn up at the same time.'

Georgie nodded. She'd expected this. 'Sure,' she said, gathering up her backpack and following Finn and Fred out of the door.

'Good luck, geniuses,' she said to them both as she peeled off towards the library.

Finn growled back at her. 'You know where we'd rather be.'

'I do. I'm just fed up that we have to waste time when...'

'Let's try to get to school extra early tomorrow,' said Fred. 'If we all try to think up a plan tonight we can discuss it then.'

'Done,' chorused Finn and Georgie.

The library was empty save Miss Brydie, the Librarian. She was known as Barn Owl - her huge round glasses slid down her hooked nose and made her appear like one of the friendlier birds of prey.

Georgie nodded to Barn Owl and sloped off towards the section where the recipe books were kept. She sat down on a beanbag with a cookbook, pondering whether there was any point in planning to make iced ginger cake when there might be no one left alive to eat it.

She flung it to her side angrily.

'Ow!' said a voice. Georgie jumped and swung round in alarm.

Vlad, the new boy who had started in their class at the beginning of term, was standing behind her, rubbing his ankle.

'Where the heck did you materialise from?' demanded Georgie. 'I thought I was alone in here.' Instinctively, she inched back away from him. There was something sinister about Vlad. His skinhead haircut exposed a skull hazed with blue veins and emphasised his dark, probing eyes.

'I was looking at the picture of the iced gingerbread,' Vlad answered, his eyes suddenly wistful, not quite answering Georgie's question. 'My mother used to make it for me.'

Something in the way he said it made Georgie think his mother must be dead.

Georgie studied him hard for a moment. She glimpsed a flash of vulnerability that made him seem slightly less sinister. 'It's not hard to make,' she said. 'You could do it yourself.'

He gave a snort. 'I don't think so.'

'Why not? Please don't tell me, boys don't cook and all that rubbish. They eat, don't they?'

'Try telling that to my father. In his world, boys definitely don't cook.'

'Women or maids do all that sort of thing, I suppose,' said Georgie sarcastically.

Vlad grinned, showing dazzling white teeth. Shark's teeth, thought Georgie.

'What're you doing here?' Vlad asked.

Georgie sighed. She got up from her beanbag and moved towards the bookshelves, hoping Vlad would take the hint and leave her alone.

'Too thick and untalented to be part of this Genius programme,' she answered acidly. 'Waiting for my cousin, Finn.'

'The swimmer!' exclaimed Vlad, his whole face brightening. 'He is brilliant. I saw him in the pool last week.'

Georgie nodded. 'Certainly is,' she answered with pride. 'Why're you here?'

'My father has something he has to do and I have to wait,' he shrugged, as if his father's movements were immutable as laws of nature.

Georgie's instant dislike for Vlad's father deepened.

'D'you play chess?' asked Vlad.

Georgie nodded. 'I do actually. My father taught me.'

'Fancy a game?' Vlad asked, a devilish glint in his eye.

Georgie was just about to decline politely when Vlad added:

'You'll be beaten, I have to warn you. I'm Russian. It's in my blood. And I'm good too.'

'Really?' asked Georgie. 'Well, I'm prepared to take that risk, if you are.'

Vlad gave a smirk as if it were no risk at all. He hurried off to get a board and pieces. He set up the game on the floor. and pulled over another beanbag.

'Black or white?' he asked.

'White of course,' Georgie answered.

'Why of course?'

Because I'm a LightFighter, she thought. She said: 'So I get to go first.'

'No prob. I prefer black anyway.'

I'll bet you do, thought Georgie.

They played so intently for the next thirty minutes that Georgie forgot she was meant to be meeting Finn and Fred outside the Achievement Centre. She also forgot her initial repugnance towards Vlad.

'Checkmate!' she proclaimed with a triumphal smile, moving her queen dramatically into position just as Finn and Fred came into the library to search for her.

Vlad shouted out something in Russian and knocked over his king. Georgie saw in his eyes a flash of fury, driven off by a sudden grin. 'Nobody beats me,' he said with a look of admiration. 'How'd you do it?'

Georgie grinned back. 'Perhaps I should be in that genius class after all.'

'C'mon Georgie. Your Mum'll be waiting,' said Finn, casting a glance at Vlad. The smile had gone now and Vlad had fallen silent. He sat, unnaturally still, thought Finn.

'Gotta go. Thanks for the game,' said Georgie.

Vlad saluted in reply, eyes returning Finn's probing stare.

Georgie waved back and walked out with Finn and Fred.

'Very chummy,' said Finn as they rounded the corner and trotted down the stairs.

'Just killing time,' replied Georgie.
'Something funny about him,' pronounced Fred.

CHAPTER NINETEEN

A Shocking ᔓ Discovery

THE NEXT MORNING, AS planned, Finn and Georgie managed to get to school a full twelve minutes early. Fred was already sitting under their acacia tree beside the cricket pitch, staring into space.

'I was thinking,' announced Fred as Georgie and Finn sat down cross-legged opposite him, 'that if we-'

Fred's next words were lost in the roar of rotor blades. They all looked up as a helicopter approached fast and low. It seemed to be heading straight for them.

They watched in amazement as it slowed to a hover, just thirty yards from them. The air screamed as its blades sliced through it and Georgie's hair streamed back horizontally from her face as if she were caught in a hurricane. The helicopter descended slowly, landing in the middle of the cricket pitch.

The blades slowed to a halt, a door opened and two figures emerged. One was Vlad.

He stalked from the helicopter like a princeling. They turned their gaze to the man walking beside him.

They gasped in shock. It was the Phoenix.

They all instinctively got to their feet and stood numb, mouths open as the Phoenix and Vlad walked towards them. They couldn't speak, or move.

Finn's thoughts whirled wildly in his head. Had the Phoenix seen them in the Fire Ark? Did he somehow know who they were? Was the man coming to kill them now, here at school? No, he couldn't be, not in front of Vlad, in front of all the other witnesses arriving at school, milling around, eyes on the spectacle of the helicopter and its occupants. Finn held his breath and kept his eyes riveted on the man. He walked like a panther, lithe, sinuous and predatory. The hairs on the back of Finn's neck stood up.

Vlad gave an infinitesimal nod of acknowledgment as they approached.

'Hi,' he said.

Fred gulped. 'Er, hi Vlad,' he managed to say.

Georgie smiled but remained speechless.

'Hi Vlad,' said Finn. His nose twitched. The Phoenix was wearing that aftershave again, so strong it was like a punch to the nose, but there was something else, another smell that was vaguely familiar.

The Phoenix bestowed upon them a smile as might be given by a King to a lowly subject.

They did not smile back.

Finn kept his eyes riveted on the Phoenix. The man paused, just for a fraction and his eyes locked onto Finn's. Finn felt a massive jolt like lightning running through his veins. He stared back into the glittering eyes. Just for a second, the Phoenix's mask of sociability slipped and Finn saw, blazing beneath, a cold, implacable evil. This man was a killer. Not just by pushing a button, but with his own hands. Finn saw murder in his eyes, the echo of murders past and the threat of murder to come. Then the Phoenix looked away, took Vlad by the arm and prowled off.

'Flipping heck!' said Georgie, after they'd passed.

'God!' exclaimed Fred.

Finn blew out a long breath, not conscious that he had been holding it since he'd first seen the Phoenix.

'Well, at least now we know who he is,' said Finn. 'I have something to tell Triton.'

'Poor Vlad, to have a father like that,' said Georgie. 'At least, I'm assuming he's his father.'

'They look alike,' said Finn. 'Same black eyes and white skin and long nose.'

'Perhaps he's the same inside,' suggested Fred. 'Like father like son.'

'I wonder,' countered Georgie. 'Vlad feels different.'

'But then we haven't seen much of him, have we?' Fred pointed out. 'He keeps himself to himself. We never seem to see him around the playground.'

'So we get to know him a bit better,' said Georgie. 'Starting now. And, as it happens, thanks to Nigella, I think may have the perfect way in.' Finn and Fred frowned in puzzlement.

Georgie got up, shouldered her rucksack and ambled over to the water dispenser where Vlad was drinking thirstily. The Phoenix himself, had disappeared.

Finn watched Georgie go. His skin was prickling with sweat, all his senses still screaming the nearness of danger.

CHAPTER TWENTY

⤳ What the Seer Saw ⤳

'COOL HELICOPTER,' SAID GEORGIE. Vlad looked up questioningly, as if testing her words.

' 'S OK.'

'Beats my school run. You'll never get stuck in traffic.'

'True.'

'So where d'you fly from then? Hardly worth it from Jumeirah or Um Suquem.'

'No, it wouldn't be.'

'Springs? Meadows? Silicon Oasis?' asked Georgie, pouring herself a water.

'Yeah, out that way,' replied Vlad.

Georgie fumbled in her rucksack. She took out what looked like a foil-wrapped brick and handed it to Vlad.

He took it with a questioning look.

'Open it,' said Georgie.

Vlad looked at the silver foil suspiciously.

'It's not a bomb,' laughed Georgie.

Vlad peeled back the foil then looked up at Georgie with a huge grin.

'Ginger cake! Iced ginger cake!' He looked utterly amazed. 'You made it yourself?'

'I like to cook,' said Georgie. 'Made a big one last

night. This is half.'

'Thank you,' said Vlad. 'I, er, I, I'm going to have some now,' he announced, breaking off a bit and popping it into his mouth.

'That is delicious,' he mumbled, taking another bite.

Georgie smiled. 'So, tell me, have you just moved to Dubai?'

Vlad shook his head. 'Lived here a year.'

'So where d'you go to school before?'

'Nelson,' answered Vlad, curtly. 'Not enough music,' he added quickly as Georgie started to frame her next question. 'My father wants me to play well. Piano and violin.'

'That was your father who just arrived with you?' asked Georgie, wishing for his sake that it weren't.

'Of course. Who else would it be?'

'Sorry. Being thick.'

'Not so thick at chess,' said Vlad.

'True,' replied Georgie with a smile.

The morning bell rang out in one long, hysterically insistent screech. 'Better get to class,' said Vlad. He bent down to pick up his rucksack. As he was pulling it on, his sleeves rode up and Georgie saw a vivid burn on his wrist.

'Gosh, that looks bad,' said Georgie. 'Shouldn't it be dressed?'

'It's just a burn. It's nothing,' Vlad snapped in a rapid change of mood. Before Georgie could say anything else, he jogged away.

Finn and Fred headed across the Astroturf towards Georgie. As they did so, they noticed The Phoenix, emerging from the school buildings deep in conversation with Mr Slavel, who was sporting a brown felt cowboy hat. Mr Slavel was scanning the playground, seemingly pointing out various pupils to The Phoenix, who turned his dark eyes upon each of them in turn.

'What're they up to,' mused Fred.

Finn watched for a moment. 'Slavel seems to be pointing out some of the guys from the Excellence Academy.'

'Probably showing The Phoenix who his son has to compete with,' suggested Fred.

'Yeah, bit embarrassing if you're a megalomaniac planning world domination and your son is just normal, isn't it,' said Finn.

Mr Slavel caught sight of Fred and Finn. He gave a choppy wave, half salute to them and said something to the Phoenix. Finn felt the Phoenix's eyes on him and again he felt a jolt. He glared back, pulse hammering in his head. For a long time the Phoenix stared at him. Finn felt his head begin to throb.

'He's a Seer,' groaned Finn, grabbing his head. 'He's getting inside my head.' Finn fought to resist him, filling his mind with images of the school swimming pool. He imagined swimming length after length, up and down, blocking out all other thought. Still he felt his head throb as the Phoenix poked and probed. He desperately tried to keep from his mind the Fire Ark and what he had seen and heard there. If the Phoenix found out…The image of the pool wobbled as if The Phoenix were pushing it aside. Finn's head felt like it was about to explode. The pain was blinding, robbing him of all control. He fell to the ground, grasping his head in his hands.

Mr Slavel let out a cry of alarm and yanked the Phoenix's arm, forcing him to turn his attention away from Finn.

The pressure on Finn's head ceased abruptly. Fred crouched down beside him.

'Finn! Finn, God, what- aargh,' gasped Fred, clutching his own head.

'He's doing it to me too.'

'Let's get out of sight,' grunted Finn, pushing himself to his feet. 'Quickly. He's too strong.'

They rushed into the nearest building - the gymnasium. Finn dropped down on an exercise mat, rubbing his hammering head.

'Are you all right?' asked Fred, sitting down beside Finn and peering worriedly at his friend.

'My head was burning. The pain, it was almost unbearable.'

'Is it better now?'

'Yeah, I've just got a normal headache now, but it's too late, the damage is done.'

'What damage?'

'I tried so hard to block him,' said Finn, biting back despair.

Fred paled. 'What did he See in your head?'

'I don't know. I tried just to think of swimming, but at the end he was pushing so hard and the image of the Fire Ark came into my head just as Slavel yanked his arm and he looked away. I don't know if he saw it,' Finn added miserably. 'I can't be sure.' He gazed up at Fred, fear flickering in his eyes.

'You tried to block him. You put up a hell of a fight, Finn. But he knows now that you have power. That you are not a normal boy. And if he did See the image of his Fire Ark in your mind, if he knows you know....' faltered Fred.

'He will seek me out and he will kill me,' said Finn. 'And anyone else he thinks I might have told which means you and your parents and Georgie and her family.'

Chapter Twenty One

❧ Trapped in the Fire ❧

FINN AND FRED, BOTH looking pale, took their seats in class just as Miss Roose was about to close the door and mark them down as late. This year, after multiple requests from his parents and much lobbying of Mr Strummer, Fred had changed classes and was now, to his delight, in with Finn and Georgie.

Georgie glanced across at them both, one eyebrow raised in silent question.

'Later,' mouthed Finn.

Fred sat at a table behind Vlad. For much of the next lesson, science, Fred stared at the back of Vlad's head, trying to See inside his mind and find out if Vlad knew anything about The Fire Ark and his father's plans. Unfortunately for Fred, Vlad loved science and was concentrating fiercely on the subject in hand; the principles of flight.

At first break, Georgie collared Finn and Fred as they hurried out of the classroom.

'What happened to you two?' she asked. 'You came in late and you both looked wrecked, you specially, Finn.'

Finn blew out a breath. He'd toyed with the idea of trying to hide this from Georgie, but she had to know.

'The Phoenix is a Seer. He locked onto me. He tried to

get inside my mind and I tried to block him, but I'm not sure if I succeeded.'

'The Fire Ark?' asked Georgie in quiet horror.

'He might have Seen it in my mind. I can't be sure.'

'So what do we do?' asked Georgie, seeking as always the practical solution.

'We find out all we can about the Phoenix, using Vlad, using whatever sources we can find and we stay on total red alert,' said Finn.

'Right, let's find Vlad,' said Fred.

The three of them searched for him, but Vlad seemed to have disappeared.

'Where the heck's he gone?' asked Fred as they scouted round the Astroturf, peering through the masses of football players. The tried the cricket pitch, the Quiet Area, the Activity Area, where Fred got hit on the head by a rogue baseball.

'Maybe he has detention or something,' suggested Georgie. 'Maybe he's in the library?'

'I'll look,' said Finn, 'there's something I want to check there anyway.'

Finn glanced round the library but there was no sign of Vlad. He slipped into a chair and logged on to Google. Quickly the screen filled with print. Finn's eyes opened wide. He speed read as much as he could until the bell rang, then he ran back down to the playground and met up with Fred and Georgie as they got to class.

'There he is!' whispered Fred as they spotted Vlad sauntering in after them. 'We searched again all round the playgrounds and I checked the loos too,' he added. 'But there was no sign of him.'

Finn studied Vlad. His eyes were glazed, faraway.

'He looks like he's in a trance,' he whispered.

'Or drugged,' added Fred.

Georgie's face creased in worry. Vlad looked like a Zombie. Totally out of it.

The next lesson was literacy. Miss Roose repeatedly called on Vlad to please concentrate young man, but to no avail. She was becoming progressively shriller, when suddenly, an even shriller note silenced her; the fire alarm. All the class jumped up from their seats with expressions of excitement and panic.

'Class, please collect your backpacks quickly and follow me in an orderly line. No running, just walk calmly please,' intoned Miss Roose, all calmness when faced with a real emergency.

'Is it a fire drill? Miss Roose?' asked Georgie, following her out of the door.

'Possibly,' came the curt answer.

Once outside, at the emergency assembly point on the football pitch, they heard the sirens of approaching fire engines, screaming like banshees.

Miss Roose urgently shouted out the class register. All twenty six children shouted back.

'All present and accounted for. Thank God for that,' said Miss Roose.

'What's the drama?' said Karl, one of the Year Six boys.

'That is,' answered Tamer Said, one of the Excellence Academy students, pointing to the west side of the gym.

Then they saw the smoke, drifting lazily in the breeze. Within half a minute, the idle tendrils had turned to billowing gusts. Threading through the black smoke clouds, hissing and writhing like snakes, were flames. They grew hungrily into a writhing mass of fire. Finn, Fred and

Georgie watched, transfixed. They could hear the fire roar. It sounded like some ravening, terrifying beast.

There seemed to be a face, thought Finn, slit eyes, a mouth. It formed, disappeared, formed, disappeared. Stayed. Finn tensed becoming hyper-aware. Then he heard, in the recesses of his mind, words, whispering like a far off wind.

Free me. Save me. Death. Burning. The Voice!

'Do you hear it?' he shouted at Fred and Georgie. He saw in their startled eyes that they did. He looked around, scanning faces left and right, but judging from their expressions, nobody else seemed to have heard anything.

Finn caught sight of the towering six foot frame of Miss Finity, their class teacher of the year before. She was standing stock still as if she had heard. She was a Light-Fighter. She too had been part of the war against Hydrus. Finn felt sure she had heard. He was just about to approach her to ask when she suddenly wheeled round and ran off towards the fire.

'Wait here,' said Finn, sprinting after her, ignoring Miss Roose's shrill cries to 'Come back here this instant young man'.

Finn caught up with Miss Finity by the side entrance to the gym.

She was trying to wrench open the door.

'There's someone inside,' she said.

'No, it's the Voice you heard. I heard it too,' said Finn.

'Exactly. There's someone in there.'

'No there isn't. It's just the Voice.'

Miss Finity shot Finn a look of sheer incomprehension. 'Finn, what the divil are you talking about? There's someone in there.'

'What did they say?' asked Finn, yanking on the door with Miss Finity. 'It's locked,' he said.

'They said 'Help me, Free me. 'They -'

She froze, from inside the gym, they both heard sobs.

'Oh my God. There is someone in there,' said Finn.

'Have you gone mad?' demanded Miss Finity. 'That's what I've been trying to tell you.'

Wafts of smoke billowed round from the front of the gym where the flames had taken hold, but now Finn saw tendrils of smoke snaking out from beneath the door in front of him.

'Why's it locked?' he asked panicked. 'The gym's never locked during the day.'

'We need to break down the door,' said Miss Finity.

The sobs stopped abruptly. 'No time,' said Finn. He thought of the stack of gym mats, just to the left of the door, where he'd been lying just an hour earlier. See Believe Launch, then he disappeared.

The gym was a smoking, stinking, burning hell. He could hardly see. His lungs burned and his throat gagged at the air he tried to breathe. He had seconds before he too would be overcome. He moved towards the flames. His eyes seemed to have cleared now and he could make out details; the wooden horse ablaze, the ropes dangling from the ceiling writhing like burning snakes, beyond them, at the opposite end of the gym, a heaving mass of flames, roaring their rage and power to the world. Then he spotted a flash of white; a school shirt, a long red plait, a body slumped on the floor. With a sound like a guncrack, the floor between him and the body burst into flames which shot ten feet into the air. You're water, Finn told himself. Pure water. He leapt through the wall of fire. He felt the searing heat, the unforgiving, horrific embrace of flame, and then he was through it to the other side. The body lay at his feet. A girl, prostrate. He gathered her up in his arms. No time to check for a pulse, to give mouth to mouth. They'd both be dead in seconds if he didn't get her out.

He stilled his roaring heart. He saw the patch of grass in the Quiet Area. He Saw, he Believed, and he and the body in his arms disappeared.

CHAPTER TWENTY TWO

❦ Pyromaniac ❧

I T WAS RANIA MANSOUR, one of the Year 5 girls. She didn't seem to be breathing. Finn sucked in a breath, bent over her, opened her mouth and blew in. He paused, blew in again, paused, blew in again, kept up the breathing, then he pressed down with both his hands on her heart; one, two three four five, then the breathing again.

Please, thought Finn, desperately, please wake up, please come back. They were quite alone, the screaming of fire engines so close, but no-one to help. Just him. Again Finn did the CPR. Nothing happened. Rania lay inert before him. In despair, Finn threw his arms to the skies. Help me, in the name of Light, help me. Give me all my powers, here now. Let me save her. He brought his arms down, pumped her chest one more time, leaned down to blow in a breath, when the air was sucked from his lips.

Rania opened her eyes and breathed. Finn raised his eyes to the heavens. Thank you, he mouthed. He lowered his head, took Rania's hand. 'You're going to be all right,' he told her.

She gave a weak smile. Finn got to his feet. 'I'm going to get the fire brigade, they might have a paramedic with them. I'll be right back.'

Rania reached out a bony hand and grabbed his wrist.

'The skinhead,' she croaked, 'he started the fire. Saw him.'

Finn gasped. 'Did he lock you in there?'

'He lit newspapers, poured fuel out of a lighter. I was in there hiding. There's a girl, Bridget, bullies me, hits me. The skinhead didn't know I was in there -,' Rania broke off into a coughing fit. Finn rushed to the water dispenser, came back with a cup which he held gently to her lips.

Rania took a few sips then continued. 'I jumped up, said hey, what are you doing? He turned round and ran towards me. I think he meant to run past me but he crashed into me and I fell back, hit my head on the floor. That was the last thing I remember. When I came round, there was smoke everywhere.'

Fury burned its own fire within Finn. 'Let me get a paramedic,' he said, running off.

Chapter Twenty Three

⮞ Lucky Escape ⮜

THE FRONT OF THE gymnasium had collapsed and the roof was dangling at a terrifying angle. Dozens of firemen were training high powered hoses inside the gym. Finn ran up to one of them and grabbed his arm. The man looked at Finn with anger, 'Get away,' he yelled over the roar of fire and water.

'Someone was in there. She needs a paramedic,' shouted Finn.

'Where? Where?' demanded the man.

'Follow me,' roared Finn.

The fireman grabbed a colleague and ran after Finn. Finn led them to the Quiet Garden, to Rania. She was lying on the grass. She sat up and smiled at Finn.

'You'll be fine now,' he said.

The firemen crouched down and began to examine Rania.

'Right. You were in the gym? My goodness, you had a lucky escape. Let's get you up, get you to hospital.' The fireman spoke into his mouthpiece.

'Ambulance. Now to JAM. Smoke inhalation.'

He turned back to Rania. 'How'd you get out?'

'He rescued me,' said Rania.

The fireman turned to thank the boy, but there was no sign of him. He had disappeared.

CHAPTER TWENTY FOUR

⚭ Mad or Evil ⚭

'WHERE THE HECK HAVE you been?' asked Georgie. 'You reek of smoke! Your clothes are all singed and there's a burn mark on your head!'

'Later,' said Finn in a voice Georgie had never before heard. 'What's going on?'

'Mr Strummer's parading around like a general in charge of an army,' said Fred. 'They're SMSing our parents to come and get us. School's out for the day.'

Finn felt he was operating at 200% of normal. The blood still powered round his veins, adrenaline burned in his body. And rage, a pure, white hot rage like none he had ever felt before. But his thoughts were clear, his mind felt radiant. He turned to Georgie and Fred.

'I've got an idea.'

He quickly whispered it quickly. Georgie's eyes widened with shock.

'Great idea!' said Fred. 'Let's do it.'

'I don't like it, Finn,' whispered Georgie.

'It's our best chance Georgie, come on. Please,' urged Fred.

'And if the Phoenix knows we know about him, it might be our only chance,' added Finn.

Georgie thought for a while, of her parents, of her sisters, of home, and of a rampaging fire, razing all before it. She turned back to Fred.

'All right. Go for it.'

Finn put his arm round his cousin and squeezed her shoulder.

Fred nodded at her with a sad smile. He pulled his new mobile from his pocket, the one wrecked by the vision was beyond repair, and called his mother.

'Hi Mum?' Fred shouted to be heard above the sirens of more fire engines arriving. 'You got the text? Good. Yeah. I'm fine, really, don't worry. Look, is it all right if I go home with Finn and Georgie? Their mum is already on the way, and she'll take me back. She says I can have a sleepover. Please Mum? Great. Thanks Mum. You're the best. Yeah. I will. You too. Bye.'

Fred clicked off with a guilty smile. He handed the phone to Georgie. 'Your turn.'

Georgie went through the same rigmarole on her and Finn's behalf, and got the same, reluctant agreement.

'She said Yes,' said Georgie, handing the phone back to Fred.

'Great,' said Fred.

Finn was shifting about, seemingly searching for someone. His eyes roved like lasers through the assembled crowd.

'How will Rooster release us when none of our parents turn up?' asked Fred. Finn seemed not be listening.

Georgie smiled. 'Like this.'

She waited until there was a milling crowd of parents.

'Miss Roose,' she called, waving at an approaching man who looked vaguely like her own father. 'There's my father. He's come to pick up me and Finn and Fred. Can we go now?'

Miss Roose glanced at the approaching man. 'Sure, sure, you can. Is that your father? He looks diff -'

'Miss Roose!' interrupted Felicia, an extremely nervous blonde from their class. 'There's my Mum! There's my Mum. I must....'

Georgie grabbed Finn and together with Fred they quietly slipped away. The man approaching gave Georgie a quizzical look before he picked up his son from a neighbouring group of children, but by that time, Miss Roose's attention was firmly occupied by the blessed Felicia.

'We can't just walk out onto the street,' whispered Finn. 'There're bound to be some teachers on guard by the gates and if they see us leaving without parents we'll be toast. Let's scoot round and hide in the cricket pavilion. We'll leave when no-one's around.'

The doors were open and it was easy to dash in and slide down out of sight onto the floor.

'So what happened?' Georgie asked Finn.

In brief, staccato sentences, Finn told her and Fred. He could scarcely speak when he told them what Rania had taught them about Vlad.

'So Vlad set the fire, then left Rania in there to burn?' asked Georgie, her voice a whisper of horror.

'Knocked her out first,' said Finn.

'Which makes it murder,' said Fred, ''cos you said the doors were locked,' he added to Finn.

'The side one was. The main one was where the fire was, so who knows? But murder is what it looks like,' he added. 'When I find Vlad......' said Finn, his jaw clenched.

'You'll do what?' asked Georgie. 'Kill him in front of everyone and end up in prison?'

'You think he doesn't deserve it?' snapped Finn. 'You didn't see Rania lying there.' He didn't tell them that he was sure she had actually been dead at that point.

'No, I didn't,' said Georgie softly, 'but we have to be smart, Finn. Find out, then act.'

Finn brooded, eyes still dark with fury. 'Hm,' was all he said. He took his water bottle from his backpack, drained it, then scrunched it up.

He glanced at his friends who were watching him concernedly. Thank God for them both, he thought to himself. He blew out a huge breath.

'I found out something interesting in the library,' he said, his voice sober once again. 'I googled The Phoenix. I found him quickly enough. There was a ton of stuff about him. Mentions his only child, Vlad, and his wife, Daria who apparently lives in Jumeirah, not somewhere out in the desert. So parents divorced I guess, and Vlad lives with his father, not his mother. But, get this. Mr Czarovich, AKA The Phoenix is a billionaire, from Russia. Made his fortune there in oil and construction. One of the things that he builds is huge underground oil storage bunkers. He's already built one in Kazakhstan, one in Iran and another one in Kuwait. Apparently he is close to finishing another one in the deserts of Dubai.'

'God,' said Georgie. 'so he's probably got disciples round the world, ready to set their fires and retreat underground.'

'Possibly,' replied Finn. 'or perhaps the other bunkers are just that. Storage for oil. A cover for the human bunker he's built here.'

'I think that's exactly what he's done,' said Fred. 'It's brilliant, in a kind of sick way.'

Minutes passed, then, suddenly, there came the sound of a helicopter approaching. They peeked out of the window and saw it set down on the cricket pitch just ten yards from their hiding place.

The Phoenix stepped from the machine and stared at the clouds of billowing smoke. His face was set in pure rage.

Vlad broke away from a knot of other children and ran towards his father. Finn watched Vlad, eyes dark with hate. Georgie saw Finn's eyes, recoiled with shock.

She turned back to watch Vlad, who was ducking and trying to pass his father to get into the helicopter. The Phoenix intercepted his son, grabbed him by the wrist and shook him. Vlad's face contorted in pain.

'The burn,' said Georgie, 'he's grabbing Vlad's burn.'

The Phoenix pointed to the smoke clouds, then yanked his son around and dragged him into the helicopter. Seconds later, they were gone.

'Yeah. What was all that about?' asked Fred.

'Vlad has a burn on his arm,' said Georgie. 'His father must have known about it but he deliberately grabbed it. Vlad looked in agony.'

'Why was he so angry with Vlad?' asked Fred.

'Because he guessed that Vlad set the fire. Like father like son,' answered Finn. 'Pyromaniacs, both.'

'It can't be the start of the huge fire, can it?' asked Georgie suddenly.

Finn shook his head. 'I don't think so. That's why his father was so furious. It wasn't part of the Plan.'

'How can he just come to school, walk around, pretend everything is normal when his father is planning to burn everyone to a cinder, all except the Chosen Ones?' demanded Fred.

'Either because he doesn't know, or because he is just as evil and mad as his father,' answered Finn. 'Take your pick.'

Chapter Twenty Five

∽ School's Out! ∽

THEY SLUNK CAREFULLY FROM school, hurried through the side streets past villas like small Italianate palaces with gleaming stucco and golden domes, past construction sites billowing with sand and diesel fumes, past ordered rows of palm trees standing sentinel like guards outside the houses they decorated. In four minutes they were on Al Wasl Road, eyeing up the taxis shooting past. Finally, Finn saw what he wanted and flagged one down. The three of them hopped in quickly and Georgie reeled off the directions.

The driver didn't question them about why they were not at school in the middle of the morning, and Finn took encouragement from that.

The taxi pulled up outside a garage on a quiet, palm-lined street just off Al Thanya. The garage belonged to friends of Georgie's parents who used it to store odds and ends - a dinghy, and Georgie's, Finn's and Fred's quad bikes and the trailer used to transport them.

Finn asked the driver to wait while he and Georgie and Fred unlocked the padlock, luckily a combination lock, not a key, and entered the garage. They closed the door quickly behind them.

'We need clothes, money, food and water,' said Finn. 'I'm going to see if I can travel back home and get us some.'

'What if your Aunt happens to be in?' asked Fred, 'and you crash land in front of her. She'll have a heart attack.'

'Mum's tougher than she looks, Fred,' interjected Georgie. 'But listen, I think she'll be at Spinneys, shopping. Go for it Finn. Just try and land on your beanbag.'

'I'll do my best.'

Rescuing Rania had given him confidence. He did believe. He saw the beanbag, bright orange and blue stripes. He imagined landing softly on its huge, yielding mass, then he gathered himself together, every fibre and sinew and particle of energy that he was, and he launched himself into the ether.

Fred and Georgie felt a suck in the air, then there was silence. They sat down on the floor of the garage to wait. Neither spoke, they were too immersed in their own thoughts. The minutes ticked past tortuously slowly and Georgie began to worry. What if her mother had been in, and Finn had landed in front of her?

Suddenly the air shimmered and then with a whoop, Finn landed before them, crouched on all fours like a cat, his backpack stuffed to overflowing.

He jumped up and grinned at them.

'I made it,' he said, 'landed right on my beanbag. Got clothes for you both,' he said, pulling stuff from his backpack. 'Snuck down to the kitchen and got water, crisps, the gingercake you made last night, George, and Fred, your favourite, pot noodles.'

'Oh no, not those. Not again,' wailed Fred between gusts of laughter. He and Finn had survived for days on nothing but Pot Noodles and chocolate three months earlier on Bone Island.

'For Old Times' sake,' laughed Finn. 'C'mon. Let's get changed. I'll bet that old taxi driver out there's getting impatient by now.'

Georgie and Fred changed into the jeans and trainers Finn had brought for them, and Georgie pulled on her long sleeved t shirt.

'Er, did you bring a t shirt for me?' Fred asked.

'Yep,' replied Finn. 'Should be in here.' He rummaged around. 'It's not here. God, I wonder where it's gone?'

'It's probably somewhere between here and home, floating down on some bewildered cyclist,' mused Georgie, and they all collapsed in laughter again. Anything, thought Georgie, to distract themselves from what they were about to do.

CHAPTER TWENTY SIX

The Park and Shop Mystery

THE TAXI DRIVER DID not look too happy about having a trailer loaded with quad bikes hooked up to his car and driving three children off into the desert, but Finn had raided his piggy bank and the sight of the crisp notes bought the driver's acquiescence.

'Er, Driver, could you go via Park and Shop on Al Wasl Road, please?' asked Fred.

'What?' asked Georgie and Finn in unison.

'It'll take five minutes,' said Fred. 'Trust me.'

'What could we possibly need in Park and Shop?' asked Georgie.

'Wait and see.'

The taxi driver pulled up at Park and Shop and Fred nipped inside wearing a mysterious smile. He came out five minutes later with a plastic bag which he grasped firmly in his hand.

'C'mon, what's in it?' asked Finn.

'Fancy a Mars Bar?' asked Fred, by way of an answer, pulling out three.

'Thanks,' said Georgie and Finn taking one each. 'And what else?' quizzed Georgie.

'Patience,' replied Fred, to a chorus of groans.

One hour and one hundred and fifty Dirhams later, the taxi driver deposited the three children, their trailer and their three quad bikes in the middle of the desert.

'How long will you be?' asked the driver. 'An hour? I can wait for an hour, but more than that and I will be hungry. My shift finishes too and I must sleep.'

Finn took out a five hundred dirham note and showed it to the driver.

'Come back to this exact spot at three a.m., drive us back to Umm Suqueim and this is yours.'

'What on earth will you be doing in the desert until three in the morning?' asked the driver.

'It's a dare,' replied Finn.

The driver seemed to agonise over this for a while.

'Your parents. What would they say?'

'They won't find out,' replied Finn. 'Not if you are here at three a.m. to bring us home.'

The taxi driver looked distinctly unhappy.

'Have you never done something your parents didn't know about, wouldn't have approved of?' asked Finn.

The taxi driver broke into a grin. 'Many, many times,' he admitted.

'Then, please. Help us. It's important,' said Finn.

Something in the urgency of his eyes must have moved the driver, for the man slowly nodded his assent.

'Three a.m sharp. Please,' said Finn, wondering if he'd ever see the taxi driver again.

CHAPTER TWENTY SEVEN

Kingdom of the Sands

THE SOUND OF THE taxi dissipated in the sand and then the desert rang with silence. They were half a mile from the tarmacked road at the end of a rough desert track. Half a mile and a thousand years from the twenty first century, marooned in time in the harshly beautiful kingdom of the sands. Skeletons of dead trees lay strewn around, casualties of the heat. The dunes reared up, witness to the power of the winds, and in the distance, blue-grey like phantoms, rose up the craggy mountains of the Jebel Hafeet.

'First off, let's cover the trailer,' said Finn, to groans from Fred and Georgie.

'Yes, yes, I know what happened last time we didn't cover our tracks,' said Fred. 'We'll do it. We'll do it. But with what? The desert's not exactly thick with foliage.'

'Look around,' replied Finn, gesturing. Fred and Georgie gazed about them, turning in slow circles. It was odd, but when you looked, really looked, signs of life abounded; green shoots strove up triumphantly through the sand and scrubby bushes dotted the sandscape.

They divided up and got to work covering the trailer. But doing it took some time, many curses and many pricked fingers from the thorny shrubs.

Finally the trailer was disguised.

'Er, one thing we didn't discuss,' said Fred, 'was how to find our way without a GPS.'

Finn had been worrying about just that. 'I have a fair idea of where our camp was. Let's get there first, then we're going to have to rely on instinct to find the Fire Ark.' Like finding one specific grain of sand in a desert of trillions, a doubting voice said in his head. Finn silenced the voice and yanked on his helmet.

Georgie and Fred followed suit then the three of them mounted their quad bikes. Finn said a quick prayer and set off, followed by Georgie, with Fred at the back.

Tearing over the dunes, dipping, swooping and sliding on a schoolday, with the sun high in a dazzling sky and a breeze cooling their faces was pure bliss, whatever was to happen next. Each of them relished the freedom. Each of them relished the beauty, told themselves to look at it, really look at it, as if for the last time.

For Fred it was the sky that did it; the huge blue expanse, stretching out forever into the infinity of space. For Finn it was the endless miles of sand, shimmering with heat, rising and falling like some golden sea. For Georgie, it was the falcon that soared above them, wheeling and diving in the ecstasy of flight.

Finn found the spot where they had camped. He dismounted, removed his helmet and blew out a massive breath of relief. He leaned back against his quad surveying the surrounding dunes.

'What d'you reckon?' he asked Fred and Georgie, who had parked up beside him.

'Since we got royally lost last time, hard to say,' replied Fred.

Georgie thought for a while, her face pinched in concentration. 'We saw the sunrise. The camp was west of it, a bit north too.'

'Brilliant,' said Finn. He glanced at the compass on his watch. 'Good job I didn't bring this camping or it'd have been fried too.' He scanned the dunes again and pointed out a route.

He turned to Fred. 'What d'you reckon?'

Fred thought for a moment, then nodded. 'Let's do it.'

Please let us be right, let us find it, thought Finn, as he accelerated off. If they got lost, they would likely die. If they got lost, Triton's chances of stopping the inferno would be that much slimmer. No pressure, he thought with a grim smile.

Chapter Twenty Eight

∞ The Leak ∞

THE PHOENIX SAT IN his study, staring at Van Gogh's Sunflowers which hung behind his desk. Unusually, he found no peace in the painting. He swivelled round in his chair to face the man sitting opposite him; broad-planed, tanned, with dark, probing eyes; black, shiny slicked-back hair; thick set, wrestler's muscular body emanating controlled violence. The Phoenix appraised him. Ivan Drax was a useful asset. A ruthless killer, practised, efficient and utterly merciless. He was a lethal weapon, but a potentially unpredictable one. He took commands but he was very much his own man. A man on some kind of a personal mission. That much was evident in the distant gleam in his eyes. The Phoenix did not like agendas that did not follow his own, but he had a strange sense, half subconscious, half the indistinct stirrings of memory, that in this case, Drax's hidden agenda might tally very much with his own.

'There has been a leak,' announced the Phoenix. 'A boy, a mere boy knows. Not an ordinary boy, admittedly. This one has power, but still, he knows and that cannot be allowed.'

Drax stiffened. His eyes gleamed with a dark hunger.

'Would you like me to kill him?'

'No. I would like you to kidnap him and bring him to me. I shall find out what else he knows and whom he has told, even if I have to fry his brain to a cinder to do so.'

Drax nodded. 'How did you find out that this boy knows?'

'Sheer luck, coincidence, the guiding hand of fate looking after me, call it what you will. I saw him at Vladimir's school. I sensed his power, considerable for a boy so young, and I became curious. I peered into his mind. He fought me, immediately. He tried very hard to resist, but of course he failed, as everyone does. I Saw what he was so desperately trying to hide. I Saw my Fire Ark. He knows.' The Phoenix's eyes hardened. 'I have no idea how he knows. It's possible Vlad told him, but then Vlad is not supposed to know. I shall have to find my son and See into his mind too,' he added with grim intent.

Drax sat deathly still. His eyes glittered with a strange anticipation. Could it be, could it really be?'

'What is the boy's name?' he asked.

The growl in his voice made the Phoenix eye him sharply.

'His name is Finn Kennedy.'

The effect was immediate. Pain, fury and an ice cold hatred blazed in Drax's eyes.

So I was right, thought the Phoenix. 'You know him, I take it.'

'Oh yes, I know him. My son, Dagmar, went to the same school. He went to JAM too,' he added. He did not want to reveal more, to risk the Phoenix's rescinding his command, selecting instead someone without a personal motive.

The Phoenix felt a flutter of contempt. Some petty schoolboy stuff, a place on the rugby team, a childhood slight writ large in the eyes of a dominant father. How pathetic.

'I'll get straight on it,' said Drax, rising swiftly to his feet and heading for the door.

The Phoenix froze him with a hand to his shoulder. 'Do not let your emotion carry you away. I want him alive and unharmed. Is that clear?'

'Crystal.'

'You know where he lives?'

'Oh yes, I know where he lives.'

'A quiet exfiltration. Do not kill the rest of the family unless you absolutely have to. We don't want to do anything to attract the attention of the police. With luck we shall have the boy back in his bed before anyone notices he is missing.'

'Back in bed with half his brain gone.'

The Phoenix smiled. 'As good as dead, would you not agree?'

Dead with a knife wielded by his own hands would be better, thought Drax. 'If he saw the Fire Ark, perhaps he has gone all the way through?' he suggested.

'If he has then he must be supremely powerful. It's possible. If you do not find him at home, then you may go through and search there, but the same rule applies. Alive, not dead. Now go. Make haste. Take a helicopter.'

Vlad, who had been eavesdropping at the door, bolted down the corridor on silent feet and hid in a loo. He cracked the door open an inch and watched the man pass. He shuddered. He could feel the violence and the hatred rising from him like heat.

Alone in his study, the Phoenix picked up the phone. 'We need to bring Operation Phoenix forward. Call all the Chosen Ones. Get them here tomorrow.' He laid the phone back softly in its cradle. Nothing and no-one would interfere with his plans.

Chapter Twenty Nine

∞ The Hissing ∞

THEY FOUND IT! THE Fire Ark! Miracle of miracles they found it straight away, guided by luck or fate, Finn didn't know.

They parked up about a quarter of a mile from where they had last left their quads, screened from the house and the bunker by three large banks of dunes. They turned off their engines and immediately set to covering the quads with whatever branches and foliage they could find.

'Great,' said Finn as they finished up. 'Let's have something to ea-'

The roar of helicopter engines starting up cut off his words.

'Quick, get under the quads,' urged Finn. They scraped themselves under, huddling amidst the thorny leaves, praying that the helicopter would not fly over head. They heard it coming closer, the engines roaring. It got closer still. Finn prayed that whoever was in it did not look down.

Ivan Drax, sitting in the helicopter, thanked the Dark Gods of fate. The revenge he craved was within his grasp. He rested his head against the headrest and smiled. In his mind's eye he saw Finn Kennedy. He planned, in painstaking detail, just what he would do. His eyes skimmed over the desert below. He saw the clumps of bushes, odd shapes, he thought, but so pre-occupied was he, so strong was his blood-lust, that he did not give them another thought.

On the ground, under the quads, seconds passed agonisingly slowly. Finally the roaring of the engines eased as the helicopter passed, some way away. Finn, Fred and Georgie stayed motionless until the noise faded, then slowly, they emerged from the thorns.

'Phew! That was close,' said Fred.

'Too close,' agreed Finn. 'I wonder who was in it?' he asked, giving an involuntary shudder.

'Who knows?' said Georgie. 'Who cares? They've gone, thank goodness. Now let's eat. We're going to need all our strength.'

Finn dug supplies out of his backpack. They sat cross-legged on the sand and ate some pot noodles and ginger cake, slurped down lots of water, and settled down to wait for the cover of night.

As the sun dipped lower their shadows lengthened and each individual ripple of sand was delineated by shadow as if some invisible hand had etched each one in black ink. Minutes passed with the only sound the singing of the wind.

Fred scooped up handsful of sand and let it run through his fingers like lost seconds. He examined the sand before letting it fall; so many colours; grains of gold, black, white, terracotta, straw, all blending together to a pale honey.

Finn sat motionless and listened to the whisperings of the wind. He lay back on the dunes to gaze up at the sky, and soon he found himself nodding off. With calculated stealth, the strange hissing sound insinuated its way into his head. The sound of his nightmares. The hissing became words, people speaking. Finn fought back, dragged himself from the nightmare and sat up with a shout.

Georgie gripped his arm. 'You all right?' she asked worriedly.

'Fine. Just a nightmare,' he said, resolving to stay awake. He ate another piece of ginger cake, grateful for the sugar high. Eyes wide open, he stared into the night.

As the minutes turned to hours the wind increased in speed and it sounded to Finn as though it were screaming in from the faraway sea. The wind drove the sand from the tops of the dunes and it blew down in plumes like snow off a mountain top. It flowed too down the sides of the dunes, like evil vapours slithering towards them. An avalanche waiting to engulf them. In spite of the heat, Finn shivered.

The sun set in a ball of fire. Slivers of red arrows shot out from where the sun had disappeared and the light began to die.

Georgie gazed fascinated by a formation of sand rocks that looked like the ruins of a lost village. She knew they were just constructs of the wind and occasional rain, but she passed the time inventing lives for the people who might have lived there. Suddenly, she froze. A snatch of conversation had just drifted to her as if on the wind. She quickly looked around, eyes searching the darkness, but there was no sign of anyone.

'What's up?' whispered Finn.

'Just thought I heard something. Words drifting, but can't see anyone. It wasn't the Voice this time. It was different. Two people, talking.'

Finn frowned into the darkness, eyes raking back and forth. 'It's funny, I thought I heard something too, when

I fell asleep. Words just cutting through the air, no-one around.'

'It was almost like tuning in to a radio frequency,' said Georgie, 'picking up a station and losing it again. That's what it felt like.'

Not to me, thought Finn. He felt that he was being forcibly invaded by the hissing and the words.

'I'm obviously on the wrong frequency,' said Fred, 'cos I didn't hear a thing.'

They all lapsed back into silence, listening for voices in the ether, hearing nothing save the screaming of the wind.

The darkness deepened. Finn glanced at his watch. Eight o' clock.

He turned to Georgie and Fred.

'You ready?'

Ready to go, thought Fred, ready to rescue, ready to spy. Ready to die. He nodded. Georgie gave a grim smile.

Together, moving in single file, they set off into the night, climbing and descending the dunes, their way lit by the moon and starlight a billion light years old.

What would those stars illuminate in a month?, Georgie wondered. The glory of the desert at night, or the smoke from the funeral pyre of a planet?

CHAPTER THIRTY

Secret Entrance

ONCE MORE, THE HOUSE shone like a beacon in the night, but this time there were no helicopters shattering the silence of the night, no cavalcades of Hummers queuing for entry to the road to hell. But there was one helicopter, glowing white, sitting on a circle of tarmac off to the side of the house.

'Daddy's home,' whispered Finn ironically.

Georgie gazed across at the house from their hiding place behind the clump of scrub. She froze as she saw the figure of Vlad pass before a window.

'So's his son.'

Finn tensed as visions of Rania's body swam before his eyes.

Georgie felt the cold fury pouring from her cousin.

'Remember what we're here for,' she said gently.

'I won't forget,' said Finn, glancing at her, murder in his eyes.

'Finn, get a grip. You're not a cold-blooded killer. You're a child of the Light, not of Darkness.'

'I know that George,' Finn replied, voice sombre. 'I'll do what I have to do.'

They huddled in their hiding place, waiting and

watching. No cars came or went. No rubbish lorries. At nine sharp they watched two guards with sub-machine guns slung over their shoulders emerge from a small, square building a hundred yards away. The guards walked round the house and up to the gaping mouth of the bunker, then they ambled into the desert, flicking torch beams like probing fingers over the sleeping dunes. After fifteen minutes of patrolling, they went back into their guard house.

An hour later, on the hour, the guards emerged and repeated their patrol. Still no cars came, no trucks.

Finn looked at his watch, glowing accusingly in the darkness.

'Ten fifteen. We're wasting time. I don't think we're going to get in the same way as last time.' He paused. 'Shall we try and Travel?'

'We're rubbish at it, you know that,' answered Georgie. 'But might as well try,' she added.

'Where'll we aim for?' asked Fred. 'And please don't say the rubbish bins.'

Finn laughed. 'Why not? They're vivid enough. Easy to conjure.'

'No way,' decreed Georgie, 'but we could do the rubbish room. Either that or the curtained off area by the stage.'

'Bin room,' said Fred. 'Don't want to risk interrupting another performance.'

Finn nodded. 'OK. Right, each of you hold on to one of my hands.' Georgie and Fred grabbed a hand and gripped tight.

'Now concentrate,' said Finn.

They all shut their eyes, saw the bin room, focused on it, believed they could get there, and launched. Nothing happened. Their faces ran with sweat so intense was their concentration, but still they stayed grounded on the sand. They tried, again and again. And failed.

'We're rubbish,' concluded Georgie, letting go of Finn's hand and blowing out a great breath of frustration. 'Not going to work.'

'There must be another entrance, or exit,' said Fred, releasing Finn's other hand. His dark hair was slicked to his forehead with sweat.

'A safety tunnel,' he went on.

'The guard house,' said Georgie suddenly. 'That's where I'd put a safety tunnel. Coming up into the guard house.'

Finn turned to her, eyes shining. 'Brilliant George. I bet you're right. Just after eleven, when the guards go on patrol, let's go and check it out.'

They drank water, ate more ginger cake, watched the moon arc slowly though the sky. The minutes dragged. Light after light was extinguished in the huge house. Finally eleven o' clock came and the gun-toting guards emerged from their guard house. They changed the direction of their patrol, walking away from the house into the desert. Then they turned and began to walk back, on a trajectory that would take them within ten yards of the bush where Georgie, Finn and Fred hid.

Georgie could hear them coming, the clink of keys, the gruff voices. She imagined their eyes raking over the hiding place, catching a glimpse of Fred's white school shirt within. She prayed none of them would move, or sneeze or cough. The guards came so close she could smell the cigarette smoke which clung to their clothes and the reek of cheap aftershave. None of them moved, or breathed. They kept their faces turned to the ground 'lest the guards catch a gleam of pale skin glowing in the branch-filtered moonlight. Finally the sound of the guards' voices faded and they breathed again.

Finn glanced at his watch. 'We've got, say seven minutes, to be safe,' he whispered. 'Ready to go?'

Georgie and Fred nodded, blood already beginning to race through their veins.

Finn was already straightening up when a sound of a door slamming ricocheted out through the night. Finn dropped back under cover. Through the small gaps in the foliage they could just see the Phoenix, marching from his house, followed by another man, almost jogging to keep up. The Phoenix headed across his garden towards the black Hummer parked on the tarmac.

There was a sudden crash as the door was flung open again, slamming into the wall, then Vlad appeared, running after his father.

'Father!' shouted Vlad, 'Where are you going? Why are you going out so late?'

The Phoenix wheeled around and stalked back to his son. 'Go back to bed. Now.'

'I want to know. You're leaving me alone in the house. I have a right to know. Or to go with you at least.'

'You have a right to what I give you. Nothing more.'

'What's happening? Something's happening. I can feel it. You must –'

Vlad's words evaporated as his father took a step towards him.

'Do I need to punish you, Vladimir? Is that really what you want?' hissed the Phoenix, voice pure menace.

Vlad took several steps backwards, then he wheeled round with a strangled sob and hurried back to the house.

'So Vlad doesn't know,' whispered Fred.

'Seems not,' replied Finn. He watched as the Phoenix returned to the Hummer, climbed into the driver's seat, scarcely waiting for the other man to get in before gunning the engine and roaring off into the gaping maw of the bunker.

'Ready?' he asked tensely.

Fred and Georgie nodded.

Finn glanced around one more time, then set off in a crouching run towards their the guardroom, dropping down on the far side of it when he got there. Fred came next, then Georgie. All of them were blowing hard with nerves. Georgie slowly straightened up and peeked through the window.

'Big room. Looks empty.'

Finn took a deep breath, cranked open the door. 'All clear.'

Quickly, they ducked inside.

Banks of screens flickered on the walls, each showing a different part of the exterior of the house, the entrance to the bunker and the surrounding area. There was a large desk bearing a computer, two telephones, a packet of cigarettes and the dregs of coffee in two cups. Two plastic chairs. A butler's tray with a kettle and a huge jar of coffee. A packet of digestive biscuits. A double door at the back of the room. Georgie approached it cagily, put her ear to it and listened. She inched it open.

'Bingo!' she mouthed, gesturing at the back wall. Finn and Fred followed her gaze. Another room, with a huge lift at the back.

'You were right, George,' whispered Finn. 'A hidden route into the Bunker.'

'But where exactly will it take us?' wondered Georgie. 'What if the doors spring open in the middle of another guard room, full of guards?'

Chapter Thirty One

∽ Transformation ∽

THE LIFT PLUMMETED DOWN so fast they felt as if they were in freefall.

Their stomachs felt as though they had shot into their mouths. They lurched nauseatedly. Down fell the lift, ever deeper.

'Is it meant to go this fast, d'you think?' asked Georgie, eyes wide.

'I went down a mine once,' said Finn. 'In South Africa with Mum and Dad. The lift went down twelve metres a second. Felt like this.'

Finally, with a gut-wrenching yank, the lift began to slow.

'That took three minutes,' said Fred. 'Two kilometres down, roughly, if you're right about the speed.'

The lift halted with a sickening judder. Finn, Fred and Georgie all held their breath as the doors opened with a sinister click, revealing not another guardroom, thank goodness, but a small chamber, about thirty feet across.

They slunk out of the lift, flicking nervous glances left and right. 'Where now?' asked Georgie.

'I say we scoot down the corridor, find an empty office next to a busy one, if we can. Hide inside and listen in. See if we can hear the Voice, or hear anyone talking about a prisoner,' suggested Fred.

'How? We can't hear through walls,' said Georgie.

Fred pulled something from Finn's backpack. 'Oh yes we can, with this.' He waggled a suction cup with wires protruding and a separate ear piece before them.

'That's what you bought at Park and Shop!' whispered Georgie, eyes wide.

Fred grinned. 'That, a periscope and night vision goggles. They're toys, of course, but they do actually work. I've got the set at home.'

'Fred, I know I've said this before,' said Finn, 'but you really are a genius.'

They hurried through a labyrinth of corridors. They heard muffled voices coming from some of the rooms they ducked down and passed. None of the voices sounded like the Voice.

They turned a corner and the corridor widened. At the end they saw a huge room, with massive screens, giant maps on the walls, huge computers blinking with lights being tended by a dozen people busily tapping away. Striding round the room, was the Phoenix.

Suddenly, behind them, they heard a door open and voices filled the corridor. They were trapped. There was a door to the right of them. Finn opened it, praying that it was empty. It was! The three of them rushed in and shut the door. There was no furniture in the room. Nowhere to hide, but at the side of the room was another door. They ran up to it on tip toe and opened it gingerly.

'Office supplies. Perfect. Get in,' said Finn.

They shut the door behind them. Moments later they heard loud voices pass by in the corridor.

They all blew out huge sighs of relief. 'Another close one,' said Fred.

'Let's just hope no-one needs a new pen or paper,' said Finn.

'Odds are they won't,' said Fred. 'Weird why they're working at this time of night anyway.'

'Suggests they're busy, doesn't it? That they have a deadline,' said Georgie ominously.

'I'm going to nip out again, stick this thing against the wall that adjoins the Control Room,' said Fred.

'Be careful,' whispered Georgie.

Fred was back in seconds. The device was already transmitting. The voice of the Phoenix came through loud and clear, that hateful demonic voice.

'-is not acceptable. You will have perfected it by tomorrow evening. We detonate at ten. There has been a leak. We have to bring it forward twenty four hours. Do you expect me to tell all the Chosen Ones that, sorry, we are not ready. Sorry, my famous nuclear scientist, Dr Bradbury just needs a bit more time?' The Phoenix's voice dripped with sarcasm and threat.

'We have been working towards this for ten years,' he hissed. 'Building bunkers, making the money to fund this venture. I have been dreaming of this moment my whole life and that's longer than you might imagine. I have a worldwide network in place and you tell me that you aren't ready?'

'I am ready, here, sir,' answered a hesitant voice that Fred assumed was Dr Bradbury. 'Our own nuclear device is primed and ready. But your idea, to hack into the nuclear controls of the countries in the region that have nuclear power, to detonate them too, that takes time. I am not a computer hacker. I rely on them for this work.'

'Get Eden and Caliban up here,' shouted the Phoenix. 'Anyone who does not meet my deadline will meet his very own deadline. The deadline of his life. Is that clear? Now get out.'

'Yes, sir. I'm gone.' There was the sound of a door opening and closing.

'Who's the leak?' asked a grim voice. 'And how far has it gone?'

'A boy called Finn Kennedy.'

The device hissed loudly, drowning out the Phoenix's next words.

There was a crackle of static then the Phoenix's voice cut in and out again. '-dealt with….. watched….. We have someone at JAM……have turned……most useful to our cause, after a little persuasion……. Agent Falcon……. briefed to go after the target…..others too, enough for a quorum…..bring me the reports.'

The Phoenix suddenly sucked in a breath as if hit by a physical blow. 'Hurry,' he rasped in a voice tight with pain. There was a crinkling of papers, a tapping of computer keyboards then the hushed quiet of contemplation.

Into the void of sound, slid words. 'Come….. Near….. -fighters….. -ee me. -ave me. -ire'

'The Voice!' whispered Finn, eyes electrified.

'Nearby!' hissed Georgie.

'Let's find him,' mouthed Fred.

They inched round the door and hurried away from the Control Room. They came to a fork in the corridor. Opposite them gleamed a huge copper door. Finn studied it. Why so huge? Why copper, not wood, and what was that smell that seemed to be emanating from the metal itself? His heart began to race. Could he be here, the Voice?

Suddenly they heard a door flung open and slam with an echoing crash. They heard footsteps, running, stumbling, desperate.

'Are you all right, sir?' called out a concerned voice.

'LEAVE ME!' bellowed the voice of the Phoenix.

In a split-second Finn turned the handle and tried to open the huge copper door. God, no, was it locked? It wouldn't budge. The ragged footsteps got closer.

Finn heaved and the door suddenly clicked open with a great suck of breath as if it were air-tight. They ducked in and pulled shut the door. They were in a cavernous chamber the size of several football pitches and maybe a thousand feet high. The walls were painted a deep ochre, like dried blood. They glowed dully in the light from the hundreds of flaming torches that ringed the walls about ten feet off the ground. The roof was domed, lined with gleaming copper, tapering to what looked like a huge funnel that led up further than the eye could see. There was a circle of white paint drawn on the sand in the middle of the chamber and, dotted around the circle were ten large copper urns which looked to Georgie like robed attendants at a satanic rite. She shuddered. The whole place felt like some kind of satanic cathedral.

'Wow!' said Fred, eyes wide with awe. 'What is this place?'

Finn started to breathe hard, as if he couldn't get enough oxygen into his lungs. The air he sucked in tasted of smoke, and of something bitter. Finn knew that smell. It was flickering round the edge of his memory like a candle in the wind, but he just could not place it. His instincts started screaming at him, so loudly that he couldn't hear what they were saying. All he could feel was danger. He looked round desperately. The urns!

'Get into those urns,' he yelled to Fred and Georgie. 'Now!'

They took one look at Finn's face, and they each ran for an urn. As Georgie scrambled up and into the urn, her trainer fell off. She was about to climb out to retrieve in when there was a great hiss as the door swung open.

There was a sound of ragged, desperate breathing, then the door slammed closed. Around the cavern the flaming torches flared. Footsteps hurried across the sandy floor.

The footsteps came closer, passed the urn Georgie was hiding in then stopped. From the middle of the circle, there came an enormous, shuddering sigh. It sounded to Finn almost like a dying breath. Then there was silence.

There was something infinitely more terrifying about the silence than the ragged breathing. Suddenly, new sounds slithered through the air; low whispers and crackles, like the sound of distant wind, growing louder, louder, becoming a roar. The roar of fire! Clouds of smoke billowed through the air and fingers of fire shot up like forked lightning.

Oh my God, thought Georgie. We're going to be burned to death. She inched upwards 'til her eyes just crested the rim of the urn.

There, standing with his back to her, arms outstretched as if in worship, was the Phoenix. Standing in a raging column of fire. Georgie bit back a scream, watching in horror as the body of the Phoenix melted away into an inferno of flame that roared up to the ceiling.

The heat, the infernal, singeing heat, like war. The air itself seemed to burn. It stole the oxygen from their lungs. It seemed to be pulling the very atoms from their bodies. They gripped the side of the urns, desperately hanging on as some awful gravity hauled at them. The pull got stronger, demonic. They fought with every living sinew, with all they had in them, terror in their hearts and eyes, but it was impossible to resist. Was this death sucking at them? No oxygen, no air, no breath….a scream, half human, the flame shuddered, condensed and disappeared….darkness…no sight….nothing….

Chapter Thirty Two

∞ Dark Fire ∞

SAND. RED SAND. HOT to the touch. Purple rocks, strewn like casualties of war. Purple sky. Luminous. Black clouds massing like an army. Thunder, rumbling constantly like an angry God. Forked lightning licking the horizon hungrily. Volcanoes of purple rock, black stratifications running down their flanks; lava tears. Yellow-grey smoke, spiralling up from the craters, thick in the air like a deadly oxygen. Spears of flame daggering through the smoke with triumphal roars. Tears, more tears, running from streaming eyes. Eyes that saw! A comet in the sky, a huge fireball ricocheting through the purple sky, burning up to a green sun. A green sun? Finn sat up. He was alive! Where the hell was he?

'George? Fred?' he tried to speak. His voice was sandpaper. He shifted in the hot sand, tried and failed to stand.

'Urgh,' moaned a voice behind him.

Georgie sat up groggily, rubbing her eyes. She opened them slowly, took in Finn, took in the landscape.

'God!'

'No,' mumbled a voice. 'I think it's the other place.'

Finn and Georgie wheeled round; ten urns, like in the Fire Ark. Leaning out of one, his black hair standing on end as if he had been electrified, was Fred. 'We're in hell, aren't we? Dead and in hell,' he said.

He pushed himself out of the urn and walked groggily over to Georgie and Finn.

Finn shook his head. 'The Phoenix is a Fire Djinn. I think this is his Kingdom, the Kingdom of Fire. We're in a parallel universe, like Triton's Kingdom of the Sea. I think the Phoenix took us with him in his slipstream when he went through a portal.'

Georgie, face ash-pale against her auburn hair, nodded. 'Felt a bit like going down through the sea into the Dark World, into Hydrus's Kingdom.'

Fred slumped down. 'Oh God. What do we do now? How do we get out? Get back to the Fire Ark?'

Finn grabbed a handful of hot sand. How would they get out? Could he travel back? Only if he could he take Georgie and Fred with him. He let the sand run through his fingers. It flickered with electricity. Tiny sparks flew as the grains rubbed against each other. Alarmed Finn threw the sand away. It flared and gave a tinny bang on impact.

'Explosive sand!' noted Fred, miserably. 'Anywhere else, I'd have said that was cool.'

There was a sudden hissing. A chattering, sibilant hissing and the air pulsated around them. Wreaths of smoke appeared and started to swirl around their bodies.

'What are these?' shouted Fred, jumping up and trying to brush them off his body.

'Smoke Djinn,' answered Georgie, shuddering. 'They were in Hydrus's Kingdom too.'

The djinn, hissing menacingly, swirled around them, thick, acrid brown-grey smoke writhing insinuatingly over their faces and bodies as if examining them, tasting them.

'They stink. Urgh!' get off, spat Fred, wheeling around, desperately trying to get them off him.

The hissing, the infernal, chattering hissing was getting inside Finn's head.

'No. Don't go,' he shouted suddenly. 'Stay here!'

'What?' shouted Georgie, alarmed. 'What are you on about Finn?'

'Don't go!' shouted Finn again, turning round, arms outstretched towards the djinn, who were clustering together, hissing madly. 'Don't tell him. Don't tell anybody!' he yelled.

Fred grabbed Finn's hand and pulled him round to face him. 'Finn, mate, you're losing it. No-one's going anywhere.'

'They are,' said Finn urgently. 'The Djinn. They said they were going to summon the Commander. And the Fire Rukhs.'

Fred and Georgie exchanged a worried look.

'I can hear them,' said Finn. 'Can't you hear them?' he asked plaintively.

'I can hear hissing,' said Georgie softly.

'Me too,' said Fred awkwardly.

'There are words under the hissing,' insisted Finn. 'I can understand them.' He watched in desperation as the djinn flew away rapidly.

'How can you understand them?' asked Georgie.

'I don't know,' said Finn. 'But I do know we need to hide. Now.'

'Or get out of here,' said Georgie.

'Let's try to travel,' said Finn, grabbing them by the hand. They stood on the red sand, under the lowering green sun, and Finn summoned all his powers, called them all to him, but nothing happened. They did not move. They tried again and again and failed.

'It's not working. We need to hi-' Finn froze.

A whop, whop, whopping sound in the sky made them all look up. Above them, flying in lowering spirals, were what looked like three gargantuan birds. They were plumed in red and orange. Their wingspan must have been thirty feet or more. Their long necks stretched out menacingly. Their beaks shimmered as if made of gold. They shrieked to one another, unearthly sounds that pierced the heart. As they opened their glittering beaks, along with the sound, out came a plume of bright fire.

They ceased spiralling and arrowed straight down towards them.

'Run!' screamed Finn. They ran, but they stood no chance. In seconds the birds were above them, scaly legs reaching down, talons splayed. Finn knew what was coming. He wheeled round, threw himself to the side, but the birds, for all their size, were agile. One threw a leg back and clamped its talons around his body. With a shriek of fire, it flapped its enormous wings and rose into the sky, Finn grasped in its talons. The other two birds captured Fred and Georgie and lifted off into the skies with them clamped in their talons.

Finn, helpless, looked frantically down. The ground was disappearing fast. They were already two hundred feet up. If he struggled, the bird might drop him. He lay still, trying to calm his breathing, to conserve energy, as the bird flew ever higher.

These creatures were, he supposed the Fire Rukhs. Half bird, half dragon. His stank. It smelled of acid and sulphur and something rancid all of its own. Its flapping wings fanned the stench into his nostrils and he wanted to gag. His mind raced feverishly. Where were the birds taking them, and why? And who was the commander?

CHAPTER THIRTY THREE

∞ Old Enemy ∞

THE BIRDS FLEW TOWARDS one of the purple volcanoes. A ring of smoke rose high in the sky from the top of the volcano, shrouding the crater. The birds flew straight for it. Finn started to gulp in as much air as he could.

'Breathe!' he yelled to Fred and Georgie. 'Get ready to hold your breath!'

They wouldn't be able to hold theirs for long, he knew. He sucked in a few final breaths and then they were in the smoke, in the thick of it. Finn closed his eyes but not before the sulphurous yellow smoke had burned his retinas. His eyes streamed and his lungs burned as he held his breath. His mind conjured images of bubbling lava, of a great crater, of being dropped into it.

The flapping eased. He found himself pitching forward. With a sudden, bone jolting thud he hit the ground. He opened his eyes. He was in the crater, on solid ground. Around him, perhaps five hundred yards away, was the tip of the crater from where he could see smoke rising. Here in the centre, there was no smoke, no wind.

The ground was like a thin crust of cracked purple concrete, littered with purple rocks. The light from the green sun cast a pall on their faces, so that Fred and Georgie looked green themselves, though that might have had something to do with being carried off by a Fire Rukh, thought Finn, who felt pretty sick himself.

He glanced up at the Rukh which had carried him. The bird met his gaze. Its red eyes were merciless. Finn could see the cruelty burning. What would the birds do now? Tear them to pieces with their golden beaks? Instead, the birds raised their eyes to the sky, and then, as if at some invisible signal, they flapped their enormous wings and spiralled up and away.

Their flapping wafted smoke towards the centre of the crater and the rotten stench of sulphur saturated the air. This must be what hell is like, thought Finn.

The air before them suddenly shimmered and thickened. They heard a laugh, and then, there on the red sand before them, materialised the body of Ivan Drax.

Chapter Thirty Four

∽ Place of Death ∾

'**F**INN KENNEDY. WELL, WELL, well,' Drax intoned. 'We meet again.' The DarkFighter smiled with a horrible hunger.

Finn remembered the last time he had seen Drax. At Hydrus's lair, in the Dark Kingdom. Drax's hand, grabbing his ankle as Finn fled, desperate to get to the wormhole, to pass back into his own world. Ivan Drax. Poisoned, unfortunately not to death. Left alive to avenge his son, Dagmar, killed when he was holding Fred prisoner. Finn flicked a glance at Fred. His friend's face was white with terror.

'I've been searching for you,' continued Drax, 'on the other side. And all the while you were making your fateful way here, to me. Jehannem will be pleased.'

'Who's Jehannem?' asked Finn.

'The Djinn of Dark Fire, or course. He sent me to look for you. He wants to See inside your head again. Tear it to pieces.'

Finn suppressed a shudder of horror. 'Where is he?'

Drax pointed to the comet burning through the sky. 'He's recharging. But don't worry. He'll be back soon. He has to go back through the Portal. Armageddon awaits.'

'How can you materialise?' asked Finn.

Drax laughed again, then as abruptly, his laugh faded and his face turned grim with hatred. 'You think you are the only one with power? I can materialise, I can See inside your mind as you think desperately of how you might escape me again. It won't happen,' he snarled, taking a step closer. 'I have waited a long time for this. Welcome to hell.'

Finn flicked a glance at Georgie. She was standing rock still, petrified like Fred. He looked back to Drax. Five foot ten, stocky, huge shoulders, all too visible muscles. They could not take him on in a fight and win. Not with their bare hands anyway. Finn, trying to keep his eyes impassive, glanced round. He needed a weapon. Desperately. Triton's voice came back to him. You are the weapon. He had an idea. He had to keep Drax distracted while he worked on it.

He flicked another glance at Georgie, trying to convey what he needed her to do, all too aware that Drax was a Seer.

Georgie cleared her throat. 'So, er how do you get through this Portal?' she asked.

Drax turned his contemptuous eyes upon her. 'You think you can escape from me?' he sneered.

'No. I realise that we can't,' replied Georgie heavily, 'I'm just curious.'

'It opens, at certain times. Or, if you have sufficient power, if you are a Djinn Lord for example, you can cut your way through,' replied Drax, his eyes still on Georgie.

Finn felt a surge of thanks for his cousin and her distraction of Drax. He cleared his mind, stared at one of the purple volcanic rocks. He focused on it. He tried to project all the violence of his loathing for Drax, of his hatred for the Fire Djinn, into the rock. He filled it. Then, with his eyes, his heart and his soul, he propelled it towards the back of Drax's head.

The rock shot through the air. Time seemed to slow.

The DarkFighter must have sensed danger because, fast as the rock, he wheeled around, tried to hurl his body out of the way. Too slow, thought Finn, as the rock dealt him a glancing blow to the side of the head. Flames shot from the rock as it tumbled to the ground. Drax, like the rock, tumbled too.

A shriek and a hiss rent the air. The smoke djinn were back, streaming agitatedly round their Commander. Finn heard their words. Kill. Kill. Kill. They whirled round in the air, closing in.

'Fight them!' yelled Finn. 'They want to kill us!'

Fred grabbed a purple rock, hurled it at one of the smoke djinn. The rock exploded. The djinn vaporised. Enraged, the others hurled themselves at Fred. He wheeled out of the way as Georgie picked up a rock and hurled it into the midst of the smoke djinn. Another explosion, and three djinn vaporised. Finn grabbed more rocks and began throwing, pounding the djinn, exploding four more. Georgie and Fred pelted the remaining four djinn with rocks until they too had vaporised. Immersed in battle, they did not see one of the smoke djinn escape.

'Result!' yelled Fred as they all cheered.

'I love these rocks,' said Finn. He gathered up as many as he could and put them into his rucksack, which soon weighed a ton.

'Nice trick with the levitating rock,' said Fred.

'Triton taught me. Or tried to teach me in the Cave of Light. I didn't manage it th -'

Finn froze. There was a roaring in the air. The comet was heading down from the heavens. Jehannem was heading back, followed by a phalanx of Fire Rukhs. Finn could only pray they hadn't seen them yet.

'Come on, let's get Drax's body out of sight, then we hide.'

He grabbed Drax's arms while Fred and Georgie took one foot each. They dragged him behind a large pile of rocks.

Finn glanced at the sky. He could already feel the heat as Jehannem got closer. There was nowhere to hide. Apart from in the smoke itself…

'Breathe!' he yelled to Georgie and Fred. 'Suck in as much air as you can. We'll hide in the smoke.'

He saw the desperation in Fred's eyes, Georgie's too, but they followed him at a run, sucking in the sulphurous air.

Into the smoke they charged, clamping shut eyes, mouths, noses. They slumped down onto the hot crust, hearts racing. Hiding in a place of death.

CHAPTER THIRTY FIVE

∽ Jehannem ∾

THE HEAT GREW, THE roaring got ever louder, there was a searing sound as if the air were tearing, then there was a series of great thuds. Jehannem and the Fire Rukhs. Landing.

Slowly, Finn allowed used breath to seep from his mouth. Thirty seconds had passed. How long could Georgie and Fred hold their breath? Two minutes max?

The roaring ceased. Finn heard hissing, scurrying, the beating of what sounded like hundreds of wings, prowling footsteps and obscene panting. He passed his hand before his eyes, as Triton had done to him below sea, then he risked opening his eyes. The smoke stung him, but not as badly as he had feared. He could just see through the acrid yellow.

In the centre of the crater burned Jehannem, a fiery mass with two red eyes burning and a slit of a mouth. He was surrounded by perhaps fifty Fire Rukhs, their red and orange feathers silhouetted against the distant ranges of volcanoes that jutted into the livid sky. Circling high above were hundreds more Fire Rukhs, so many that they almost blocked out the sky. Finn saw two pale yellow moons which seemed to have just risen. Around each one was a huge, dark meniscus. The green sun appeared to be setting. The sickly yellow light doused the crater like a nuclear pall.

Around the feet of the Fire Rukhs on the crater scuttled hordes of rats covered with red scales. Their eyes burned red, as if they were rabid, but instead of foam, their mouths bubbled with what looked like lava. Finn shuddered. Prowling round the crater, necks slung low, shoulders powerful, was a huge pack of what looked like hyenas, red-eyed like the rats, mouths drooling lava. Prowling and slithering after the hyenas were creatures with the head and upper body of a lion and the tails of serpents. Their forked tongues flickered from their mouths, spouting flames.

Jehannem started to hiss in the universal language of djinn. The rats stopped scurrying. The Fire Rukhs stood motionless as sentinels. The hyenas froze. Finn listened. And understood.

'My creatures of fire, noble rukhs, fire rats, firenas, chimeras. The moment is near. In a few hours of earth time, on your morrow, we shall launch Operation Phoenix. Not since the beginning of time will there have been such destruction, such death as I am about to unleash. This will be the war to end all wars.'

There was a great roar, flames leapt from the beaks of the Rukhs and lava dribbled obscenely from the mouths of the rats and firenas. The creature Finn guessed was a chimera spat a blade of fire that sliced through a purple rock, exploding it, detonating three fire rats.

Jehannem laughed. 'Bombs, fires, volcanic eruptions will assault the earth. The Sacred Veil that separates our universe from planet earth will be breached.' The thunder roared as if in approval and a huge fork of lightning whipped down and struck the crater top.

'The portal shall be permanently open to you, the beings of dark fire,' continued Jehannem. 'Any living thing that you find there will be yours to devour. I have a new gene pool of humans - the best and the brightest. The true Chosen Ones. We shall let them live, for our own amusement if nothing else. The rest shall die. Creatures of Fire, tonight we shall inherit the earth and all in it.'

Finn gasped back his horror. He felt Georgie flounder beside him. He turned to her. Her face was a horrible green. She was passing out from lack of air. Finn grabbed hold of her, prized open her lips with his fingers, put his own mouth to hers and blew in a stream of his own air. He felt Georgie revive. Her eyes flew open for a moment. She nodded at him. He turned to Fred who slumped suddenly on the sand. Finn blew air into his mouth too until he saw his eyes flicker and consciousness return. They had to get out of here, they had to escape. Finn could feel his own lungs burning. He had little air left.

The fire creatures were roaring, belching fire. Finn could feel the heat searing him. He began to feel dizzy.

A voice cut in, with a shrill hiss. Finn could dimly hear it.

'Attackers. Two boys, one girl. One boy was special. He attacked the Commander, then they all attacked us. Killed all but me. I fled, and only returned when I saw you arrive, Master.'

'A boy? What boy?' hissed Jehannem.

'With an aura. A boy of power.'

'Where is he?' roared Jehannem, eyes burning round the crater.

'They must have escaped Master, down the volcano.'

'Find them!' bellowed Jehannem.

There was a collective screech, and a monstrous flapping of wings as all but a guard of ten Fire Rukhs took off to search. There was an obscene growling, a slithering of tails and a scurrying of feet as the firenas, the chimera and the fire rats hurried off through a rent in the crater wall.

Finn could just see other firenas, perhaps those with a superior sense of smell hanging back, circling round, snouts scenting the air as they hunted down and found the prone body of Ivan Drax. There was much barking and growling, then Jehannem swooped down to his Commander, scattering the firenas. A hand reached out from the burning mass of Jehannem's body. It swept back and forth over Drax. The Commander sat up abruptly, retching violently.

'Who attacked you?' snarled Jehannem.

'It was the Boy. Finn Kennedy,' groaned Drax.

'I think you had better tell me who, exactly this Boy is, how you know him, and how he managed to beat you in a fight,' commanded Jehannem, flaming mouth tight with rage and contempt.

'He is the Prince of Atlantis,' replied Drax, wiping vomit from his mouth. 'A supremely powerful LightFighter. He is the Boy written of in the Prophecies, with sea blood in his veins. Three months ago, in the Dark Kingdom of the Sea, he outwitted Hydrus, drugged him, lured him into a bottle with the Pearl of Wisdom. Trapped him in the bottle. He is here to fight you. He will try to stop you,' warned Drax.

Jehannem roared with fury. 'No-one shall stop me. No Boy. No Prince. Find him! Kill him! Now!' he screamed to his DarkFighters. 'And the other two. Kill them all!'

He turned back to Drax, eyes narrowed. 'Who were the other two? Do you know them as well?'

Drax nodded. 'Georgie Sherwood and Fred Adams. LightFighters too, not as powerful.'

'We shall kill them just the same. Wait for me in the Ring of Urns,' Jehannem ordered Drax, before soaring up and away from the volcano.

Finn's eyes were closing. There was no more air in his lungs. Beside him, Georgie and Fred lay prone. Hang on, thought Finn, just hang on, a few more seconds. He forced his eyes open. He could just see Jehannem burn off into the sky and Drax de-materialise. He could just see the remaining Fire Rukhs spiralling up and away until the crater was quite deserted.

Finn grabbed Fred and Georgie's hands, yanking them back to consciousness. With a superhuman effort, he dragged them from the smoke and collapsed on the crater. All three of them lay there, chests heaving, desperately sucking in lungsful of toxic air which had never tasted so sweet.

Chapter Thirty Six

∽ The Hunt ∽

JEHANNEM LED HIS BAND of DarkFighters in the hunt. He burned through the air, red eyes searing the earth as he sought the fugitives.

The Fire Rukhs spiralled up and down through the sky, screeching with menace, spewing forth fire; all but a few. These few did not screech, did not belch fire, but they hunted, even more urgently than the others.

The firenas, the chimera and the rats split into two parties. One raced down the side of the volcano, slithering on the lava scree so that they descended fast as an avalanche. The other party snuffled round the volcano, noses and eyes prying into any hiding place, seeking out the humans.

Jehannem watched the green sunset sending out sparks of green and blue over the sandscape. Time was running out. He called down his chief Fire Rukh, Jadwa.

'Keep searching. If they are here, find them. Finish them. I must go back through.'

Jadwa nodded, eyes gleaming at the prospect of human flesh.

Jehannem landed in the centre of the ring of Urns. Drax was sitting there, awaiting his command.

'Come through with me. Seek the Boy on the other side. He might already have passed through if he is as powerful as you claim. If he has, he can do untold damage. He must be killed. Immediately. Adams and Sherwood too. Kill all three of them. Redeem yourself.'

Drax bowed his head, sure that the pleasure of killing the boy and his friends would yet be his.

Jehannem gazed at the volcano summit from which he had flown. He flared, then disappeared. Drax was sucked through with him. All that remained was a haze of grey smoke.

CHAPTER THIRTY SEVEN

Djinnish

A KIND OF LURID DARKNESS fell over the volcano. The ever-present thunder rolled menacingly overhead as lightening forked around them.

Finn quickly told Georgie and Fred all he had heard Jehannem saying.

'How come you can understand what he says, what the djinn say?' asked Fred.

Finn shook his head. 'I don't know, but I can. The night after the vision, or the early morning rather, when I finally got home, fell asleep at Aunt C's, I had these nightmares. I heard hissing. I heard Djinn. I had the nightmare every time I fell asleep. I didn't understand what it meant till we got here, and I heard the hissing, and I understood it.'

'Thank God you do,' said Fred. 'By the way,' he added. 'Thanks for saving my life. I was dimly aware of mouth to mouth.'

'Yeah, tell anyone I kissed you and you're dead,' said Finn with a grin.

'Thanks from me too,' said Georgie.

Finn nodded, all too aware of how close they had all come to death, and how death waited for them on the plains below.

Finn glanced at his watch. 'We have to get back through into the Fire Ark. It's midnight. Operation Phoenix will happen tonight, if we don't stop it.'

'How do we get back through?' asked Fred, rubbing his head ferociously.

'Shall we head for the urns, see if we can get back through there, somehow or other?' suggested Finn.

'Can't think of a better idea,' said Fred.

'Me neither,' said Georgie.

Finn ran back into the smoke to search for his backpack. Mercifully, he found it quickly, tripping over it. He ran back out into the air, shouldered his backpack with a groan.

'These volcanic rocks weigh a ton,' he exclaimed.

'But they make great weapons,' said Fred, as he and Georgie gathered as many of the smaller ones as they could cram into their jeans' pockets.

'Let's skirt around away from here,' said Finn as they exited the crater through the rent. 'We don't want to use any obvious routes.'

They tried to move round the top of the volcano, but each step they took, the lava scree sent them descending about twenty feet. Sidestepping was exhausting, it would have been much easier just to go with the flow, but they persisted until they felt as if they were off the main route.

'Let's do some scree-running, shall we?' suggested Georgie.

Finn and Fred nodded. Georgie set off, taking huge jumps down the scree, which obligingly accelerated under her foot, till soon the three of them were thundering down the slope.

Georgie prayed that no-one would hear them, that the rumble and blast of other volcanoes and the constant background thunder would shield their own noise.

In minutes they were approaching the plain. The lava scree hurtled below their feet and Georgie wondered how they would ever stop without being smashed to pieces as the scree hit the plain. There was no way to slow it, they just had to keep going.

Dimly she could make out a darkness at the base of the volcano, a sort of shimmering blackness. She braced herself, said a quick prayer, then she found herself tumbling into water, down deep, deep, deep. So deep, would she never stop descending? The water seemed heavy too, almost wilfully dragging her ever deeper. She kicked frantically, flailing her arms, fighting the liquid that seemed determined to hold her under. A body crashed into hers. She grabbed onto it. Finn or Fred? Felt muscled, like Finn. She kicked again, felt him kicking too, and gradually, their descent slowed and they began, agonisingly slowly, to rise. She felt another great splash above her, stuck out her arm and caught hold of a body hurtling down. Fred! She gripped on tight, immediately she and Finn began to descend again.

Finn kicked out, desperate now. This was not water. This was not buoyant like salt water, or neutral like sweet water. It seemed to be some malevolent liquid actively seeking to drown them, to pull them down. Finn opened his eyes but could see nothing save a purplish black. He kicked frantically, summoning all his remaining strength. Beside him he felt Georgie kicking too. Once again, their feverish descent slowed and they began to ascend through the hostile water.

Fred kicked too, thanking God that someone's arm, was it Georgie's or Finn's had crashed into him and grabbed him. He tried to kick, to help them fight for the surface, but at that moment took a blow to the head from one of the lava rocks that had raced down the volcano with the scree. Stars exploded behind his eyes and he blacked out.

Georgie felt his arm go limp. She grabbed hold of him more tightly, and desperately kicked out for the surface. Up, up, up they went, so slowly, so grudgingly did the water let them pass. She was short of breath again. Her lungs were searing. She fought down panic. Not again. Please not again.

Just then, her head broke the surface. She flipped over, drew Fred's head onto her chest above water.

Finn, blinking off the putrid water, saw Fred's prone body and kicked hard for the shore, dragging Georgie. There was a bank, perhaps ten feet high. He let go of Georgie for a moment. He swam to the bank, searching for handholds, for anything. It was sheer rock. There seemed to be no way out. Georgie was trying to push Fred up, but each time she pushed, she just went under. Finn wheeled round in the water to go to her aid.

'Well, well, well,' said a voice. 'So this is where you got to.'

CHAPTER THIRTY EIGHT

Unak and
Total Eclipse

FINN FROZE. GEORGIE GAZED up in horror. Peering down at them through the gloom was a Fire Rukh. With the weight of Fred on her, Georgie went under again.

The great bird stretched out a talon. 'Climb on,' it said in a deep, raspy voice.

Finn gazed around wildly, searching for an escape. He took hold of Fred so that Georgie could stay above water, but he could see how exhausted she was. Fred was still unconscious. They desperately needed to get onto dry land.

The bird could fry them all, there in the putrid water. Finn stared at it. Into its eyes. They were green, not red like the other Fire Rukhs.

'I'd hurry it up a tad if I were you,' said the bird.

Finn took a decision. He lifted Fred up. The Fire Rukh extended his leg down over the water, grasped Fred in his talons then laid him on the red sand. Next he took Georgie, then Finn.

'Who are you?' asked Finn as the bird released him. 'How can you speak to us?'

'I am Unak. I am a Fire Rukh. I am also a LightFighter.'

Fred, tended to by Georgie, suddenly regained consciousness. He saw the giant bird and screamed.

'Quiet,' hissed the Fire Rukh, scanning the skies, 'You'll alert the DarkFighters.'

'Ssh, Fred,' said Georgie. 'He says he is a lighFighter.'

'I am a LightFighter,' said the Rukh, green eyes flashing.

Finn studied the creature. He stared fiercely down his golden beak at them, massive wings folded neatly at his side, talons retracted. His face was battle-hard, terror-inspiring, but his nobility shone through in his eyes.

'Why are you here then?' Finn asked. 'This is the Dark Kingdom.'

The Fire Rukh nodded gravely. 'About a year ago, the Fire Djinn of the Light, our Lord Vulcan, was dethroned. He has not been seen since. We think Jehannem kidnapped or killed him. We also think Jehannem has conjured a charm preventing a successor to Vulcan from ascending to the throne. So the Fire Kingdom of the Light is leaderless. Shortly after Lord Vulcan disappeared, Jehannem launched an assault against our kingdom. Without a leader we fought badly. We were in disarray. Fifteen of us Fire Rukhs were captured by Jehannem and his Dark Army. He brought us to here. We are his slaves,' he added bitterly. 'He cast more charms, he stole our fire. Now we are just common air breathers.'

'How can you speak English?' asked Georgie, feeling a pang of sympathy for the proud but defeated bird.

'I am part Djinn. I can metamorph. I have been a human boy.' The Fire Rukh raised his head and scanned the skies. 'Enough talk. They are looking for you and they will kill you when they find you.'

'We need to get to the urns,' said Finn. 'We need to pass back through into the Fire Ark, and stop Jehannem blowing up our world.'

'Any damage you do to him, helps us. But we must hurry. A Portal opens when the two moons are in total eclipse.' Unak raised his head to glance at the two moons which were already overlapping. 'We have just minutes. I will fly you there, but I can only take one at a time.'

Fred lay in Unak's talons, flying over the red desert. The great bird suddenly wheeled away. 'Dark Rukhs,' he said, 'flying in at ten o' clock.'

Fred looked to his left. About five Rukhs were flying straight at them. Unak spiralled to the ground and landed. He closed his wings and sat back on his talons, concealing Fred.

Fred, surrounded by feathers felt horribly claustrophobic.

He heard a great flapping, followed by thuds. The other birds landing.

There was a series of ear splitting squawks that sounded like an argument. This carried on for a minute, then there was a great whopping sound as the Dark Rukhs took off. Unak stayed still for a while, then slowly stood.

'That was close,' said Unak. 'They wanted to know why I wasn't searching. I had to pretend I had injured my wing, was resting,' he said, sounding affronted.

'Let's go,' he added, extending his great wings and flapping upwards. 'Time is short. I don't want to have to leave one of you behind here in the Dark Kingdom.'

Fred shuddered at the thought.

Minutes later Fred saw the dull, coppery gleam of the urns. Unak circled once over them. They were deserted. Unak landed softly, released Fred and immediately took off again.

Fred hid behind a pile of rocks and waited for Unak to return. He watched the moons, inching ever closer to total eclipse. Around him the night darkened as he waited and watched, wishing, desperately that he could slow down time.

Four minutes later, Unak returned with Georgie. She and Fred waited together, anxiously watching the moons. They could hear the screeches of Fire Rukhs some distance away. They could just see them circling high in the sky about half a mile west.

Georgie froze. 'I hear something,' she mouthed.

Fred nodded, turned, dread in his eyes. A whisper of paws upon sand, the stench of carrion in hot air. Around the rocks slunk three firenas, teeth bared, the blood of a recent kill still dripping obscenely from their mouths.

Georgie and Fred scuttled back. Georgie tripped over a rock and fell. The lead firena sat back on her haunches, snarling, eyes on Georgie, measuring the distance, preparing to pounce. Georgie closed her fingers over the rock that tripped her. She raised her hand and hurled the rock as the firena leapt. The rock crashed into the firena's head and exploded. Georgie yelped as its fiery blood sprayed over her, but the beast fell dead. Enraged, but newly wary, the other two firenas circled, heads low, snarling. Fred grabbed rocks from his pockets and frantically hurled them. The firenas dodged and the rocks exploded harmlessly on the sand.

Georgie grabbed her rocks from her pocket, aimed them, missed.

'Fred, they'll see the explosions, the circling Fire Rukhs.' The two firenas edged closer. Georgie and Fred had used up their supply of fire rocks. They scrabbled desperately for more. They found little ones, hurled them. It was getting darker, harder to see, harder to find the rocks.

Georgie glanced up. The larger moon had almost completely covered the smaller one.

'Oh God,' she whispered, 'the eclipse. It's nearly total.'

There were no more rocks within reach. The firenas seemed to know this for they were edging ever closer, so close, Georgie and Fred could see the blood lust gleaming in their red eyes.

Suddenly the firenas froze. There was a great flapping sound, then, like an arrow from the sky, a bolt of colour shot down.

'It's Unak and Finn!' shouted Georgie.

Unak rammed his beak into one firena, instantly breaking its neck, while Finn had taken a rock from his backpack and hurled it at the other firena. The explosion threw the creature off its feet. It fell to the sand, quivering in death.

Unak landed, unfurled his talons, and released Finn.

'Run,' he urged. Get in the centre. The moons have eclipsed.'

Fred looked up. The two green moons had become one. Silhouetted against the, was a pack of Fire Rukhs, descending at speed.

'Fire Rukhs!' screamed Fred. 'Go Unak. Fly away.'

Unak glanced up then took to the skies.

'Run!' he screamed, as he soared upwards.

They sprinted, Georgie, Fred and Finn. They screamed to a halt in the centre of the circle. Please let us be in time, prayed Georgie, eyes on the screaming Fire Rukhs, descending on them like a band of demented Furies. Nothing happened. The Fire Rukhs would be on them in seconds. Then the air shuddered around them. They felt that pulling, the awful pulling that seemed like every molecule in your body was being compressed by a hundred tons.

They felt the terrible heat, slamming through the air, searing their faces. They welcomed it as it stole the air from their lungs, singed their eyebrows, waged war once again on their bodies. The pull grew stronger, unbearable, a demonic gravity dragging them through universes, out of the Kingdom of Fire, away from the outstretched talons of the Fire Rukhs just inches from them, back to earth.

CHAPTER THIRTY NINE

∾ The Code ∾

'THANK GOD!' EXCLAIMED FRED, pushing himself up shakily from the floor of the Fire Chamber. 'Back to earth. To our earth.'

'Thank Unak,' said Georgie. 'Without him we'd be stuck in that awful stink hole.'

Finn nodded. 'I hope he got way from those other Rukhs. We'll repay him, somehow. Right now, we have to get out of here. Get back to Shell Beach, tell Triton. Operation Phoenix happens at ten tomorrow. We've got less than twenty four hours to stop it.'

'Let's go,' said Georgie, hurrying out of the circle of sand.

Hearts pounding, they retraced their steps to the lift room. Luck was with them and they met no-one in the snaking corridors.

Finn glanced at his watch. 'One a.m. The guards should be out doing their rounds. The lift'll take a few minutes. We should have time.'

Fred pushed the button. They heard a high pitched whine as the lift powered down to them.

'Someone's gone up before us,' said Finn. 'When we got out, the lift stayed down here.'

'Think they're still in the guard house?' asked Fred.

'Let's hope not,' replied Finn, eyes looking round for a weapon. There was nothing. Save himself.

With a great whooshing sound, the lift slowed to a halt and the doors pinged open. They stepped in and pushed A for ascend.

Their stomachs lurched into their mouths again as the lift ascended with sickening speed. They were down so deep, it still took them nearly three minutes to reach the surface. The lift pinged again and the doors opened onto an empty room.

Finn checked his watch. 1.06. Nine minutes or so until the guards came back.

They hurried across to the connecting door. Finn stuck his ear close and listened.

'All clear.' He tried the handle. It didn't budge. He tried again, pushed his shoulder against the door and heaved, but the door stayed shut.

'The door's locked,' said Fred, pointing to the light panel flickering to the left of the door. 'We need an entry code.'

Finn felt the misery of it sweep over him like tidal wave. He let it, for one brief moment and then he rammed it down. He forced his mind to think. He had an idea, hovering somewhere beyond the fog of exhaustion in his brain.

Fred was muttering: 'What can it be, what can it be?'

Georgie was gazing straight ahead, her face pinched in concentration.

Finn looked at his watch. 1. 07. If they didn't come up with something soon they would have to go back down in the lift.

Code. Code. Think, Finn yelled into the void of his own mind. Who would set the code? The Phoenix or one of his minions? If it were one of the minions it could be anything and they would never get it. But if it were Jehannem. What would he choose? Something personal. Something relevant. Finn thought of the articles he had read about Czarovich on Google. Igor Czarovich. Russian. Born in 1968, on the fifth of November. Gunpowder, treason and plot. Finn stifled a cry and tapped out 05111968. The door clicked. Finn pushed and it opened.

'Yes!' hissed Finn, punching the air with his fist.

CHAPTER FORTY

Blood on the Sand

THE GUARD ROOM WAS empty. The bank of camera screens flickered accusingly at them. Finn glanced at his watch. 1.09

'We have to move. Now guys.' He listened then cracked open the main door an inch. His eyes scanned back and forth across the sweep of sand; three hundred yards to the bushes. No sign of the guards, but Finn knew they could be completing their circuit any minute now.

He turned to Georgie and Fred. 'Ready?' he whispered. They nodded, grim-faced. Finn pushed the door open for them. They slipped out, ducked down and ran across the open ground. Finn shut the door silently behind him and sprinted after them, soon over-taking them.

They were half-way to the bushes when there was an eruption of sound:

'Hey you! Stop!' shouted a guard, appearing out of the darkness.

They ran as fast as they could across the open ground, but the guard, tall, fast and super fit, was gaining on them. His calls had drawn another guard who was now sprinting directly at them.

Fred suddenly tripped and went sprawling on the sand.

In a few strides, the first guard had caught up with him. He threw himself down on Fred and held him squirming. Finn whirled round to go to help Fred.

'Run!' Finn yelled to Georgie. 'Get back. Tell Triton.'

The other guard was feet away from Finn. Finn wheeled round again, dodged, stuck out a foot, and the guard went sprawling. Finn rushed towards Fred.

'No!' Fred screamed at him. 'Go. Get help. You must. Please!' he roared desperately.

The shouting had brought other guards running. There must have been ten of them approaching at a sprint from three hundred yards away.

'I'll be back. I promise,' Finn called to Fred, before turning and sprinting after Georgie.

His cousin was stumbling her way to cover. She was nearly at the bushes. Finn caught up with her, grabbed her arm, and dragged her beyond the bushes and on up the sand dune.

They were half way up when suddenly there was a roar of gunfire.

Finn and Georgie froze. The guards stood lined up on the sand pointing their rifles at them.

'Stop or we will kill you!' shouted one.

Finn saw murder in his eyes, knew the threat was no bluff.

He grabbed Georgie's hands. Bikes! he yelled in his brain, seeing every millimetre of the quad bikes with a kind of hyper clarity. Now!

He heard the burst of gunfire, felt a searing pain on the side of his head, then the air was sucking at them, yanking them out of the moment, blasting them forward.

One millionth of a second later, they landed on the sand by their quad bikes. Their bodies lay crumpled. Neither moved. Under the light of the moon, the sand turned red.

Chapter Forty One

⤂ Unmarked Grave ⤃

'WHO ARE YOU?'
    'Why are you here?'
    'Who sent you?'
'Did someone send you? Did they? DID THEY?'

The South African marched round the guardroom, his hobnailed boots beating out an angry tattoo on the floor as he barked out questions at Fred. Fred didn't hear the questions. All he could hear, playing over and over again in his head, was the sound of gunfire.

Finn and Georgie must be dead. If they were alive, then why weren't they in here with him? He hadn't been able to see what had happened because the guard who had caught him had pushed his face into the sand, but he had heard the gunfire and when he had screamed out for Finn and Georgie there had been no answer.

He wanted to die himself, he wanted to find whoever had shot them and kill them in return. Beside what had happened to Georgie and Finn, his own capture seemed irrelevant and he gave no thought to escape.

He turned to the guard, eyes on the weapon slung over his shoulder. If he could just get it off him. But how? The man looked like a tank. His muscles bulged out of his short-sleeved shirt and his neck seemed to grow directly out of his shoulders. He was angry, but, oddly, he seemed afraid too. He was sweating profusely. The back and underarms of his khaki shirt were dark with sweat and his face ran with it.

There was a loud rapping at the door.

The guard swore quietly and approached the door nervously.

A man dressed head to toe in black with short spiky black hair stood in the doorway. His eyes, filled with hatred, passed over Fred and back to the guard. 'He's on his way,' he said urgently. Then more quietly. 'We need to work out a story. He'll kill us if we say we let two of them get away.'

'They didn't get away, Sergeant Raven,' whispered Tank Man. 'They vanished into thin air.'

'Yeah. Mr Czarovich is really gonna buy that one. I'm not even sure I buy it myself and I was there.'

'We saw them. There were three of them. Two vanished.'

'No,' said Sergeant Raven, his voice cold with menace. 'There were not three. No-one vanished. What we saw was just the one kid. We captured him and what we need from him, in the next minute, is a story about why he's here and why he was alone. Do what you like - beat the hell out of him. Just get the story, make it fit and do it now or we're both dead.'

Fred gave a shout of elation. So Georgie and Finn had got away! They were alive and they had vanished. They must have travelled. This time it must have worked. Now he knew what he had to say.

Tank Man returned and kicked the door closed behind him. He bunched his hands into fists. His eyes were slits of violent intent.

'I got lost,' said Fred quickly. 'I was running away from home, just wanted to spend the night in the desert, you know, scare my parents a bit, but then I just seemed to be going round and round in circles. I-'

Tank Man slammed his fist down on the table between them.

'Just went for a little walk into the desert and got lost. I don't think so.'

'Quad bike. I took my quad bike at midnight. We live in Diamond Oasis so it wasn't that far.'

Tank Man moved back to his seat and looked at Fred quizzically.

'Quad bike. Running away. Mmm. You were alone then?'

'Totally alone,' lied Fred.

Tank Man smiled. 'Excellent.'

Seconds later, the door behind them swung open and in walked Jehannem, in his manifestation as Czarovich, flanked by four scared-looking guards and Sergeant Raven. Tank Man jumped to his feet and saluted. He too looked sacred. Jehannem ignored him and focused on Fred, who lowered his gaze to the floor. Anything to avoid looking into the eyes of a Dark Djinn.

The Djinn studied Fred, then he reached out his finger, pushed up Fred's chin so that Fred was forced to look into his eyes.

'You!' spat the Djinn. He whirled round to the guards. 'Leave us,' he commanded.

Nervously, the guards backed out. Fred could see fear in their eyes, fear for him.

The door closed with an awful finality.

'Fred Adams,' hissed the Djinn. 'You have been busy. You and your two friends. Where are they now?'

Fred said nothing. He stared at the floor.

'Where is Finn Kennedy? Where is Georgie Sherwood?' repeated Jehannem.

Again, Fred said nothing. He felt his head burning as the Djinn Looked in. Jehannem gave an awful smile.

'You know what I can do to you. No-one will come to help you. You are quite alone here. Quite helpless. If you do not tell me everything you know, I shall be forced to pick apart your brain.'

Still Fred said nothing. He tried to cast his mind away, back to his bedroom. He saw his telescope in his head. He imagined being there, peering into it, seeing the glory of the stars. That was where he would send his mind, high up and away, out of reach, just as Mr Violet had taught him, all those months ago.

The Djinn laughed. 'Very clever. You have a brain. Perhaps I shall preserve you.' He grabbed Fred's wrist. 'There is another way to make you do my bidding, without destroying your mind. And you could be a useful companion for Vlad.'

Fred felt the fingers grip his wrist ever tighter. Then he felt the burn, an indescribable, horrific heat. Pain, and searing sadness as he drifted away, as everything he was, everything he believed in drifted far away. With a scream he slumped to the floor.

The Djinn turned away with a sneer of contempt. How these humans lamented their lives, their beliefs, their trite morality. What was belief but a piece of cloth with which they clothed the nakedness of their stupidity? They could have had truth instead, the truth of all he knew, a knowledge of millennia, but still they gripped onto their tiny lives, the meagre knowledge of years.

He called in the guards. Fred watched from the ground.

'Which one of you caught him?' asked the Djinn.

The South African stepped forward nervously.

'He was alone, you say?'

The man pulled at his tie and nodded.

Jehannem smiled. 'You lie.' He took a step towards the guard, who must have seen something terrible in Jehannem's eyes, for he backed away, shaking horribly.

'No. Please, please,' he pleaded. 'Let me explain.'

'Too late!' spat Jehannem. With the speed of a viper striking, his hands snaked forward, grasped the man's head, jerked it sideways with an awful, sickening click. The man fell to the ground, neck broken, mouth fixed in the rictus of death.

Jehannem turned to the other guards. 'Dispose of him. And get the helicopter up,' he said, voice calm. 'We are looking for two more children. Another boy and a girl. Find them, unless you want to join your colleague here in an unmarked grave.'

CHAPTER FORTY TWO

∾ Race against Time ∾

FINN'S EYES SHOT OPEN. All he could see was a red blur. Pain flared at his temple. He reached up to rub his eyes and his hands came away red with blood. He shook his head, sucked in a few deep breaths and slowly his vision cleared. The first thing he saw was Georgie, lying prone beside him.

'Oh God, George,' he moaned. He bent over her, saw her chest rising and falling with breath and said a silent Thank You.

He wiped the blood from his hands onto his shorts, then gently shook Georgie's shoulder.

'George. Wake up.' Nothing happened. He shook harder, alarm drumming in his heart. 'George. Please. WAKE UP!'

Agonising seconds passed. Then suddenly Georgie's eyes flew open. She locked onto Finn's face.

'Argh! Finn!' she pushed herself up and reached out for his face. 'You're covered in blood.'

'It doesn't matter. We've got to get out of here. Now. If we don't get away we'll never save Fred.'

They both pushed groggily to their feet. A wave of pain rocked Finn and he nearly passed out. He braced his hands on his knees and took a few more deep breaths.

'Finn, I think you were hit by a bullet. There's a bit missing on your ear,' said Georgie in a horrified voice.

'It's a flesh wound. C'mon George. We have to move.'

'Let's try to travel again,' said Georgie. 'Get straight to Shell Beach and Triton.'

Finn nodded. He took Georgie's hand and together they both focused all their thoughts on Shell Beach. Finn gripped Georgie's hand so hard it went white, but seconds passed and nothing happened. Soon both of them were pouring with sweat, but they stayed immobile on the sand.

'Damn!' said Finn. It's not working this time. Why -' suddenly he fell silent.

'What is it?' asked Georgie, looking ashen.

'Helicopter. Starting up. Searching for us. Let's get out of here. No lights.'

Finn roared off on his quad bike, cresting the dune so fast his bike flew into the air. It landed ten feet away, bounced sickeningly, then sped off down the other side. Georgie followed, speeding faster than ever before. She hit a mound of sand, and her bike flew into the air, tilting alarmingly. She hung on desperately while the bike landed on two wheels, bucked and finally steadied. Concentrate, she yelled to herself, eyes straining to see in the light of the moon.

They heard the roar as the helicopter took off. Finn prayed it would start the search for them in the wrong direction.

Together he and Georgie raced on through the darkness. As their eyes grew re-accustomed to the dark they were better able to see the folds and ridges and small, scrubby bushes in the sand so they went faster still.

The whine of the helicopter faded and soon they could no longer hear it above the throb and roar of their own engines. Finn felt his hopes soar. They raced up and down and round dunes until they found level ground. Finn prayed that they were going in the right direction. He scanned the dunes around him, slowed up and gazed at the stars. He made a quick adjustment to the route, then sped on along the flat sand. A few more miles, he reckoned. If the driver was waiting for them, they had a chance.

On and on they roared through the darkness, hands numb, eyes burning from staring so hard. Finn checked the time. 3.08. He had bidden the taxi for three a.m. Would the driver stay the extra minutes, that's if he had even returned for them in the first place?

Finn strained his eyes. After about five minutes, he thought he could make out the form of a car in the darkness. Then he saw head-lights flick on in the distance and the car began to move. He accelerated, desperately trying to close the gap between him and the car. The taxi! It was the taxi. But it had turned around to drive away. The red tail lights winked at Finn like mocking eyes.

'No!' he yelled, pushing the bike to full speed so that it jumped and tilted over the ground terrifyingly. 'Look in your mirror!' he screamed. 'Look in your mirror!'

The taxi continued to drive off and Finn and Georgie continued to scream after it. Then, suddenly, as if the driver had heard or sensed them, the taxi slowed to a stop. Finn and Georgie whooped with delight.

They caught up with it and broke into the most enormous smiles when the driver stepped out.

The man's smile froze on his face when Georgie and Finn removed their helmets.

'Oh my Good God!' he said, rolling his head. 'What has happened? Your face, blood! Blood everywhere!'

'Silly me. I tripped and fell, cut my ear on a cactus, that's all. Thanks for coming back,' said Finn, trying to sound casual.

The driver nodded. 'I waited for fifteen minutes. I was thinking it was some sort of prank you have been pulling on me.'

'But you waited and then we got here just in time,' said Georgie. 'Thank you so much.'

'And where is your friend?'

'We're going back to get him later. Can we hitch up the trailer?' Georgie asked.

'He is left alone in the desert?' asked the driver, with horrified eyes. 'All alone in the desert?'

'Not alone. He is with people. He's OK,' answered Finn, terrified that the driver would call the police who would then take them in for questioning and hours would be lost.

'Please can we hitch up the trailer?' asked Georgie. 'We need to get home.'

The word home seemed to do the trick for the driver got back in his car and reversed up to the trailer which Georgie and Finn hurriedly uncovered, ripping their hands with thorns in their haste. They hooked it up to the taxi, pushed their bikes up onto it and secured them in record time.

Finn glanced at the darkened sky, looking for lights, but there was no sign of the helicopter. He and Georgie got into the taxi and collapsed in exhaustion against the back seat. The driver drove off. In ten minutes, they were back on the tarmacked road with a phalanx of early morning cement lorries and oil tankers heading for Dubai.

CHAPTER FORTY THREE

Five million Dollar Killer

J EHANNEM WAITED IN THE guard room with Seargent Raven while the helicopter searched for Finn and Georgie. He wore a mobile phone attached to his belt, with a tiny earpiece and a small microphone at his mouth. On the surface, he looked like what he pretended to be; a successful business man. But, now that he knew, Fred could sense the Djinn underneath. It was in the terrible stillness as he stood and stared out of the window into the darkness as if he could see something invisible to the rest of them. It was the stillness of a creature that knew he could unleash monumental destructive power at any moment. It was in the sense of untrammelled power that emanated from the man, a power that people would have attributed to his billions. It was in the evil glittering in the dark eyes; an evil that knew no limits, an evil that would turn the planet into an inferno and erase all life from it, save his few Chosen Ones. Unless, somehow, he and Georgie and Finn could stop him. Fred could smell him, underneath the expensive cologne he seemed to shower himself in. Underneath that, still detectable, was the whiff of sulphur.

Fred turned away and stared out of the opposite window, thinking of Georgie and Finn, praying that the helicopter would not find them.

He suddenly felt burning in his head. He looked up to see the Djinn staring intently at him.

The Djinn's phone rang, breaking the silence.

The Djinn looked away. 'You've found a quad bike?' he asked, speaking into his microphone. 'One quad bike, but no children,' he hissed. 'Keep searching.'

He turned to Sergeant Raven.

'Take the boy to the Control Room and stay there with him. I'll be there shortly.'

Raven looked surprised. 'Er, to the Control Room, Sir?'

Jehannem smiled slyly. 'I think his LightFighter friend, Finn Kennedy, with his misbegotten notions of friendship will come and try to rescue Fred. I have taken measures to ensure that Kennedy is dealt with, and I might put another in place. But, just in case he manages to elude my people, I shall keep Fred near me. He shall act as the perfect bait. I've been told that this Prince of Atlantis has powerful blood. I'm feeling rather thirsty. I'd rather enjoy killing him myself.' Jehannem barked out a laugh that chilled Fred's blood. 'Besides,' continued Jehannem, 'you don't think Fred could get up to any mischief, do you? He's burned. He's my slave, like the others. Now go.'

Jehannem watched Raven lead a passive Fred from the room. Then he turned to his mobile and rang another number. A backup plan. He always liked to have at least one.

The sharp, high-pitched voice answered on the third ring.

'Talk to me.'

'I have a job. An urgent one. I shall have the pictures downloaded to you shortly.'

'I am busy,' said the voice.

'Five million dollars,' said the Djinn.

'In that case, consider it done.'

The Djinn hung up. Five minutes later he was in his house, in his study, rifling through drawers. After a few minutes, he found the JAM yearbook. He quickly flicked to the class photos. He smiled as he found the faces of Finn Kennedy and Georgina Sherwood staring back at him. He scanned the images and e mailed them, as promised. He sat back, satisfied. If anyone could find them, and kill them swiftly and efficiently, it would be the Assassin. She had never failed, so far.

CHAPTER FORTY FOUR

The Plan

THE TAXI DRIVER LEFT Finn and Georgie at the garage. They paid him his five hundred dirhams which he looked at guiltily, then quickly accepted with a smile. Finn closed the garage door behind them and slumped on the floor, leaning back against a surfboard. Georgie found some bottles of water and handed one to Finn while she downed another. The water washed out the taste of sand from her throat. She poured some over her face and it came away brown with sand and grime.

'Right,' said Finn after he'd gulped back his bottle. 'We need to go and tell Triton everything, then we need to go and rescue Fred.'

He told Georgie his plan. She smiled in anticipation, adding refinements here and there. Finn looked at her in wonder.

'You're keen to do this. You're actually keen to do this.'

Georgie looked at him with eyes that blazed with purpose.

'We have to rescue Fred. I can't bear the idea of him there, the Djinn's prisoner. And as for taking on Jehannem, if we do nothing, we die. Doing something, even if we die doing it, has to be better.'

'We won't die doing it,' said Finn, managing to keep his voice steady. 'We beat Hydrus, the Dark Sea Djinn. We'll beat the Dark Fire Djinn,' he added, getting to his feet, 'and we'll rescue Fred. C'mon. Better try to clean ourselves up and get ready for school. We have a meeting to keep.'

'Think school will be open, after the fire?' asked Georgie.

'For once in my life I can only say I hope so,' replied Finn.

'So who's the Dark Agent we heard Jehannem speaking about, care of Fred's listening device?'

'Someone he turned,' mused Finn. 'Suggests a former Lightfighter.'

'Miss Finity!' they said in unison.

'I hope not. Not her,' said Georgie.

'We'll try and find out. Remember what Mr Violet taught us? How to See?'

'Read people's minds? Of course. I still try,' said Georgie, 'not very successfully.'

'Well, we can try it on Miss Finity, can't we?'

'Yeah, we can, but remember, Jehannem will still be hunting us, in his world, and ours. So if she's a DarkFighter now, we don't want to get too close to her.'

'She, or whoever this DarkFighter is if it isn't her, won't kill us in the middle of JAM,' said Finn.

There were dark corners, bathrooms, thought Georgie. There was always a way for a killer who was sufficiently determined and desperate.

Chapter Forty Five

☞ Too Close ☜

SCHOOL WAS OPEN. THE gymnasium was a charred mass of warped steel and blackened brick, but it was some distance away from the other school buildings which had not been affected. The stench of smoke hung heavy in the air.

Georgie and Finn found their way into the cricket pavilion and sat down to wait for the helicopter, praying that Vlad would come to school today. At seven twenty they heard it. Finn and Georgie looked at each other in relief. Minutes later, it hove into view. It landed bang in the middle of the cricket pitch. The blades slowed and the figures of father and son emerged.

They walked past so close that Finn could smell Jehannem's aftershave. Vlad looked dejected. He walked, eyes downcast, a half step behind his father.

One minute later, after dropping Vlad on the Astroturf, the Dark Djinn returned.

I will kill you, like I killed the other DarkFighters, thought Finn as he peaked through a crack in the door. I will kill-' suddenly, the Djinn whirled round and stared straight into the pavilion. He seemed poised to walk over, but a security guard wandered up at that exact moment and greeted the Djinn with a shy Good Morning.

The Djinn spat a reply before wheeling round and heading for the helicopter. With a great roar, the machine rose from the ground and sped away.

'Phew!' said Finn exhaling heavily. 'That was close. I think he sensed me. I was thinking about him.'

'He's a Seer,' said Georgie. 'You can't afford to think about him when he's close by. Now let's get out of here. I'd feel a heck of a lot safer in our classroom.'

CHAPTER FORTY SIX

∞ Miss Finity ∞

THEIR FIRST LESSON THAT day was science.

'Write a letter to your Mum and Dad,' whispered Finn, passing Georgie a piece of paper torn from his science book.

'I'm writing one to them too, and to my own parents, and to Fred's,' said Finn, eyes grave.

Georgie nodded. She took the paper and gazed into space. What do you write? Dear Mum and Dad, I might never see you again. Sorry, but there's something I have to do? Or, Sorry Mum and Dad. I just have to go away to sort something out for a few days. See you soon? The callousness of what they were doing to their parents, for the second time, almost overwhelmed her. Then she thought of the Fire Djinn, of Operation Phoenix and her resolve hardened. She began to write.

The bell sounded for first break. Finn and Georgie shadowed Vlad as he left the class.

'Will your father be picking you up today?' Finn asked.

Vlad shook his head. 'He said he was going to be really busy. He's got something big on. Lots of people coming in to town this evening.'

Finn and Georgie exchanged a look. 'The Chosen Ones,' mouthed Georgie.

'So who's picking you up?' asked Georgie.

'The pilot,' answered Vlad, eyes narrowing in suspicion. 'Why?'

'Thought we might ask your father if you can come round to my house sometime,' improvised Georgie. 'No matter. I'm sure I'll catch him another time.' She walked off with a casual wave. 'See you later,' she called.

Finn followed her. 'He's suspicious,' he noted.

'Wouldn't you be, with a Fire Djinn for a father?'

'True,' acknowledged Finn with a smile.

'Talking of suspicions, I've got to go and find Miss Finity, give her our letters.'

'What if she is the Agent?' said Georgie, horrified.

'I'll try and See into her mind first. When I saw her yesterday outside the gym, she seemed normal. No evidence that she'd been turned.'

'I don't like it, Finn. Jehannem said he'd turned someone here. He suggested a LightFighter. Who else could it be?'

'I don't know, but that doesn't mean it must be her. We need her, George. And we have to trust someone.'

'We trusted Mr Violet,' replied Georgie sadly.

'I'll be careful, George. I promise. You be careful too. Stay out in the open. Go and find someone to hang out with. Preferably a crowd.'

Finn took the letters and ran off. He knocked at the staff room door. Miss Frisbee, the school counsellor, opened it with a look of surprise.

'I really need to see Miss Finity,' Finn said loudly, trying to peer around the door. 'Is she here?'

'Finn, you look upset. Calm down now. Take a deep breath,' intoned Miss Frisbee.

'I need Miss Finity,' said Finn, almost shouting now.

'Finn, really -' began Miss Frisbee.

'Lairt me through' said a determined Scottish voice. Miss Finity appeared from round the door. She was an imposing presence with her height, her long, beak-like nose and her sharply intelligent grey eyes. Finn prayed that she hadn't been turned. She had been a formidable ally. She would make a dangerous adversary.

'Thank you,' Miss Finity said briskly to Miss Frisbee.

'Now, Finn, if it's about that wretched fossil you lairt in my class last year,' said Miss Finity, guiding Finn away from the curious eyes of the staff room.

'Lairt's go in here,' she said quickly, opening the door to the empty music room. She closed the door softly behind them and turned to face Finn. The sea glass pendant hung from her neck. Finn remembered Triton's words when he had given him and Fred and Georgie their pendants: *No-one evil can wear it. It will protect you from the Dark Ones.* Finn looked up into her steely eyes. He heard the Phoenix's voice in his head. *We have turned someone at JAM. They're most useful to our cause.*

He drew on his powers to really See, but he detected no guile, no concealment, no evidence whatsoever of being turned. He made up his mind.

'It's happening again,' he said. 'This time it's fire. There's a Fire Djinn and he's planning to incinerate the planet.'

Quickly he told Miss Finity everything. She listened in silence, sucking her breath in when Finn told her how Fred had been captured and he and Georgie had been shot at.

Finn handed her three letters. 'Please give these to Georgie's and Fred's parents when they come to pick us up today.'

She took the letters. 'That I will,' she said gravely. 'I will for my part summon as many LightFighters as I can, and we too will wairk out our own plan.'

'Great. Thanks,' said Finn.

Miss Finity nodded. Her grey eyes sharpened. 'Don't trust Vladimir. Use him, but never trust him. He's the son of a Dark Djinn. There's dark blood in him.'

'I won't trust, don't worry,' replied Finn. 'Are there any more DarkFighters in the school?' he asked.

'Wairl, since Georgie killed Mr Gusting, and Fred disposed of Dagmar Drax, that's the two biggest ones gone.'

'But there could be more?' pressed Finn.

'Ach, there're always more. So, yes, Finn. There're more, but who, exactly, I canna say.'

'Are there any more LightFighters?'

'Wairl, there cud be. But not that I know of. Why d'yu ask?'

'Just curious,' replied Finn.

'Now, du yu have a mobile phone?'

'I do,' replied Finn.

'Here, take my number. Keep me posted. And give me your number, please.'

Finn remembered Georgie's voice: we trusted Mr Violet.... He knew that with his mobile number Miss Finity, with the right technology, could track him down wherever he was.

Finn had looked and Seen nothing. But still, the faintest of doubts flickered in his mind. He pushed it down, recited his number then headed for the door.

'Good luck,' said Miss Finity, shaking Finn's hand.

'Thanks,' replied Finn. 'Good luck to you too.' He turned to go. Suddenly Miss Finity's fingers closed around his arm like a vice.

'Be careful Finn. Be very careful.'

Finn pulled his arm free. 'I will,' he said, quickly stepping through the door and out into the hallway, wondering whether what he had seen in Miss Finity's eyes was threat or warning.

CHAPTER FORTY SEVEN

Vladimir's Choice

THEY NEEDED TO WAIT for the end of the school day, and for darkness. Lessons passed interminably. They seemed like the biggest waste of time. Georgie, exhausted and desperate to get on with their plan, wanted to shout:

'Don't you know what's coming? Don't you know what's just round the corner? A nuclear inferno! Annihilation!' But of course they didn't, couldn't know. Children and teachers went about their daily business in blithe ignorance.

Georgie and Finn spent the day constantly looking over their shoulders, searching for the Agent, always staying near other people, going to the loo in a crowd.

At last, two fifteen came and the school bell rang. This last bit was the most painful. Georgie's and Fred's mothers would be there to collect Georgie, Finn and Fred. Instead they would find notes left for them at reception.

It was also the most tricky part. Finn and Georgie hurried across the classroom and took up position, flanking Vlad as he left the class.

He flicked a nervous glance at them, but said nothing, just looked ahead, dark eyes brooding.

Miss Roose led their class out through the snaking corridors, downstairs, yelling at them to 'Walk not Run.' Finn flicked a glance across at Georgie. She nodded.

'Hang on a second, Vlad,' she said, taking hold of Vlad's arm. 'I want to show you something.'

'What?' he demanded impatiently.

'Come and see,' smiled Georgie. 'It's just around the corner.'

'Look, my pilot's waiting. Another time.'

'I don't think so,' hissed Finn, grabbing Vlad's other arm. 'I suggest you come with us now.'

Vlad laughed. 'And what if I don't? What if I say No, and go to Strummer and tell him you are bullying me. What if I ring my father now?' He pulled out his mobile. Like a viper striking, Finn snatched it.

He leaned in towards Vlad. He moved his grip so that he was grasping Vlad's burn.

'Ow, you're hurting me,' yelled Vlad.

Finn tightened his grip.

'If you do not do exactly as we say, then I shall tell the school, tell your father, tell the police that you knocked out Rania Mansour, left her to die in the gymnasium,' said Finn, his eyes blazing with threat. 'So make your choice Vladimir.'

'My father will go ballistic, he'll kill me if I'm not on that helicopter,' said Vlad.

Finn smiled dangerously. 'I rescued Rania from your fire Vlad. I saw her nearly dead, thanks to you. You don't co-operate, I might kill you myself.'

Vlad saw the cold, calculated fury in Finn's eyes. He paled. 'What do you want me to do?'

'Leave, quietly with us. Do exactly what I say. Do not

try anything. Do not try to get away because if you do, I will chase you down and you will wish you'd never met me.'

Vlad nodded.

Finn, Georgie and Vlad slipped away in the crowds of milling students, heading for the back entrance. Finn kept his hand on Vlad's shoulder, just in case Jehannem's son should try to run away.

They nearly bumped into Mr Slavel, who was leading a group of students off towards a luxurious-looking coach. Finn frowned. The Excellence Academy! There was to be a party tonight, an award ceremony. He hadn't been paying attention when Slavel had got all the members together the other day, but he dimly remembered mention of a party, and being given an envelope with the details. Where was it? Where was Slavel taking them, he wondered? He quickly tagged along at the end of the queue. Slavel spoke to the security guards, gestured to the snaking queue of students, pointed to the coach, and exited the school. Finn, Georgie and Vlad followed in his slipstream. Before Slavel could catch sight of them, Finn hurried them past a row of parked cars and into a side street. They walked quickly, leaving the school and the milling pupils behind.

'Are you going to tell me what this is about?' asked Vlad.

Finn smiled grimly. 'You wouldn't believe me if I did.'

'So where are you taking me?'

'Wait and see,' replied Finn.

They snaked through the side streets until they emerged on Al Wasl Road close to Safa Park.

'Right, let's get a taxi and get as far away from here as we can. They'll be looking for us,' said Finn.

'I hate doing this to my parents,' said Georgie. 'They and Fred's parents are all going to go frantic.'

'My father will too when he hears I'm not at the helicopter,' said Vlad. 'At least you have a choice,' said Vlad. 'You could go home to your parents.'

'No we couldn't,' replied Georgie with infinite sadness.

'Send a text to the pilot,' said Finn. 'Tell him you've gone round to a friend's place, that you'll meet him at school at the cricket pitch at seven. That should buy you a few hours.'

Vlad shook his head. 'Not with my father. He'll go nuclear.'

'Let's hope not,' said Finn. 'Give me the phone. I'll write the text.' Finn tapped out a message. 'What's the pilot's name?' he asked, 'and don't even think of lying to me. I'll see it in your eyes.'

'Ahmed,' replied Vlad.

Finn stared at him for a moment, then sent the text. Then he dropped Vlad's phone into a bin.

'What are you doing?' shouted Vlad.

'I'm ditching your phone because your father's men will use it to track you, or me if I have it on me.'

Vlad looked at him wide eyed. 'Why on earth would they do that?'

'Don't pretend your father isn't the kind of man to do exactly that,' replied Finn curtly.

Vlad just looked away, dark eyes brooding.

They took a taxi to Mall of the Emirates and meandered with the thronging masses hunting down retail nirvana. They killed a few hours before hunger drove them to Starbucks. They ordered coffee and croissants.

Vlad muttered something under his breath, then sunk his teeth into his croissant. His teeth were, Finn noticed, brilliantly white. Like a shark's.

Finn sipped at his coffee, ignoring his croissant. He felt uneasy. His gaze flickered around the room. Georgie and Fred's parents would be hunting for them. Jehannem would have his guards out hunting too. Hunting to kill. He'd thought hiding in full sight was the best and safest policy. Now he wasn't so sure. All his senses were screaming danger.

He jumped to his feet.

'Let's get out of here. Quick. I've got a bad feeling.'

They hurried from the café and into the crowded mall. Georgie turned to say something to Vlad. He ducked his head down so that he could hear her. At that precise moment, eyes swept over them. Failing to spot their target, they swept on and away. Vlad straightened up a second later.

'No sign of Vladimir in Emirates Mall,' said a voice, speaking into a mouthpiece, eyes raking over the people sitting huddled at the tables in Starbucks. 'I've hunted up and down. No sign of Kennedy or Sherwood either. Where now? OK. Ibn Battuta. I'm on my way.'

Finn, Georgie and Vlad descended the escalator and left the mall by the taxi rank. They caught a taxi which sped off round the corner seconds before the chauffeur-driven Hummer pulled up to collect three of the Phoenix's body guards.

'Where are we going?' asked Vlad. 'Why are you dragging me around like this?'

'Wait and see,' growled Finn.

Their taxi dropped them at Shell Beach. The waves

were huge. They crashed onto the shore with great roars, as if at war with the kingdom of land. Immediately Finn began to feel better, as he always did when he was near to the sea. He wished he had his surf board. He wished he could just run into the waves and escape for ten minutes.

Darkness was falling and there were few people on the beach. They hid on the rocks by the Fisherman's Village.

'Do you remember, just three months ago,' said Finn, 'saving this place.'

Georgie nodded.

'What d'you mean, saving this place?' asked Vlad.

'Long story,' replied Finn. 'Another one you wouldn't believe.'

'Look,' snapped Vlad. 'You've basically kidnapped me, held me prisoner for hours. When are you going to tell me what this is about?'

Finn turned to him. 'You really want to know?'

Vlad faltered, as if he had seen something in Finn's eyes he would rather not have.

'Er yes, I really want to know,' he answered falteringly.

'Well, be prepared for a bit of a surprise,' said Finn darkly. 'You know Fred, our friend, the boy with dark hair. Brilliant at maths. In our class?'

'Yes. He wasn't at school today.'

'That's because your father's men captured him last night. In the desert.'

'Captured? What're you talking about?' asked Vlad, indignantly.

'See this,' said Finn, turning so that Vlad could see the bloody wound on his ear. 'I got this last night, running away from them, with Georgie. The guards ordered us to stop, and when we didn't they opened fire.'

Vlad was shaking his head in disbelief. He jumped up. 'You're mad,' he said.

'Sit down,' said Finn, pushing him to the ground. 'And listen.'

Finn told him, the whole terrifying story; Operation Phoenix, the plan to raze the earth and all its occupants, Fred's capture.

Vlad raked his fingers through his hair. His face had turned pale with shock. He kept shaking his head as if refusing to let in Finn's words.

'No. It can't be true. It can't be. You're making this up. Why? Why would he do this?'

'Who were all those people arriving the other night?' demanded Finn. 'It was like an invasion wasn't it, helicopters and Hummers and Range Rovers everywhere. Where did they all go?'

'Into the oil facility,' replied Vlad shakily.

'Oil facility.' spat Finn scathingly. 'Yeah sure. That'll really get the hotshots flying in.'

'Business meeting,' said Vlad. 'That's what Father said it was.'

'You don't hold business meetings in an oil bunker, Vlad,' said Georgie. 'You hold them in some fancy hotel. Unless of course you wanted to show your clients where they were going to live for the next eighteen months or two years of their lives.'

'Have you ever been down there, Vlad? demanded Finn.

Vlad shook his head. 'He won't let me.'

'No, I'll bet,' said Finn. 'There's a complete city down there, with shops, a hospital, a school. That's the school where you'll be going. When all your friends here have been burned to bits. He's built an ark down there. A Fire Ark he calls it, for him and the Chosen Ones who can pay him one billion dollars each.'

'Chosen Ones,' mouthed Vlad, looking as if he remembered something.

'You know, don't you?' asked Georgie. 'You know something's not right.'

'But why?' Vlad asked incredulously. 'Why would he do that?'

'You really want to know?' asked Finn, his voice like a whiplash, his eyes narrowed with fury.

Vlad quailed under Finn's glare.

'I'm going to tell you anyway, because we need your help, to get Fred back, to stop your father,' said Finn.

'Have you ever heard of Djinn?' asked Georgie.

'Spirits,' answered Vlad. 'Supernatural creatures. Myths.'

Georgie shook her head. 'Not myths. They've believed in them in Arabia for thousands of years. Because they're real. Spirits, below angels, above demons. They can shape shift. They can become pillars of smoke. Birds. They can also transform into humans.'

'What's this got to do with my father?' asked Vlad.

'He's a Djinn,' spat Finn. 'A Fire Djinn.'

Vlad stared at Finn, unmoving, almost unseeing. He sat like that for a long time, then he dropped his face into his hands. He was muttering something through his fingers.

'Not human. My mother always said. She left him. When I asked why she said because he was inhuman, but I heard her screaming at him one night. Not human, she called him.'

'Where is your mother?' asked Georgie softly.

'Jumeirah. She has a villa on Beach Road. He tries to keep me from her. He hates her for leaving him, but I'd rather live with her than him. He wants me with him, keeps me with him. If I don't do what he says, he, he -' Vlad faltered. His fingers went to the burn on his wrist, scabbed over now.

'He burns you,' said Georgie.

Vlad nodded. The movement was so slight it was almost undetectable. Georgie saw in it all his pain, and his shame. She pretended not to see. 'I thought it was a Chinese burn. He twisted his hand round…..'

'It's a real burn,' said Georgie.

'My mother…' said Vlad.

'Will die,' replied Finn, 'unless you help us.'

Vlad raised his eyes and locked them onto Finn's. 'Against my own father.'

'Yes,' replied Finn, voice softer now, but face implacable. 'Against your own father.'

Vlad did not reply. He stared up at the sky, fists clenched, eyes clouded with turmoil. Finn peered at him. He saw tumult, anger, shame and something else, burning beneath the storming emotions, something that he could not identify, something that sent a spike of unease crackling up his spine.

'Now, enough talking,' said Finn. 'We are going to summon Triton, the Sea Djinn of the Light. That's why we are here.'

Vlad opened his mouth to ask another question, but Finn froze him with a look.

'We need to focus.'

He and Georgie gripped their sea glass pendants and called out in their minds to Triton.

'We are on Shell Beach. Please, come to us now.'

Vlad stuck his hands in his pockets and fingered his spare phone. If he could slip away, just for a minute, ring his father. There must have been a terrible misunderstanding. His father's men wouldn't have shot at them, his father couldn't be planning to annihilate the world, and his father was not some kind of fantasy creature. Finn and Georgie were obviously dangerously deluded.

'I'm just going to have pee round by those rocks,' said Vlad. 'Back in a sec.'

Finn, eyes fixed on the sea, waved his arm in assent. 'Yeah, sure. Go on. But don't try to run away Vlad. It wouldn't be a smart move.'

'I won't run away,' replied Vlad. 'I promise,' he added, veiling his grin.

He hopped across the big stones, crouched down out of sight, took his spare phone from his pocket and dialled.

CHAPTER FORTY EIGHT

∽ Betrayal ∽

THE FIRE DJINN STUCK his mobile to his ear and listened to the voice of his Head of Security in disbelief.

'My son has gone missing, now, today, this day of all days and you call me and let me know three hours later?'

'We thought we could ffffind him,' stuttered the man.

'Have you checked his mother's?'

'Yes, that was the first place we went. She's gone frantic too.'

'How touching,' hissed the Djinn. His voice deepened and slowed so that it sounded like lava grinding over rocks. 'Find me my son. You have one hour.'

'Yes sir.' The threat was left unsaid. Sixty minutes of life remaining unless he found the son.

The Djinn clicked off the line and immediately his phone rang. His face contorted with rage when he recognised Vlad's number.

'You had better tell me where you are and you had better make this good or you will learn a whole new type of suffering.'

'I'm with some people, Father. Deluded people,' whispered Vlad, his voice veiled by the crashing of the waves.

'They're enemies, father. They forced me to go with them.'

'Where are you?'

'Shell Beach,' answered Vlad, his voice quailing at the violence in his father's.

'Stay there. Who are these people?'

'Georgina Sherwood and Finn Kennedy.'

The Djinn smiled.

'Really? Finn Kennedy? Well, well, well. That's most convenient. You've done well, Vladimir. Better than you know. Keep them there. Do not let them go.'

'Er, I'll do my b -'

His father hung up abruptly. Vlad pocketed his phone. How did his father know of Finn and Georgie? Why did he sound so keen to get them? His voice had been full of a strange kind of hunger. Vlad stared into the night, emotions swinging between fear and triumph. What had he done?

The Djinn rang his Head of Security and barked out his instructions.

The South African listened carefully.

'Right, Sir. I'm on my way.'

He glanced at his watch. He pulled out of Ibn Battuta and accelerated down Sheikh Zayed Road. Every speed camera clocked him as he sped past at two hundred kilometres per hour, horn blazing, weaving lanes.

Next, the Djinn rang the Assassin.

'Dae, I take it you haven't found them?'

'Not yet.'

'Allow me to make it easy for you. They're both on Shell Beach.'

Dae smiled. She hauled on her steering wheel and pulled a U turn on Beach Road. 'I'm by the Village Mall.

I'll be there in ten.'

She drove carefully back up Beach Road. The last thing she needed was to be stopped by the police. She parked up on Shell Beach by the big mosque and stepped from her black Range Rover. Her slim, powerful legs were clad in black leggings, over which she wore a voluminous black t shirt finished off by black trainers. She glanced around, assuring herself that no-one was watching as she reached into the boot. She pulled out her revolver, checked the safety catch and slipped it into the holster she wore beneath her t shirt. She added a spare magazine. She adjusted her scarf that hung artfully round her neck. The seams were sown with weights and two lead weights hung at either end, enabling her to use it as an African lynch cloth if need be.

She pulled on a pair of sun glasses to veil her eyes. They were dark, free of make up, watchful in her pale, oval face. They were also merciless. She had made her first kill at sixteen, when a man was foolish enough to attack her younger sister. Her father, who had left his Korean home-land to move to Dubai before Dae was even born, had believed that his sons and daughters alike should know the principles of self defence. Dae had proven an adept pupil, quickly outstripping her older brothers, gaining her black belt in Tae Kwando by the age of twelve. She had trained and improvised ever since.

She combined her skills with a taste for vengeance. Soon killing became for her a dispassionate and highly lucrative business. She still killed for free when any severe injustices came to her attention, but most of the time she was employed by a shadowy group of the world's business and crime potentates, and the odd politician.

Her family knew nothing of her covert operations. They employed her as Sales Manager for their textile manufacturing business. It was a good cover. She could fit international assignments around her trips to visit textile buyers around the world. Local assignments were easily accommodated.

Dae locked her car and walked quickly onto the sand. Her outfit made her look like an innocent woman out for a walk or jog. It also enabled her to run if need be, without attracting attention.

Her eyes scanned the beach. She'd received the photos earlier on her e mail. She had memorised the faces; one boy, one girl. She hoped they were enjoying the last few minutes of their lives. Dae smiled to herself, sublimely confident. She never failed.

CHAPTER FORTY NINE

ಹಿ The Truth ಲಿ

FINN WATCHED AND WAITED, summoning Triton over and over. The waves crashed around the rocks sending spray high into the air. Vlad slunk back and sat triumphantly gazing out to sea. His father's men would be here soon. Then they'd see just how brave Finn Kennedy was, with all his lies and his insane threats.

The tide seemed to be coming in very fast and the plumes of spray soon soaked them. Even though the air was warm, the wind was cool and they became chilled.

Finn stared at the undulating water, seeking a shape, seeking a form. He was beginning to feel uneasy. He had that hunted sensation again. The back of his neck tingled with fear. He kept glancing round as if expecting to see someone or something in the shadows, but there was nothing there, just this nebulous fear that refused to go away.

Vlad kept turning round too, glancing uneasily over his shoulder. He was seriously getting on Finn's nerves.

Finn turned back to the sea. The light from the moon silvered the dark water, and something else….. suddenly Finn sat bolt upright, staring hard. He heard Vlad gasp. There, in the waves, was Triton. He rode up on a wave, then dragged his body onto the rocks so that only the tip of his tail was left in the sea.

'You came,' said Finn smiling.

Triton bowed his head and smiled gravely. 'Hello Finn. Of course I came.' He turned to Georgie and smiled at her. 'Hello Georgina.'

'Hello Triton.' Georgie beamed at him. Whatever else was going on in the world, seeing Triton here before her, with his magnificent, noble face, and his eyes, radiating goodness, made everything instantly better. He was like a piece of the sun captured here on earth and she basked in his glow.

Triton reached out and took her hand. She felt his power stream into her, electrifying her. When he took his hand away, hers glowed, as always, with phosphorescence,

Triton turned to Vlad. His smile faded. 'And who is this?'

Vlad was staring at Triton with a look of sheer amazement. 'It's true!' he muttered, over and over. 'You were telling the truth.'

Finn glared at him. 'Of course we were.' He turned to Triton.

'This is Vladimir Czarovich.' Finn paused. 'His father is the Phoenix. His father is a Fire Djinn.'

Triton's eyes widened. Light seemed to pour from them as he scrutinised Vlad. Finn saw anger, he saw understanding and he saw pity flicker across Triton's great face.

'Why is he here?' the Sea Djinn asked softly.

'He's come to help us,' said Finn. 'I have a plan.' Quickly he told Triton.

Vlad was mumbling, struggling to speak. When Finn had finished speaking to Triton, he burst out, 'My father, he's not a djinn. He's can't be. He's just a man.'

Finn shook his head. 'We saw him transform,' he said, 'he passed through a Portal into the Kingdom of Dark Fire. We were dragged with him.'

'So you've met Jehannem,' mused Triton. 'You know his name means Hell in Arabic. That's what he represents, here on earth. Hellfire. He is immensely powerful. He's over two thousand five hundred years old.'

'Two thousand five hundred?' repeated Finn, astounded.

'Can't he die?' asked Georgie.

'He has died, several times, and each time he has been reborn as a Phoenix.'

'Can't he die properly, and stay dead?' asked Georgie.

'Not so far. But all djinn die, sooner or later, so unless he's found some secret source of eternal life, he should too.'

'Perhaps he's like the sun,' whispered Georgie. 'Perhaps he'll burn for millions of years.'

'Even your sun will burn out one day, Georgie,' said Triton. 'He's a Dark sun. Dark fire. The fires of destruction. They burn quicker.'

'And the Fire Djinn of the Day, where's he?' asked Georgie. 'We met a Fire Rukh, a LightFighter called Unak. He helped us escape from the Kingdom of Fire. He told us that Vulcan had been missing for more than a year. He thought that Jehannem had killed or imprisoned him, then erected a charm to stop any successors. He was holding a lot of Fire Rukhs of the Light as slaves.'

Triton hissed in a breath. 'I thought as much. None of us has seen or heard of Vulcan for a long time. All our worlds need him, desperately. Vulcan is sun fire. Gold fire.

Cleansing fire. He makes Jehannem look like a child. He is ten thousand years old. His own fire cleanses him. He is the fire of light that legends say will grant eternal life to those who bathe in it.'

Vlad sat silently beside them, eyes fixed on Triton. He was shivering, as if with cold.

Finn suddenly stiffened. All his sense were screaming danger. He glanced round but saw nothing. Triton too was scanning the darkness.

'DarkFighters approaching. Finn, stay with me. We need to talk further. You must go,' he said to Georgie and Vlad. 'Now.' He took Georgie's hand again.

'Your bit of the plan is brave beyond measure. Good luck, Georgina.'

Georgie nodded.

Triton turned to Vlad and took his hand.

As he did so, both Triton and Vlad flinched. Triton frowned at Vlad and turned his wrist.

'What is this?' Triton asked, staring at the burn.

'M..m..my father burnt me,' Vlad managed to say.

'Many times?' asked Triton.

'When I do not do as he wishes.'

'He controls you, with the burn,' said Triton. He reached up his fingers and very gently laid them on the burn. Before Vlad's astonished eyes, the burn healed and new skin grew over it. Vlad let out a cry, as if something were flying out of his mouth.

'Go,' urged Triton to Georgie and Vlad. 'They are already at the other end of the beach. Run.'

'Goodbye Triton,' said Georgie, 'bye Finn.' She grabbed her cousin in a fierce bear hug, wondering fleetingly if she would ever see him again.

'Good luck, George,' said Finn. 'Don't trust Vlad,' he whispered. Georgie gave a slight nod. 'Good luck yourself,' she said, then she grabbed Vlad's hand and ran. They scrambled over the rocks and into the cover of the Fishermen's village.

'Come,' said Triton to Finn. 'Hurry.'

Finn sucked in a couple of deep breaths, rushed into the water and climbed onto Triton's back. With a lash of his great dolphin's tale, Triton swam away, and dived down under cover of the sea.

CHAPTER FIFTY

⚬ Dae ⚭

'C'MON,' WHISPERED GEORGIE, PULLING Vlad along between the shacks of the Fishermen's Village.

Vlad seemed to be in a state of shock. His eyes were glazed and his movements were heavy. Georgie wrenched at his arm.

'Come on. We have to get back to JAM. Your helicopter should be there, waiting.'

Vlad's eyes widened and he seemed to recover himself. 'OK OK,' he replied, speeding up.

They ran through the gate and out onto Street 2B. Neither of them noticed the figure in black, jogging quietly along the pavement a hundred yards away.

A taxi rounded the corner and pulled up directly in front of them. It disgorged a family of five onto the pavement outside their villa.

'Can you take us to JAM?' Georgie quickly asked the driver. He nodded, wordlessly.

They slipped in and slammed the door behind them. Georgie sank back on the cracked plastic seats, never knowing that she had been seconds away from a silenced bullet in the brain.

'Phew,' she said, blowing out a sigh of relief as the taxi turned onto Road 31A. 'That was lucky. I think we've got clean away. I wonder who the DarkFighters were, how they were onto us?' she mused. 'It must have been your father's men.'

Vlad's eyes flicked with jagged guilt. He shrugged as if, really, how could he possibly know.

On the dark pavement, Dae cursed, but luck was on her side too. Another taxi arrived, depositing guests at the same villa. Dae hopped in and told the driver to catch up with the taxi driving off ahead of them.

'Slot in two cars behind it when it gets to Beach Road,' she said, in imperious, slightly American-accented English. The driver was about to complain about being given silly instructions and no advance warning of their destination. Then he saw the woman's eyes as she took off her sunglasses. He flinched, swallowed his words and promptly followed her commands.

Ten minutes later, their taxi dropped Georgie and Vlad at JAM then roared off into the night. As the sound of its engines faded away, Georgie felt suddenly stranded and horribly exposed. The school and the neighbouring streets were deserted, eerily silent. This would be the perfect place for a kill. She glanced round, fear prickling along her neck. There was no sign of any Darkfighters, of anyone at all, but that gave her no comfort.

'I hope your helicopter's there,' she said to Vlad. 'If it is waiting on the cricket pitch, its engines must be turned off.'

'It'll be there,' said Vlad. 'I'm sure.'

'Hellooo!' called Georgie. 'Anybody there?' She rattled the main gates. They were locked.

Vlad called out too. 'Hello! Hello! Open up!'

A school security guard appeared from the building, rubbing his eyes as if he had been asleep.

'What are you two wanting?' he asked. 'School is closed till tomorrow. Go home.'

'My helicopter. Should be here,' mumbled Vlad.

'Helicopter?' The guard raised his eyes to the sky. 'Yes and my helicopter will be here soon to take me back to India. Go on. Go away home.'

'It will,' insisted Vlad. 'I said I would be here at seven. It picks me up every day at two fifteen normally. But I was busy…,' he added lamely.

'I work nights. I have no idea what goes on here during the day. I suggest you -'

'Wait!' said Georgie, cutting him off. 'Listen. A helicopter!'

The distant whine of the helicopter vibrated through the darkness. Soon they could see the lights as it approached. It circled the school once, then landed.

'See!' said Vlad to the astonished guard. 'I told you.'

She still had time to walk away, thought Georgie. Just catch a taxi back home, end her parents' agony. In fact, a taxi was just pulling up twenty yards away, a black clad woman getting out, paying off the driver. She could take that taxi, get far way from here, go home to her parents, to her sisters. Then what? Leave Fred in the clutches of Jehannem, stand back and do nothing while the clock ticked time to oblivion?

She turned back to the guard. 'Please let us in,' she said to him. 'We need to be on that helicopter.'

'What is your name?' the guard asked Vlad.

Vlad paused for a moment, as if unsure. 'Vladimir

Czarovich,' he said, falteringly.

'Wait here while I go and investigate,' said the guard, walking off.

Dae dropped to her knees, taking aim. At that moment, a rubbish lorry careened round the corner and accelerated up to the school. Two men got out and began to laboriously empty the bins stacked up on the road.

Dae bent down over her trainers, as if engaged in nothing more sinister than tying her laces. She concealed the revolver in the belt beneath her billowing t shirt.

'Right, just spin your pilot a line about how I'm coming for a sleepover OK?' said Georgie.

Vlad nodded.

'But when we get to your house, I'll need to stay out of your father's sight. He's hunting Finn and I'm sure he knows my identity by now, so he'll be hunting me too.'

'So why on earth are you coming with me to my own house if my father's hunting you?' asked Vlad.

'Because I have no choice. I have to try to do something, to free Fred, to stop Jehannem. What, exactly I am going to do I don't know yet. I'll just have to make it up as I go along and you'll have to help me.' Georgie looked Vlad hard in the eye.

'You are going to help me, Vlad, aren't you?'

Vlad felt sick. How could he explain that he had already told his father that Georgie Sherwood was an enemy, that he was leading her into a trap?

Vlad looked terrified, thought Georgie. Guilty too. But then he was going to betray his father, wasn't he?

'Think about your mother,' urged Georgie. 'Think about saving her, and the rest of the planet while you're at it.'

A new light seemed to switch on in Vlad's eyes. 'I will,' he said determinedly, fingering the patch of new skin on his wrist. 'I will.'

The rubbish lorry's engines roared loudly as the driver accelerated away. Dae steadied her arm for the shot.

'Please!' came a voice in the darkness. 'Please, come this way. Apologies. Very many apologies.'

It was the guard, rushing to unlock the gate, beckoning them in and through, relocking the gate after them.

Georgie took a deep breath, gripped Vlad's hand and squeezed.

'Good luck,' she said.

'Good luck yourself,' Vlad replied, face pinched with fear.

Dae stared into the empty darkness, her eyes black with fury, her heart hot with shame. She had failed.

CHAPTER FIFTY ONE

The Palace of the Djinn

THE HELICOPTER WAS WAITING like a giant bird of prey. The pilot glowered at Vlad as he approached. Vlad ignored him as he ushered Georgie in first, motioning her to put on headphones. He climbed in after her and put on his own headphones.

'Where the hell have you been?' shouted the pilot, turning in his seat to harangue Vlad. 'Your father has organised a major search party for you and you stroll up as if everything's just dandy, and who the hell is this?'

The pilot jabbed a finger at Georgie.

'Ahmed, calm down,' replied Vlad. 'I've rung my father and he knows I'm fine. And this is my friend, er, Tanya, my only friend in this blasted school. She's coming for a sleepover.'

'A sleepover? Tonight? Are you mad?'

'Probably,' replied Vlad. 'Now fly me home.'

Ahmed shot him another venomous look before turning back to the controls.

Moments later, Georgie felt as if her stomach had been ditched on the ground as the helicopter lifted up off the grass and pitched forward into the night.

Georgie looked down at the glittering lights of Dubai, spread out below her. In the distance, she could see Burj

Dubai glittering like a knife in the darkness. What looked to be miniature cars sped along Sheikh Zayed Road.

Soon they left behind the lights of Dubai and flew in darkness over the desert. Georgie and Vlad sat in silence, lost in their own nightmares.

Georgie suddenly gave a start. Other lights beamed through the darkness of the sky. They seemed to be coming from all directions. Helicopters! Dozens of them, converging around the glittering house that now came into view. Jehannem's house. As they got closer still, Georgie saw the Djinn, standing, arms outstretched to the sky, welcoming the swarms of helicopters. Welcoming the Chosen Ones.

Their own helicopter hove round to the back of the house and landed neatly.

'Get out. Hurry!' urged the pilot. 'I have to fly back to the Burj to collect another VIP.'

Vlad and Georgie ducked out, ran across the landing pad and headed in through the back of the house.

Their feet were loud on the marble floors. Their reflections skittered past ornate gilt mirrors that seemed to adorn every wall. The house smelled of wax polish, cigar smoke, the Djinn's aftershave, and, under it all, the rotten-egg, sulphuric whiff of Djinn. But there was no-one about.

All they could hear was the roar of the helicopters. It sounded, thought Georgie, like war.

'Get me out of sight somewhere,' whispered Georgie.

'My bedroom,' said Vlad. 'Follow me.'

He led Georgie up a flight of marble stairs. He gasped suddenly. 'They're gone!' he exclaimed.

'What's gone?' asked Georgie.

'The paintings. They were on the walls. There were Picassos, Rembrandts, a Monet.' Vlad was aghast. 'He loved them. I did too. Someone must have stolen them.'

Georgie looked at him sadly. 'They'll be in the Fire Ark I think, so they don't burn.'

Vlad looked wildly from the blank walls to Georgie. He ran a trembling hand through his hair. Georgie knew that his old world was crumbling, and the new world that replaced it was one he did not want to believe in.

Vlad turned away and set off down a long hallway, hurried to the last room and beckoned Georgie inside. He closed the door behind him and blew out a sigh.

Georgie flicked off the light and walked over to the window overlooking the front garden. Jehannem was standing there, arms still outstretched to the skies, welcoming the helicopters as they disgorged the kleptocrats and the war criminals, the elected rulers and the crime lords.

Georgie turned back to Vlad, standing immobile in the darkness.

'Does your father have a study here, an office?'

Vlad nodded. 'Yeah. Works in it a lot.'

'Good. Who else is in this house?' she asked. 'There must be an army of people to keep it clean and look after you and your father.'

'There is, but they come in to cook and clean when my father or I summon them. They live in a building under the ground, out of the way. My father doesn't like to have them around.'

'I'll bet. Wouldn't do to have them see him transforming into a column of fire.'

Vlad turned away, but not before Georgie had seen the

flash of misery in his eyes. Whatever Jehannem was, he was also Vlad's father.

'OK Take me to your father's study please, think up a good excuse for being there in case anyone pitches up.'

Georgie followed Vlad back down the hallway, down the stairs and to the opposite end of the house. They saw no-one.

Vlad opened a gleaming mahogany door and flicked off the light. Georgie followed him in and pulled the door behind her. It clicked shut with a whoosh of air. The room suddenly felt claustrophobic. Georgie swept her eyes round. The lights from outside filtered in, allowing her to see a desk, several leather sofas, a drinks cabinet and several televisions.

'Where would he hide things?' she asked Vlad. 'In his desk, or does he have a safe?'

'I don't know about a safe. I have seen him locking things up in his desk though.'

'And the key?'

Vlad gave a little smile. He walked up to a clock, opened the back and carefully removed a sparkling silver key.

'Devious,' said Georgie, as Vlad turned it in the lock.

'He leaves me alone for ages, with no-one. Nothing to do.' He shrugged. 'I spy on him. A bit. Now and then.'

'Well done you,' replied Georgie, feeling a pang for Vlad and the twisted world in which he lived.

Vlad pulled open the desk drawer and stood back to allow Georgie to sit down and examine the contents.

She pulled out a red leather file. Inside were sheet upon sheet of numbers, with names of what appeared to be banks, and then the names of the faces she had recognised outside. Bank payments. She put them back in the folder and flicked quickly through other sheets. More numbers. What did they mean? She picked out three of the pages that looked the most significant to her. One was headed with a splodge of red. Blood, Georgie wondered, or red ink? She folded them and shoved them into her jeans pocket.

She glanced up as Vlad gave a start.

'What's wrong?' she asked.

'Thought I heard something. Get over there, behind that screen.'

Georgie quickly put the red file in the drawer and pulled it closed, then she hurried round behind an ornate Japanese screen, just as Vlad was opening the door and peeking out into the hallway.

Georgie glanced about her; another desk, a fax machine and a copier and scanner. Nowhere to hide, but… on impulse, she pulled the sheets of paper from her jeans, photocopied each one, hid the photocopies inside her shoes and pushed the originals back in her pocket.

Just as she had finished, she heard the door close softly and Vlad's footsteps approach.

'No-one there,' he said. 'But time to get out.'

'I'm with you,' replied Georgie.

Back in Vlad's bedroom, Georgie paced in the darkness, figuring out a plan.

'We have to get into the Fire Ark, the two of us. We have to try to find Fred, and get him out.'

Vlad scratched his eyebrow. 'My father has his Hummer on standby, with the driver inside. I could try to ask him to take us in, say that my father was coming later.'

'And when your father finds out you've taken his Hummer and gone inside which you are absolutely forbidden to do, what happens then?'

'He better not find me,' replied Vlad vehemently.

Georgie rubbed her hands over her eyes. She felt trapped. She was deeply uneasy about using Vlad and trusting him, but she really had no choice.

'All right. Let's go and nab your father's Hummer.'

Vlad nodded, but his eyes looked tortured. 'What's going to happen, Georgie? You don't really think we can stop this, get out of this, do you?' he asked, his voice so quiet Georgie had to struggle to hear him.

She looked straight into his eyes. 'Mad and wild as it sounds, Vlad, I do think we can stop this. I do think we can get out alive. I have no idea how, just that we will do it and we will figure it out. If we don't think that, then we might as well give up now. Is that what you want to do?'

Vlad glanced at the patch of skin where his burn had healed. It glowed green with phosphorence. He blew out a great sigh. 'No. I do not want to give up.'

'Good,' said Georgie with a smile. 'Let's go.'

The Hummer stood gleaming under a floodlight. The driver, who must have been well over six foot, leaned against the door, smoking.

'Good,' whispered Vlad. 'He'd never be lounging around if he thought my father was about to need him.'

Vlad strode up to him with an air of urgency.

'Hi, Hans. My father wants me and, er, Tanya inside, then he wants you back for him.'

Hans dropped his cigarette and ground it out thoughtfully. 'You're not allowed in there.'

'Well not normally, but tonight's a little different. Better hurry. Don't want to keep him waiting.'

'He said to get us to the Control Room,' said Georgie in an imperious voice. 'Doctor Bradbury is waiting for us there.'

'You know Dr Bradbury?' asked the driver incredulously.

'I met him last time I was down there,' said Georgie, ransacking her brains for other names. 'I know all those guys, Bradbury, Eden, Caliban.'

'How come you got in and not Vladimir?' asked the driver.

Georgie pasted on a smug smile. 'You'll just have to ask Uncle Igor that, won't you? Now come on. Hurry up. Please. We don't want him angry. Do we?' demanded Georgie.

'Get in,' said the driver, opening the door for them.

The door slammed with a thud of finality. They drove across the sand, shielded from the front of the house by the bank of Range Rovers and Hummers waiting to chauffeur the Chosen Ones from their helicopters to their new home. Georgie took one last glance at the night sky, bejewelled with stars, before the Hummer turned onto tarmac and drove into the great maw of the bunker.

Down they went, round and round, deeper and deeper on the road to hell.

The deeper they went, the more intense became the look of disbelief on Vlad's face. They finally levelled out and drove through the miniature city. The supermarket which had been bare just days ago was now stocked with rows of fruit and vegetables on stands outside. All ready for the Chosen Ones, thought Georgie. For Armageddon.

Vlad leaned across to Georgie, his face tight with anger.

'He lied,' he whispered so Hans would not hear. 'My father. He lied about everything.'

'I'm sorry.'

'I couldn't really believe it, what you and Finn said. I knew something was wrong, something odd was going on, but this…' he waved his arm around.

'This is real,' whispered Georgie. 'And his plans to exterminate everybody and everything on the face of the earth are real too.'

'I'll help you,' whispered Vlad through gritted teeth. 'I'll do whatever it takes.'

CHAPTER FIFTY TWO

The Limits of Power

IN THE CAVE OF Light, Finn told Triton everything.

'The Chosen Ones are arriving tonight. Armageddon happens at ten,' he concluded.

'You have done well, Finn. I salute you. I will muster my Kingdom, but there is one thing you must know, Finn, my friend. We are creatures of the sea. We cannot spend much time out of the sea, or we will weaken quickly and die.'

Finn blinked back his amazement. 'But, but I thought you could transform into anything you wanted.'

'We can, but we cannot inhabit those forms for long outside the sea. What this means, Finn, is that we have about one hour's fighting time. More than that, we die.'

Finn sucked hard on his conch of air. He had never thought of Triton as vulnerable, as fragile in any way. It was impossible to think of him dying, or able to fight in Finn's own world for only a short time.

'That's why Jehannem had to get through to the Kingdom of Fire. Drax mentioned that he was recharging. So he is vulnerable too,' mused Finn.

'But if he makes an inferno of earth, he can recharge here, he won't need to pass through into his old Kingdom,' observed Triton grimly. 'I cannot put out word to the Kingdoms of Air and Rock,' he added, 'because there are traitors there, and if any plan we make is told to Jehannem, then we are lost before we start. So we will fight, the Kingdom of the Sea, and the Kingdom of man in the persons of you, and Georgie and Fred too, when you find him and release him.'

'You think he's still alive?' asked Finn, falteringly.

Triton held his gaze, nodded.

Finn read hope in Triton's eyes, but uncertainty too.

'I need to hurry back,' said Finn. 'And find Fred. I'll also try to do as much damage as I can, sabotage the detonation. Somehow. I don't know how, but I'll figure something out.'

Triton nodded. 'You will find a way. We will get there at about nine thirty to help. Look out for us then. Be ready. We will either go in by this emergency lift you told me of, or by the tunnel. Now, ride on my back to the shore, then travel from there.'

Finn glanced sharply at Triton. Did he know of his disastrous attempt to travel back before? Triton just smiled at him, eyes impervious.

'Come on Finn. Get on my back.'

Finn took a few deep sucks on the conch, draining the last of its oxygen. Then he dropped the meteoric stone and climbed onto Triton's back. In seconds they were hurtling through the sea.

Triton slowed about two hundred yards off Shell Beach. He rose up from the water cautiously and peered through the darkness.

'The DarkFighters have gone. But be careful Finn. I'll take you in, and then, from the shallows, you must travel.'

'All right. I will.'

Triton surfed in to the shallows on the crest of a wave. Finn saw to his relief that the beach was deserted. He slid from Triton's back and gazed into eyes that now revealed faith.

'Bye, Triton.'

'Goodbye, Finn. This is war now. Again you enter the battle. May the powers of Light go with you. May you fight with all you are and all you can be.' Triton raised his arms to the sky, then lowered them slowly to place them on Finn's head, like a blessing.

Finn felt the power. He felt it flow into every bone and muscle and sinew. It warmed him, gave him courage. Still he tasted fear in his mouth, but he knew that was good. Fear would sharpen him.

'I'll see you again Triton. Soon.'

'I know it,' said the Sea Djinn.

Finn steadied himself, readied himself to Travel, readied himself for war.

Chapter Fifty Three

∽ Illegal Entry ∽

H ANS, THE DRIVER, KEPT glancing nervously at his watch.

'Just leave us by the main entrance and we'll find our own way,' said Georgie.

'Are you sure?' asked Hans, clearly relieved.

'Absolutely,' replied Georgie. 'I know my way perfectly well, even through Vlad doesn't.' She gave Vlad a haughty look, just for good measure.

Vlad replied in kind. 'Look you little self-satisfied prig. Just because father -'

'Enough!' said Hans plaintively. 'No squabbling, please. Look, here we are,' he said with evident relief.

'Thanks,' said Georgie, leaping out.

'See you later,' said Vlad.

'I'm going to have to hurry,' muttered Hans. 'If your father is waiting for me he'll crucify me.'

'Maybe just fry you,' said Vlad bitterly.

The driver gave him a strange look, then executed a rapid turn and sped off, tyres screaming.

'Right,' said Georgie, straightening her shoulders. 'Hold your head high. Look like you own the place and one day you will. That's what Fred's parents always said to him,' she explained to Vlad. 'Act like you belong, and everyone will think you do.'

Vlad gave a snort. 'I'm meant to belong. In theory, this place does belong to me, in part. I'm his son, for God's sake!'

'Would you want it to belong to you?' asked Georgie.

'No. Of course not.'

'Right. Well let's go.'

Together they walked up the flight of steps leading to the enormous door.

'Looks like a museum,' said Vlad.

'Yeah, only the artefacts will be human and other animals, and they'll be alive,' replied Georgie.

There was a small door cut into the enormous door. Georgie banged on it.

'Open up. It's Tanya and Vladimir. Hurry.'

Footsteps sounded on the other side of the door, which suddenly swung open to reveal a gun-toting guard.

'Master Vladimir,' he said in surprise.

'Hi,' replied Vlad. 'May we come in?'

'Who is this?' asked the guard.

'She is my cousin, Tanya.'

The guard seemed to hesitate for a split second, then he stood back to let them through.

No-one challenged them as Georgie led them through the hallways. They passed a couple of women wheeling along a caterer's trolley of steaming dishes; they passed men in suits with briefcases. A wild-looking man with bushy hair that looked like he and it had been subjected to an electric shock, overtook them muttering under his breath. Everyone they encountered seemed to be in a great hurry, eyes pre-occupied, brows furrowed. They showed no interest in the skin-headed boy and his elfin companion.

After a number of wrong turns, Georgie stiffened. She slowed down and peeked round the corner of one corridor. She quickly pulled back.

'Control Room's at the end.' She gulped back her nerves. 'Are you ready?' she asked Vlad.

He nodded. His heart felt like it was slamming into his ribs it beat so hard. 'Are you?' he managed to ask.

'I think so. C'mon. Let's go.'

Chapter Fifty Four

∞ The Burning ∞

GEORGIE AND VLAD WALKED side by side down the corridor toward the Control Room. Just as they approached the door, it swung open and a woman emerged, pushing a trolley of empty plates and coffee cups. Vlad and Georgie stood back to allow her to pass and then nipped in before the heavy door swung shut.

Georgie scanned the room; televisions banked up in rows of ten, showing flickering images of the desert, of city streets, of green pastures; computers - dozens of them, and people bent over them, feverishly tapping in commands, and, right in the centre, sitting next to the frizzy-haired man, deep in conversation with him, was Fred. Georgie wanted to cry out and rush across to him, but instinct held her back.

'What the hell are you doing here?' barked out a voice. An angry looking man with close-cropped black hair strode over to them. 'What is this? A kindergarten?' he demanded.

'I have every right to be here,' replied Vlad, managing somehow to hide his nerves, 'and so does my friend,'

'Does your father know?'

'Of course he knows. We wouldn't be here otherwise, would we?'

'Wants you to have ringside seats for the show, huh? Wants you to see the burning,' replied the man with obscene relish. 'Everybody up in smoke.'

There was a hiss of something that sounded like disgust from the man beside Fred. 'Leave him alone, Sergeant Raven,' he burst out.

Sergeant Raven laughed at him, lips curled with contempt.

Georgie and Fred locked eyes. Georgie tried to transmit a dozen questions in her look; Are you alright? What have you found out? What is happening?

But Fred's eyes revealed nothing. He had the same, glazed, zombie-like expression she had seen on Vlad, but at least he didn't appear to have been physically harmed.

'Go and sit with the other child then, and stay out of our way,' said Sergeant Raven.

Vlad and Georgie took their chance. They walked over, pulled up some chairs and sat by Fred.

'Hi,' said Fred, trying to conceal a smile.

'Hi,' replied Georgie and Vlad.

'So, what's happening here?' asked Vlad.

The frizzy-haired man turned round in his chair to face them. He had electric blue eyes of startling intelligence. He rubbed at his wrist. Georgie saw the livid burn and flinched.

'We are preparing to start the countdown,' he answered. His voice seemed to waver between horror and excitement.

'How long is the countdown?' asked Georgie, striving to sound casual. 'There're still lots of the Chosen Ones above ground and making their way down,' she continued.

'This isn't some little tripwire,' answered Frizzy Hair indignantly. 'The countdown lasts two hours. Then, at ten tonight, we begin nuclear meltdown. We will send up a signal, a tower of fire so high it will be seen for hundreds of miles all around by the naked eye, and it will also be relayed by live TV feed to our agents all around the world. This will be their signal to detonate. All together we will detonate a thousand nuclear bombs, tens of thousands of conventional bombs, and we will achieve our target,' he concluded, his voice sounding strangely mechanical as if he had banished all emotion.

Georgie wanted to gag. 'Really,' she managed to say.

'Really,' Frizzy Hair answered. 'Fred here is assisting me. Mr Czarovich thinks he is bright. Thinks he needs a real education.'

Georgie swallowed back a gasp and gazed into Fred's eyes. He looked back at her, then down at his own wrist. Georgie knew what she was going to see; the burn, fresh and livid. So Fred too, was under the Fire Djinn's control. She felt a wave of misery, followed by rage.

'Right,' said Sergeant Raven, marching across the room towards them. 'Enough talk. Back to w-'

The door to the Control Room crashed open. In strode Jehannem, eyes blazing. He marched up to Vlad, who cowered down in his seat. The Djinn snatched up Vlad's wrist and gripped it hard. Abruptly, as if stung, he let it go. Slowly, carefully, with his finger tips, he turned Vlad's wrist this way and that, examining it.

'Phosphorescence!' he hissed. 'The mark of the Sea Djinn. You rang me from Shell Beach, told me you were with Sherwood and Kennedy. You didn't mention Triton.' Jehannem leant so close to his son that his spittle flew onto Vlad's face. 'My own son, consorting with my enemy, letting him undo my mark. So you think you are cured, do you? This is the cure boy. This and only this.'

Jehannem, face red with rage, grabbed his son's wrist, gripped it so hard he almost snapped it.

Vlad screamed in pain. His whole body shuddered and writhed in agony, but still the Djinn gripped him, malice contorting his face.

Smoke billowed from Vlad's wrist, gradually easing. Vlad's body ceased its wild thrashing. The Djinn released his son and Vlad collapsed to the floor, sobbing quietly. Everyone in the room turned away, apart from Georgie, who watched in horror. Sheer hate rose in her like a fever.

Jehannem glared down at Vlad. 'Now you are mine.'

Vlad lifted his eyes to his father. They were dead, the eyes of a zombie.

'What did you tell Triton?' asked Jehannem.

'I told him nothing,' replied Vlad.

Jehannem studied his son, saw the truth in his face. He grunted and turned away.

His eyes widened in surprise when he noticed Georgie. The girl was alive! Dae had failed.

'Why is she here?' Jehannem asked Vlad in a silvery whisper.

Vlad's eyes flickered from Georgie back to his father. Georgie could see him struggling. Now he was controlled again. He would not be able to lie to Jehannem.

'She's my friend,' Vlad answered.

'Really? And I ask again, why is she here?'

'To keep me company. I was lonely.'

Georgie felt a surge of affection for Vlad. He had told his own truth, omitted the lie. Along with the phosphorescence, some semblance of Triton's cure must have remained within Vlad.

The Djinn turned his eyes back to Georgie. She felt

his mind probing hers, like hot slivers of arrows stabbing her brain. Georgie grabbed her head; a Thought Thief. She filled her head with images of her bedroom, with longing to be there, lying safe in bed, far from here, far from madness, far from evil.

The Djinn barked out a laugh. 'Oh, the poor baby misses her home.' Jehannem shot out his hand, grabbed Georgie's wrist and gripped it.

Georgie had never before felt such pain. The burn seemed to fill her body. She heard herself crying out. She couldn't help it. Then she felt something flooding her veins, a kind of passivity, acceptance. Everything would be fine, as long as she listened to him. Did everything he said, did everything he said, everything he said…

The Djinn moved away. Georgie felt her own self drifting up and away. Come back, she wanted to call, please, please, come back. She was losing herself, she knew it and there was nothing she could do. She thought of Finn, of her parents, of her sisters, of everyone on the planet dying, consumed by fire. No, it couldn't happen. It couldn't. She must stop, she must stop….An idea tugged at her mind, out of reach, like herself, just drifting away.

Suddenly she saw Triton in her mind. She saw him handing her and Fred and Finn their sea glass pendants. That was it! She nearly cried out. With the fingers of her good hand, she reached down under her shirt for the pendant. She glanced around to make sure no-one was watching, then she pulled the pendant over her head and held the sea glass to her wrist. There was a hissing noise, which she covered up with a coughing fit. Smoke rose from her wrist, but it had been smoking before anyway, so she hoped no-one would notice. The pain was indescribable.

She felt as if her body were a battleground. Her very blood seemed to be fighting itself, bubbling through her body in revolt. She wrapped the string round her wrist and kept the pendant pushed hard into the burn. Then, second by second, the pain abated, and slowly, incredibly slowly, Georgie felt herself returning.

The Djinn too returned.

'So, my former LightFighter,' he whispered to Georgie, his eyes slits of evil. 'Welcome to the Dark World. Now you shall help me in my battle with the Light. You too shall betray your Sea-bound master. I shall put you to work, just like little Fred here. Nothing like the sweet pleasure of corruption, I find. So, tell me, what did you tell the Lord Triton?'

'Nothing,' answered Georgie.

'Does he know about my plans?'

'What plans?' asked Georgie, eyes wide with feigned innocence.

'Is he coming here?' demanded the Djinn. 'Is he going to try to stop me?'

'Stop you doing what?' asked Georgie.

Jehannem scrutinised her. Georgie hoped he didn't try to read her mind, but would be content just with her answers, believing her incapable of lying, burnt as she was, loyal, supposedly only to him.

'So what were you doing there? Why was my son taken there?'

'To be cured,' answered Georgie.

'Where is Kennedy? Where is the Prince of Atlantis?' hissed Jehannem, his frustration growing. 'He will know. You are just a hanger on. No wonder you know nothing.'

'I do not know where Finn is,' answered Georgie, truthfully.

Jehannem whirled back to his son. 'Where is Finn Kennedy?'

'He went with the dolphin/man,' replied Vlad mechanically. 'He went down into the sea.'

The Djinn sucked in a breath. 'Sergeant Raven,' he called. 'I think the Kingdom of the Light might be on its way. We must prepare for war.'

CHAPTER FIFTY FIVE

The Power
of Sea Glass

FINN LANDED HEAVILY IN darkness. His right shoulder crashed into a wall and he bit back a curse. His heart was roaring and he felt the blood pounding in his ears. He held still, trying to listen. He heard nothing, save a background throb and hum - the Fire Ark breathing.

Slowly, he straightened up, using his hands as feelers; shelves, lots of them, and papers, boxes. The storeroom! He had made it! He inched forward to where he thought the door was. He could see the faintest crack of light creeping under it. His fingers found the handle, then very gently, he cranked open the door just enough to peer out.

The room was deserted, but the muffled sound of voices came to him. He dropped down to the floor and leopard crawled to the door. He inched up until he could look through the glass panel half way up it. He could just see the door to the Control Room.

Suddenly it opened and Georgie emerged. She'd made it! thought Finn, elated, but then he saw that she seemed to be weeping. Finn felt his heart contract with rage.

He watched her cross the corridor and enter the loo opposite. With a quick glance to check there was no-one else around, he hurried after her, praying that there was no-one inside.

Georgie was alone, bent over the sink, washing her face. She glanced up as the door opened.

'Finn!' she exclaimed. 'You're here!'

Finn grabbed her in a bear hug. Georgie hugged him back fiercely, then drew away with a smile.

'You made it, then. Well done George. But how on earth did you manage to get into the Control Room, and then just stroll out of it again, free as a bird? And is there any sign of Fred?' Finn garbled, desperate for information.

'Let's hide in the cubicle,' said Georgie. 'There's a lot to tell you.'

Locked inside the cubicle, Georgie filled Finn in as quickly as she could.

'Fred's alive. He's here in the Control Room. He's got pally with this nuclear scientist with mad grey hair called Professor Bradbury. Bradbury told me everything,' continued Georgie. 'At ten exactly, there will be a column of fire generated from here, so high that it will be seen for hundreds of miles and will be relayed on TV to their agents around the world. It will act as a signal to the others to begin detonation in a kind of chain reaction all around the world.'

Finn grabbed Georgie's hand to shake it.

'Well done G-' he stopped as she winced in pain.

'What's wrong?' he asked concerned. 'He gently took Georgie's wrist and pulled up her sleeve. He saw the sea glass pendant embedded in the burn.

'What the hell-'

'He burnt me. Jehannem. He's burnt Fred too. And Vlad. It was too horrible for words. Everything that's me seemed to leach out of me, leaving this shell that just wanted to obey him. I felt as though my soul were dying. Then I remembered the sea glass Triton gave us. It reverses the burn. It's even more horrible at first. It felt like my whole body was on fire, battling itself, then it got a bit better.'

Finn clenched his fists with rage so tight his nails scored into his skin.

'Well done, George,' he managed to say. 'But what about Fred? He must be under Jehannem's control now. And Vlad.'

'I'm going to go back in there and put Fred's pendant on his burn.'

'And Vlad?'

'I don't know. I daren't take my own pendant off until I feel stronger. When I do I'll try to heal him too.'

'He'll betray us. He'll have no choice.'

Georgie remembered Jehannem's words to Vlad - you phoned from the beach - Vlad already had betrayed them.

'I know,' she replied.

'I have to go,' said Finn. 'Tell Triton about this column of fire.'

Georgie nodded. 'I'll try and figure out if and how the detonation sequence can be sabotaged.'

'Good luck, George.'

'Good luck, Finn.'

Finn turned away from her. He conjured the image of Shell Beach, the spot where he had left Triton. He smelled the tang of salt water, he felt the breeze on his face, he heard the call of the *Muezzin* from the fishermen's mosque, he saw the moonlight dancing on the waves, and he saw the noble face of the Sea Djinn, unfathomable eyes beckoning him. There was a great rush of air and he was gone.

CHAPTER FIFTY SIX

⌾ Bleeding Nose ⌾

GEORGIE HURRIED BACK TO the Control Room. No guard had been sent to accompany her to the loo, because clearly the Djinn believed that once he had burnt you, he made you his creature, obedient in all ways. She smiled grimly. She would let him think that, then use it against him, but first she had to try to cure Fred and Vlad.

She knocked on the door to the Control Room. Sergeant Raven opened it with a scowl and let her in. She smiled sweetly.

'Thank you. I'm wondering, would it be possible to have some food? A few sandwiches and some juice perhaps?'

'What is this, a restaurant?' he demanded.

'No. This is Arabia and I am your guest and I am asking for some hospitality.'

A bark of laughter cut across the room.

'Get her what she asks for, Raven' commanded Jehannem. 'At least she has some spirit,' he added, turning on his heel and leaving the room with a flourish.

'Yes, sir,' answered Sergeant Raven, adding, when the Djinn was out of earshot: 'The world's about to be annihilated and my job's babysitting. Great. Just great.'

Georgie sat quietly in the corner, watching Fred talking animatedly to Frizzy Hair, trying to see how corrupted he had become. He seemed fascinated by Frizzy Hair, by his words, by the images he was seeing on screen. Georgie craned her neck to see. Factories in some big city. She suspected these contained not machinery, but nuclear warheads.

Why was Fred ignoring her, Georgie wondered. Was he playing a role, trying to pump Frizzy Hair for information, or, now that he had been burned, was he simply indifferent to her? Had the fire burned off their friendship as well?

Georgie watched and listened, trying to learn what she could.

Vlad got up and came to sit by her.

'See what happens when you try to resist my father?' he asked in his zombie's voice.

Georgie nodded awkwardly.

'He is the one with power, true power. Not Triton. My father,' Vlad added vehemently. His eyes glowed strangely. They seemed to veer between hatred and adulation. They focused suddenly on Georgie as if seeing something they hadn't noticed before.

'You are a plotter. You are trying to stop him. You-'

'I am a friend,' said Georgie, laying her hand gently on Vlad's arm. 'I am your friend. I made you iced ginger cake, remember? I beat you at chess...?'

There was a hint of a smile in the dark eyes. 'You did, didn't you?'

'I'm sure you'll beat me, next time,' replied Georgie.

The door opened with a bash and the food lady re-appeared pushing a trolley laden with sandwiches and jugs of apple and orange juice. Georgie jumped up, glad of the interruption. She waved a hand and the woman weaved her trolley awkwardly between the work stations. It would have been much easier for Georgie to move to the woman, but she wanted her snack served in as discreet a part of the room as possible.

'Thank you,' said Georgie. 'Sorry about all that weaving.'

The woman was almost bent double with age and hard labour. She looked up at Georgie in surprise, as if kind words were a foreign language. She bore a name badge; Hilda. She studied Georgie for a moment, and now it was Georgie's turn to be surprised. For a few, brief moments, the woman's eyes blazed with intelligence and purpose, and then, as if a screen had come down, they once more became dull, bovine. The woman unloaded the snacks and juices onto Georgie's table then awkwardly wove her way out.

Vlad helped himself to a Coke and a jam sandwich. He wandered over to the other side of the room, a thoughtful look in his eye.

Georgie walked apparently casually up to Fred and tapped him on the shoulder.

'Time for a snack, Fred. You need to keep your strength up.'

Fred glanced up at Georgie absent-mindedly. Georgie tried to communicate with her eyes the memory of their friendship, of all they had been through together. Something must have got through to Fred, or perhaps he was just hungry, for he got up and followed her.

Georgie handed Fred a sandwich. It was Marmite, his favourite.

He returned it to the plate.

'Don't tell me you'd prefer pot noodles,' said Georgie, striving to keep her voice jokey.

A distant light seemed to come on in Fred's eyes as he remembered. It was enough for Georgie.

'Are you wearing your sea glass pendant? The one Triton gave to you?' she whispered.

Fred looked puzzled, as if he were struggling for that memory too. 'Yes,' he answered at last.

'Take it off, discreetly,' whispered Georgie, biting into a sandwich in case anyone was looking.

'Why?' asked Fred.

'Please, Fred. Please just do as I ask.'

'But I'm busy. I need to go and help Professor Bradbury. He needs me.'

Georgie felt despair flood through her like a sickness. Fred had been corrupted. Well, she would un-corrupt him. Whatever it took.

'Fred, look into my eyes,' mumbled Georgie through a mouthful of tuna sandwich.

'In the name of the LightFighters, and of Triton, and of your friends, Finn Kennedy and me, please take off your sea glass pendant.'

Fred blinked once, then slowly pulled at the leather thong around his neck. He took it off and handed it to Georgie.

She took hold of his wrist and wrapped the leather thong around it several times.

'What're you -' Fred began to ask.

'Sssh,' cut in Georgie. She quickly pushed up his shirt and exposed the burn.

She risked a quick glance around. Everyone was pre-occupied. She had to act now.

She punched her own nose hard. Blood gushed out, just as she had hoped. Fred looked at her open mouthed. 'Wha-' he said, just as Georgie plunged the sea glass pendant into his burn. Fred let out a howl of pain, as she had known he would. He tried to pull his arm free, but Georgie clamped the pendant to the burn. They both crashed to the floor. Georgie yanked Fred under a table. Fred tried to roll away, but, with a superhuman strength she didn't know she had, Georgie kept him and the pendant in place. Under the table, she saw the smoke rise from the burn, she saw the agony on Fred's face, and then half the room seemed to be upon them, standing by the desk, screaming down at them.

'Don't you ever hit me again, you bully,' shouted Georgie, keeping the pendant in place.

'What!' Fred managed to gasp. 'Hit you? I -'

'Get up and come out from there,' screamed Sergeant Raven, 'before I hit both of you.'

'Not until he's said sorry,' said Georgie, still holding the pendant in place. She saw Fred's eyes changing before her. The Fred she knew was coming back.

'I am going to count to five,' said Sergeant Raven.

'Leave us alone. This is between me and him,' Georgie shouted back, desperately trying to buy more time.

'For God's sake! I'm going to just shoot both of you if that's what it takes to get some peace in here. We're trying to plot nuclear meltdown and you two are seriously getting in the way of things.'

You have no idea, thought Georgie.

'Keep it in place,' she mouthed to Fred, pointing at the sea glass.

He nodded, as comprehension dawned. Georgie prayed that enough of the real Fred had returned. She let go of the pendant just as hands clamped round her ankle and dragged her out from under the table. She just caught sight of Fred pushing the pendant further into his burn and then pulling down his shirt sleeve over it before she was unceremoniously yanked to her feet. Blood still poured down her face from her nosebleed but she was delighted. She tried not to let it show.

'Go and clean up,' ordered Sergeant Raven. He reached under the table and yanked up Fred, who had Georgie's blood all over his school shirt too.

'Hell and damnation. You go and clean up too, if you can be trusted to go to the lavatory with this girl and not kill her.'

'Sorry,' mumbled Fred, averting his eyes. 'Sorry. Won't touch her again. I'm sorry.'

'Off you go. Both of you. And hurry back.'

Georgie hid her smile. He thinks we're controllable!

Vlad watched them go, his eyes narrowed in suspicion. Absently, he rubbed at his burn, removing more of the phosphorescence.

Georgie and Fred walked from the room, crossed the corridor and found the unisex loos blessedly empty.

Fred doubled up. 'God! That hurt like hell.'

'It was hell,' replied Georgie. 'It was a battle between good and bad right there inside your body, and your body, with the help of Triton's sea glass expelled the evil that Jehannem had burned into you.'

'Hellfire,' mused Fred. 'That's what it felt like, the burn, and the cure.'

He looked warily at Georgie. 'D'you think it's gone? All of it? I felt so different. I felt caught up in it all, like all I wanted to do was obey the Djinn and -' he swallowed back an anguished sob.

'Do you think it's gone,' asked Georgie, softly.

Fred went very still. 'Yes,' he answered slowly. 'I think so. I hope so.'

Georgie nodded. She turned away and splashed cold water over her face, hoping that the small, stubborn doubt that she felt did not show in her eyes.

She straightened up, dried her face and turned to Fred.

'So, what did you find out?' she asked him.

Fred was mopping his face and clothes with paper towels. They came away stained with Georgie's blood. He dropped them into the bin. Georgie looked at them and felt momentarily sick; the gash of red against white. She dabbed at her nose.

'The man with the frizzy hair, Professor Bradbury, is programming all the arming codes into the nuclear warheads around the globe. Then, just after the fire signal from here goes up, he will input the detonation sequence and copy it across for each warhead.

Georgie twisted her hair round her finger.

'What happens if no signal is sent up from here?'

Fred looked puzzled. 'I'm not sure. That's meant to be the trigger. But it's symbolic I guess. I think there are other bunkers in the region. When the occupants of those see the tower of fire, they'll set off their own detonation programmes, so, I s'pose, if they don't see a tower of fire, they won't detonate.'

'But the detonation here will still happen?' queried Georgie.

'I suppose so,' answered Fred.

'So we need to stop the Djinn from detonating and we need to stop this tower of fire.'

Fred raised his eyebrows at Georgie and gazed skywards.

'Not asking much, are you?'

Georgie let out a peal of laughter. Fred, the real, wry, dry-humoured Fred, seemed to have come back.

'C'mon. Let's go back in before they come and check that we're not killing each other,' said Fred.

Georgie nodded. 'You continue to act like you're the Djinn's creature, yeah, and I will too.'

'Sure,' replied Fred. 'What're we going to do about Vlad? Shall we try and cure him?'

'Soon as we get the chance. He's getting dangerous. It looked like part of him stayed loyal to us even after his father burned him, but that effect seems to be wearing off now. He-'

The door swung open and Sergeant Raven stood glowering before them. Georgie's heart slammed into her ribs. How long had he been outside? Had he heard anything?

'What are you doing?' he demanded.

'Cleaning up,' replied Georgie. 'Making friends again.'

'Ah. Touching. Get back in the Control Room. Now,' he hissed, eyes sharp with suspicion.

CHAPTER FIFTY SEVEN

∾ Traitor ∾

SERGEANT RAVEN STEPPED ASIDE and watched Georgie and Fred leave the loos. As they were crossing the corridor, Georgie stopped. There were voices coming towards them from round the corner. Children's voices, many of them, crying softly, weeping, shouting.

Georgie stopped in horror and waited. Seconds later, Mr Slavel appeared, followed by a miserable gang of children. Georgie looked at them in horror. They were all from JAM.

'The Excellence Academy!' whispered Fred.

They spotted Georgie and Fred and started shouting to them.

'Georgie! Fred! You're here too. We've been kidnapped. Help us. Please, do something. I want to go home. Help, please.'

The different voices, the same pleas, hammered like blows at Georgie's heart.

'You're never going home,' said Mr Slavel in a dreamy voice. 'We all belong here now. This is home.'

'No!' screamed Francesca, a brilliant linguist who spoke fluent Arabic and Italian as well as English. She broke free from the group and ran to Georgie. Georgie hugged her, held her while she sobbed, but she could say nothing. Under the scrutiny of Sergeant Raven, and Mr Slavel, and the machine gun-toting guards who stood at the rear of the group Georgie had to appear to be the Djinn's creature.

Francesca pulled back and stared at Georgie. 'Say something!' she yelled. 'Say something. Tell us it's not true. Tell us we'll go home.'

All eyes settled on Georgie. 'It is true,' she said dully. 'This is home. We belong here now.'

'No!' screamed Francesca, pushing Georgie roughly away. Georgie stumbled backwards, feeling sick. I will help you, she said silently to herself. I promise.

Mr Slavel took hold of Francesca's arm and pushed her back into the group. He turned and regarded Georgie and Fred. His eyes were different. He was not the old Mr Slavel. Georgie glanced down, saw the burn on his wrist, turned away, sickened. She saw Jehannem's plan. He was the mystery benefactor behind the Excellence Academy. He'd got Slavel to set it up, bring in the children, then he'd burned Slavel and ordered him to kidnap the children and bring them here. She remembered the luxury coach. Slavel herding the children aboard. They thought they were going to a special party. An award ceremony. And they ended up here. Genetic material for a Dark Djinn. They were the next generation. The parents of tomorrow. All stolen from their parents today. Georgie could have wept.

Mr Slavel turned his attention back to the children.

'Right, follow me, and stop that snivelling.'

'Traitor,' hissed Francesca as she passed Georgie.

Shame burned through Georgie, but she looked at each child who passed her, seeing the despair, the abject terror in their eyes.

I will get you out. I will stop this, she mouthed to herself.

As she headed back to the Control Room she was calm as those in the grip of a truly enormous anger can sometimes be. The anger to change the world. The anger to save the world. She vowed to do whatever it took.

CHAPTER FIFTY EIGHT

⤜ Star-speckled Night ⤛

FINN LANDED ON SOFT, moonlit sand. He quickly sucked in a few deep breaths, glancing round to make sure he had not been seen. Thankfully, no-one was about on this part of Shell Beach. He could see movement way down the other end, but they would not have seen him materialise as if from the ether, he knew that. His own eyes had grown sharper over the months, and he knew he could now see what normal humans could not. Another one of the gifts he had once fought against. He embraced it now.

He waded into the water and dived under, undulating his body, breaking the surface in a butterfly stroke. He swam out to about fifty yards from shore.

Triton, he called in his mind. Triton, I'm here. I have news. Please come.

Seconds turned into minutes as Finn waited. He began to feel a sick dread in his stomach. What if the Sea Djinn didn't come? How could they possibly beat the Jehannem without him? You beat Hydrus alone. You and Georgie and your parents, don't forget that, said a voice in his head.

At that moment there was a ripple in the sea before him, then Triton's great head with his mane of hair rose from the moon-silvered water.

'Greetings,' said the Sea Djinn. 'Tell me all.'

Hardly pausing for breath, Finn told Triton everything he had learned from Georgie. The Sea Djinn thought for a while.

'This is what I shall do,' he declared.

Finn listened to his plan, then smiled with savage approval.

'Where exactly is the Fire Ark?' asked Triton.

Finn gave the GPS co-ordinates of his original camp.

'It's somewhere near there,' he said apologetically. 'By a great huge house which'll be lit up like a birthday cake.'

Triton nodded. He touched Finn's forehead. Finn felt the power pulsing into him.

'May luck go with you,' said Triton, eyes grave, then he was gone.

Finn gazed out over the sea. It had become more turbulent, choppy waves worrying the surface. It was time to go, to return to the Fire Ark.

Finn took a few moments, savouring the feel of the water on his limbs, the enormity of the star-speckled night above him. He pulled himself up quickly. There was no room for yearning, or he could end up travelling to the stars themselves. He turned his mind to the stationery cupboard, deep underground; papers, pencils, pens, that dry, slightly woody smell, the darkness of the cupboard. He saw it. He felt it, and then he was gone.

CHAPTER FIFTY NINE

∽ The Voice ∞

JEHANNEM PACED AROUND THE Control Room, hissing out questions.

'You. Bradbury. When was the last time you checked the Cryo Room?'

'Er, two days ago, Mr Czarovich, Sir.'

'Two days. You moronic imbecile. Go and check it immediately.'

Fred, listened in. Cryo Room. What could that be?

He turned to Professor Bradbury. 'Shall I come and help you?' he asked, eyes innocent.

Professor Bradbury frowned at him for a moment. 'Yes. All right. I don't see why not.'

Professor Bradbury walked towards the door. Casually, Fred followed him. Georgie saw him going out of the corner of her eye. Now what's he up to? she thought.

She noticed Vlad watching Fred, his eyes narrowed. Vlad got to his feet, looking towards his father. He opened his mouth to say something, but Georgie was on him before any sound came out.

'Vlad,' she called out excitedly, 'let's find a chess set shall we? Have a re-match. You're Russian, remember. You have to win.'

Vlad reluctantly dragged his gaze away from his father to Georgie.

'Course, I might just whip your ass again,' said Georgie, hands on hips.

Vlad gave the ghost of a smile. 'Let's see, shall we. Father?' he called out. 'Is there a chess set down here somewhere?'

Fred held his breath until he was safely outside the Control Room. They turned the corner and Professor Bradbury bumped straight into Sergeant Raven.

'Idiot! Watch where you're going,' spat Raven. His eyes narrowed. 'Where are you going? And where're you taking him?' he cast a look of contempt at Fred.

'Mr Czarovich asked me to check the Cryo Room. Fred's coming along to help me.'

'To help you? That little squirt!'

Fred felt his face flush with humiliation.

'He is tomorrow's generation. He needs to learn. Educate the young, that's what Mr Czarovich says and that's what I'm doing.'

'Exposing him to operational secrets is what you're doing,' shouted Sergeant Raven with such force that the spittle flew from his lips and landed on Professor Bradbury.

The Professor stepped back and turned his brilliant blue eyes on to the other man.

'And just what do you think he's going to do with any operational secrets he discovers? Run away? Escape from here through a hundred tons of steel gate at the entrance? And let's say by some miracle he did escape. The planet will be in cinders in a matter of hours. Or are you worrying that he is going to communicate his learnings telepathically, or twiddle his ear and point his watch at the sky and send a radio signal to a bunch of aliens who will come to rescue him? I don't think so Sergeant Raven. And, in case you'd forgotten, he's been burned, so he's not going to want to betray us, is he?'

And that, thought Fred, is where you are very wrong.

Professor Bradbury turned to Fred. 'Come on. Let's go. We're wasting time.'

They edged round the glowering Sergeant Raven's bulk. Fred could feel the heat of the other man's stare burning his back as he and Professor Bradbury walked away.

'He's horrible,' said Fred.

The Professor turned to him. 'He's a bully, and I don't like bullies.' He pushed back his cuff to check his watch. Fred noticed the burn. Could he heal him, he wondered, and, if he did, what sort of person would the Professor be restored to? Fred felt that his original nature was good, but what if he resisted being healed, after all, the pain was excruciating. What if he told Jehannem? If he did, Fred and Georgie would be exposed.

Fred resolved to just watch him, and learn.

He padded along the corridor after the Professor, not yet daring to ask him any questions. The route they took was unfamiliar to Fred, and he tried to memorise the twists and turn and different forks.

The Professor stopped abruptly in front of a huge steel door. On the side was a control panel. Fred inched closer and watched the Professor's fingers move across the panel.

59297. Fred was sure those were the numbers. He immediately committed them to memory.

The great steel door clicked and swung open. Fred was hit full in the face by a blast of icy air.

'Hurry,' said the Professor. 'We can't spend long in here, or we'll freeze.'

Fred followed the Professor into a huge, vaulted room. The floor was tiled black. The walls were painted white. Standing in the centre of the room was a huge pillar of ice well over fifty feet high and thirty feet in diameter. Above it was a huge metal mouth and it seemed to be anchored within a similar metal mouth at its base.

The ice was cloudy.

'What is it?' asked Fred. 'What's it for?'

The Professor shook his head. 'Haven't a clue. I just know that I have to check it every day, ensure that none of the ice has melted. Mr Czarovich is most particular.'

'Odd,' said Fred, rubbing his arms to stay warm, 'when there's nothing in it.'

'Say that again,' replied the Professor, shivering. 'I have to check the control panel. You can wait outside if you're too cold.'

'No, it's OK. I'll stay.' Fred turned away from the column of ice and watched the Professor walk across to a computer screen and peer closely at the readings on it.

Fred heard something. In his head. He wheeled round and saw a flash of blue in the ice.

'I, I -' he stammered.

'Silence,' said the Voice.

The Professor turned round to Fred.

'You all right?'

'I'm freezing,' he managed to say.

'I've finished up. Let's go.'

'I'm here. In the ice. I am -'

Fred felt dizzy. He had found the Voice.

CHAPTER SIXTY

Find the
Lightfighter

FINN LANDED IN THE stationery cupboard. He took
a few moments to gather his breath, to listen, then
he cranked open the door. As he did so, his foot
brushed something on the floor. He bent down to pick it
up. Fred's periscope. He must have forgotten it. Brilliant!
He eased into the room and crouched at the far end and
set up the periscope so that he could keep watch on the
Control Room.

He could see Jehannem pacing. Then Fred and the
frizzy grey haired man he assumed was Professor Bradbury
appeared in the corridor. Finn ducked down until they had
passed by. Fred seemed jaunty, elated even. Finn wondered
why. He watched them enter the Control Room where
Professor Bradbury seemed to be reporting something to
Jehannem. The Djinn nodded curtly, then with a crash of
the door, left the Control Room followed close behind by a
thuggish-looking man with cropped black hair.

At the same time, Finn heard shouts, then loud
sobbing, then pounding footsteps. Round the corner came
Fereed Abbas, the school's best sprinter, running at full tilt,
followed by a crowd of other children Finn instantly recognised from JAM.

'Halt!' shouted the Djinn, stepping into Fereed's path. It was almost as if there were some kind of force field around the Djinn because Fereed seemed to collide with the empty space before him.

'Where do you think you are going?' hissed the Djinn, focusing on Fereed.

Fereed stared at him with a mixture of fear and defiance, then Mr Slavel came panting round the corner.

'Sorry, so sorry Mr Czarovich, Sir. They tried to escape. Fast runners you see. Someone tripped me up going into the bunk room and he -'

'Shut up,' hissed Jehannem. He turned back to Fereed and like a viper striking, snatched his wrist, held it and burned him.

Finn felt Fereed's scream almost splinter his brain as the boy writhed in agony. Finn saw his eyes, almost blind with pain, and then, gradually as the pain receded, all life seemed to ebb away leaving a vacancy.

Finn clenched his fists until the skin turned white. He stared at the Djinn with pure loathing. Suddenly Jehannem released Fereed's hand and wheeled around. He approached the room where Finn was hiding. He would be there in seconds. Finn took hold of the periscope, thought of the stationery cupboard, saw its every feature, and travelled to it just a fraction of a second before the Djinn opened the door. Finn crouched on all fours and held his breath, waiting.

'What's the matter, sir?' asked a low, tough voice which barrelled through the air.

'I felt something,' came the Djinn's sibilantly evil voice. 'There's a LightFighter somewhere, Raven. I'll bet it's Finn Kennedy. Find him and bring him to me. Remember what

I said. He has power. Kill him if you have to, but I would quite like to have him alive. It would be quite something, would it not, to corrupt a Prince of Atlantis, enlist him to the Dark side.'

'It will be my pleasure, sir,' replied the other man.

Finn heard footsteps, heard the door slam closed. Silently he sucked in breaths. That had been too close. He would have to veil himself now. He waited until he was sure that Jehannem and Raven had gone, then he inched open the door and walked, blinking, into the light.

Using Fred's periscope, he scanned the Control Room. Jehannem had not returned there. Neither had Raven. Finn paused, heart racing as an idea hit him. He smiled. The time for caution was gone. He straightened up, left the room and strode confidently towards the Control Room.

He stood outside the door, waiting. He turned at the sound of wheels behind him. A woman, almost bent double over a tea trolley. She glanced up at him and her eyes flew wide with surprise.

'Ah. The Boy of the Prophecy. You have come,' she said with a smile. Finn looked beyond the wrinkled skin, the dowdy housecoat, the missing teeth, and saw only the brilliance of her eyes, shining at him. He knew a Light-Fighter when he saw one.

He read her name tag; Hilda. He grinned back at her. 'Wish me luck, Hilda.'

'All the luck of the Light to you, young Prince. Like to go in?'

'You bet.'

The tea lady tapped out the code and the door to the Control Room swung open.

In walked Finn.

CHAPTER SIXTY ONE

∽ To War ∽

JEHANNEM STOOD IN HIS Fire Chamber, summoning his powers. His blood burned with excitement. His dream, the dream he had harboured for two thousand years, would soon be reality. The world would be aflame. The bombs would rock the magma. The atmosphere itself would shudder. The Sacred Veil would be breached. Billions of humans would die. He, Jehannem, would rule, alone, unchallengeable.

In ten Fire Arks around the world, DarkFighters awaited their signal - the huge column of fire. Those in the Middle East would be able to see it with their own eyes from their underground telescopes. Those further away would see it relayed on the special television screens. The Chosen Ones waited for destruction to be wrought in their name. Everybody else went about their business, unaware that they were living out the last minutes of their life.

Just off Shell Beach, about one hundred yards out to sea, there was a disturbance in the water; an enormous whirlpool. From the middle of the churning water, Triton erupted, immediately changing from the man/dolphin into a tornado of air. Swept up in the air current were Triton's Albatrosses of War. One hundred of them. They flew with

Triton, in his slipstream, gaining height. The palm trees on Beach Road clattered wildly as they soared overhead. A man on his motorbike screamed in alarm as he felt the air suck at him and almost pluck he and his machine from the tarmac. But the tornado passed by, streaking higher into the dark sky, accelerating over the steel and glass and concrete of Dubai to the sands of the desert. To the Fire Ark. To War.

CHAPTER SIXTY TWO

Professor Bradbury's Revelation

FINN SMILED AS ALL the heads in the room swivelled to look at him. He felt eyes upon him, probing, searching. Be grey, he told himself. Veil yourself.

He hunched his shoulders, drew in his chest, imagined himself swathed in a blanket of grey so that his eyes, his skin, his hair, his mind, his heart, everything was grey. Eyes turned away as he did so, save a few pairs.

'Not another blasted kid,' said the gruff voice. Finn wheeled around to see Raven emerge from behind a towering filing cabinet, glaring at him. He sucked in a breath of air. He thought the man had gone off with Jehannem.

'Who the hell are you?' demanded Raven, crossing the room in a few powerful strides.

'Er, I'm Stan,' replied Finn. 'Mr Slavel sent me in here 'cos I'm terribly good at maths. He says I'm a p p p p prodigy,' stuttered Finn.

'What's seven thousand four hundred and ninety nine divided by eighty six?' demanded Raven.

Finn nibbled at his nails for a few seconds. He had absolutely no idea. 'Eighty point four,' he answered decisively.

'Right,' replied Raven, who clearly had no idea either, but like most people was impressed by confidence. 'Get over there with the other prodigy and stay out of my sight.'

Finn gave a modest smile and shuffled over to where Fred and Georgie were sitting.

Vlad hurried across to Finn. 'How did you get here? Has he burned you, my father?' he demanded, reaching out towards Finn's wrist.

'Course he has,' said Georgie, grabbing Vlad's own wrist. 'Right here, like yours. He wouldn't be in here otherwise, would he?'

'I don't trust you,' said Vlad. 'Any of you. I'm going to call my father and -'

'I wouldn't call him for a few minutes,' warned Finn. 'After he burned me he told Slavel he wanted to talk to him alone for five minutes and he warned the guard with him not to interrupt him.'

'Five minutes,' hissed Vlad. 'And I want to see your burn. Now.'

'I'm going to be sick,' said Finn dramatically, putting a hand over his mouth. 'I've wanted to vomit since he burned me.'

'Professor Bradbury'll help you,' said Georgie, flicking a glance at Finn, trying to communicate her plan. She pointed to the frizzy haired man. Finn gave an infinitesimal nod, then lurched over to Professor Bradbury.

'Please, the loos, where are they, take me there or I'll-' Finn stared to make retching noises.

'I'm a nuclear physicist,' muttered Professor Bradbury, 'not a physician.'

'Please,' garbled Finn. 'I'm going to be sick on you.'

That got a response. Professor Bradbury jumped to his feet, grabbed Finn and helped him from the room.

Once they were in the loos, Finn risked a quick glance

round. Empty. Brilliant! He quickly pulled off his sea glass pendant, straightened up, wheeled round, and grabbed Professor Bradbury's wrist.

'Hey! What are you doing?' exclaimed Bradbury as Finn clung on to his wrist and held the sea glass to the burn.

Professor Bradbury began to scream. With his free hand, Finn clamped his hand over Bradbury's mouth. The Professor writhed and flailed against Finn, but Finn held on as smoke rose in the air, as the acrid stench of burning skin and blood filled his nostrils. Finn used all his strength, desperately clinging on as Professor Bradbury fought him.

After a while, the man stopped screaming, then he stopped struggling. Finn saw a new awareness light up the Bradbury's eyes, then he sagged and fell to the floor. Finn went with him, still holding the sea glass in place.

'My God,' said Professor Bradbury in a voice laced with horror. 'What have I done?'

'You have input the entry code for a series of nuclear explosions,' answered Finn. 'And now you are going to go back in that room with me and input the abort code. And don't tell me there isn't one. There has to be.'

Professor Bradbury looked at Finn with eyes empty of all hope. 'I don't know it,' he said. 'Only that man, that monster....he is the only one who knows it.'

Finn felt a wave of despair threaten to engulf him. He fought it down.

'Let's get back in there and figure out the abort code, or invent a new one, or sabotage the computers, or something!' he yelled, racing towards the door.

CHAPTER SIXTY THREE

The Final Countdown

JEHANNEM SLID BACK INTO the Control Room for one final check. Vlad looked up from the chessboard. He was losing again. This girl beating him, she was not his friend. Not a friend. An enemy. He jumped up, knocking the chessboard to the floor. Pawns and knights and queens rolled across the marble like casualties of war.

'Father! She's a traitor,' shouted Vlad. 'This one,' he yelled, pointing to Georgie. 'She's trying to stop you. She's an enemy. She stole something from your desk.'

The Djinn approached Georgie with his eyes fixed on her. She felt the burning. She tried to escape in her mind, conjuring visions of her bed again.

'What did you steal from me?' hissed Jehannem. Georgie noticed his eyes. They were like pools of fire, flickering, raging with madness and evil.

Georgie said nothing.

'She put them in her jeans pocket,' shouted Vlad. 'Check her.'

The Djinn reached out to Georgie who flinched backwards. She would not let this creature touch her.

She took the folded sheets from her pocket and handed them over. The Djinn looked at them, and his eyes narrowed in fury.

At that moment, Professor Bradbury entered the Control Room. Finn slid in behind him then ducked down as if to tie his shoelace. He stayed there, crouched down under a table, trying to hide his presence in a veil of grey so that Jehannem would not sense him. Luckily for him, Jehannem's fury was a potent distraction.

'The abort codes,' intoned Jehannem, reading the numbers. He looked back up at Georgie. 'You actually stole the abort codes.'

He refolded them and tucked them into his pocket. He turned to move away and Georgie began to let out a breath, but then his hand lashed back through the air and hit her full on the mouth, knocking out a tooth.

It lay bloody against the marble floor. Georgie breathed out hard, willing the pain away, remembering what she had to do, her hatred building like a nuclear fire of its own.

She stifled a smile as she remembered the copies of the abort codes she had secretly made and hidden inside her shoe.

'Treachery is punishable by death,' said the Djinn, eyes on Georgie. 'You know that, Miss LightFighter. I need to make a little fire shortly. Let's see just how well a Light-Fighter burns, shall we?' he snarled.

Frantically, Georgie tried to veil her thoughts as she made her plan. She had just seconds, she knew that. Fortunately, Jehannem turned away and approached Sergeant Raven on the other side of the room.

Georgie turned and saw Professor Bradbury standing a few yards behind her. She knew from the haunted, horrified look in his eyes that Finn had succeeded in healing his burn. She glanced towards Vlad, who was watching her with a twisted smile that mingled satisfaction and a semblance of regret. Suddenly, the bulk of the tea lady, Hilda, filled her vision.

'Cup of tea dear?' Hilda asked Vlad, blocking Georgie from his sight as she did so. Georgie took her chance. She stepped backwards towards Professor Bradbury, bent down and slipped off her shoe. Her fingers shook wildly but she grasped the folded paper, straightened up and shoved it into Professor Bradbury's pocket. He gave an infinitesimal nod and began to ease forward towards his computer. He flicked a glance at Jehannem, who was eyeing up the TV screens with Sergeant Raven.

Georgie, Fred and Finn, from his hiding place watched Professor Bradbury inch towards his computer. He sat down at his seat, took out the piece of paper and began to type in the numbers.

Suddenly, the Professor's computer began to beep loudly. Everyone wheeled round to look. The Djinn screamed with rage and together with Sergeant Raven, sprinted towards Professor Bradbury.

Hilda, who had moved stealthily into position since pouring Vlad his tea, shoved her tea trolley directly into their path. They crashed into it and rolled on the floor, boiling tea pouring over them. Professor Bradbury did not take his eyes from the screen, save to glance at the remaining numbers. Ten more. Just a few seconds more. The Djinn was on his feet again, slipping on the wet tea, but running now, nearly there, closing on Professor Bradbury like a battering ram. Just a second before he made contact, a siren screamed out and Professor Bradbury sat back. When the Djinn collided with him and smashed him to unconsciousness, he was smiling. He had aborted the bombs.

CHAPTER SIXTY FOUR

The Cryo Room

FRED SLIPPED FROM THE Control Room. Everyone was distracted by the mayhem inside and it was easy. But now he had to find his way across the building to the Cryo Room and that would not be easy and he did not have much time. Jehannem could still unleash his tower of fire and all the other Fire Arks would detonate. Right, left, right, right left. He followed the map he had drawn in reverse in his mind, praying he had not made a mistake.

Four minutes later, he was there, outside the cryo Room. He took a deep breath and tried to recall the code he had seen Professor Bradbury tapping in. 59297. He hoped. There was a click. Fred pushed. The door swung open.

'Yes!' whispered Fred. The cold hit him like a fist in the face, but he didn't step back, he pulled the door close behind him and he rushed in.

The column of ice stood before him, shimmering. He stole one quick look at it then hurried across to the control panel. He took a few moments to study it, saw the + and the - signs. He crossed his fingers, then began to press the + sign again and again.

He waited. Nothing happened. But how could it? He knew the principles of science. A block of ice that size would take weeks to melt unless attacked with a blowtorch, which he didn't have. He dragged his hands through his hair. There had to be something else he could do.

He studied the control panel again. There was nothing. No magic button that would thaw the ice in seconds. Fred was beginning to shake with cold.

He turned and walked up to the ice column. He placed his hands on it, then touched his forehead against it. The cold burned him as surely as any flame. Cold fire. With shaking hands he pulled out his sea glass pendant. He held it to the ice. Seconds ticked by and Fred began to despair. How much longer could he keep this up? He was shaking so violently his legs threatened to buckle and his teeth were chattering so wildly he kept biting his tongue. Still he held on, pressing his hands and the pendant into the ice. He could feel himself slipping into unconsciousness. He ground his teeth, screwed up his face, desperately fought to stay awake. But he was slipping. Slipping away.......

CHAPTER SIXTY FIVE

❦ Djinn meets Prince ❦

JEHANNEM STOOD ABOVE PROFESSOR Bradbury's prone body. He shouted over the hysterical screaming of the siren.

'So, we have more than one traitor in our midst?' He began to pace around as scores of security guards ran into the Control Room. He silenced their shouted questions with a raised hand.

'So brave, so very, very brave. And so futile.' His lips snarled and he gave a shrill, high pitched laugh. He kicked Professor Bradbury's body out of the way and sat down at his computer. Georgie slid up to Professor Bradbury and felt for his pulse. It was still beating, but faintly. She eased off her sea glass pendant and slipped it inside his shirt, pressing it to his heart.

Jehannem tapped in a series of commands then stood up. He looked down at Georgie, tending to Professor Bradbury and let out a snort of contempt.

'Don't bother trying to save him. He'll be dead soon. You will all be dead soon. You see, while I cannot reverse the abort code for the detonation of the nuclear weapons, I can add in one more command.' He laughed again. 'I planned ahead, for just such an event as this. Nuclear bombs will not detonate in this Fire Ark today, but conventional ones will. The Fire Ark is booby trapped. The entrance is being sealed as we speak with a thousand ton metal door. The emergency lift has gone into lockdown. In twenty minutes, the bombs will explode.' He turned to Georgie.

'You have proved strangely immune to my burn. But you have achieved nothing save your own death and that of everyone in this Fire Ark. Not quite as much of the planet will burn as I had hoped, but enough. Soon this place will be a pile of rubble and the death of your school friends will be on your hands. I shall go now to send up my signal, my column of fire. The other Fire Arks will see this and they will detonate their own nuclear bombs. In another thirty minutes, this Fire Ark will be consumed by fire and rock. But you will not have to wait for death since you have sought it, so foolishly by fighting me. I have a more immediate death planned for you.'

He grabbed Georgie's arm, pulled her to her feet and began to drag her towards the door. She just had time to yank back her pendant and conceal it in the palm of her hand. Professor Bradbury suddenly sat up, blinking, muttering. Georgie gave him a faint smile.

She turned to see Finn step into Jehannem's path, his eyes blazing.

'Let her go. Now.'

The Djinn's eyes opened wide. He let go of Georgie's hand and gave a mock bow.

'Well, well, well. Finn Kennedy. The boy of the Prophecy. The Prince of Atlantis who fought and conquered Hydrus and his Dark Army. I wondered when you would pop up.'

'Hello Jehannem,' spat Finn.

'You would use my name,' hissed the Djinn.

'Let her go,' Finn repeated.

'Oh I don't think so. I was just about to take her away and incinerate her. I shall take you at the same time. You shall not conquer me.' He laughed, then reached out his hand. Finn saw the flickering flames dance obscenely round Jehannem's finger tips, as if he could no longer conceal his nature.

'I will enjoy burning you, Prince of Atlantis, and then killing you,' he intoned, eyes consumed with hate.

'I don't think so,' said Finn.

He grabbed Georgie's hand, summoned all his powers, cast his mind to the surface, to the bush by the dunes overlooking the Djinn's glass palace, and then he and Georgie disappeared.

Chapter Sixty Six

∽ Column of Fire ∽

EHANNEM SCREAMED IN FURY. Everyone in the Control Room cowered and covered their ears as he roared his rage to the skies. Then he stalked from the room. Down the corridor he went, heading for the Fire Chamber.

He opened the huge copper door, strode to the centre of the circle. He stood there, stilling his breathing, summoning his power. This was the moment of all moments. There would be no going back now. No room for distractions. The last minutes of normal life on earth were ticking away.

He raised his arms and smiled as smoke began to pour from him, dark and viscous, curling and billowing into the air. Flames erupted from his body. Soon he was a towering column of flame. He waited until the flame grew, till it was almost filling the Chamber, then he exploded up through the roof.

Finn and Georgie sat in darkness behind the thorn bush. The ground before them trembled and ripped then flames erupted and shot up into the air like some satanic missile. Just like the Vision, thought Finn and Georgie. The inferno built and swirled until it became a roaring tornado of fire, screaming its fury and power up towards the heavens. It must have risen for miles. The blackness of the desert was torched into blazing, blinding light.

Jehannem whirled his limbs of fire like a dervish in the throes of ecstasy. He danced and he gloried in his element. Freed of the shackles of a human body, freed of everything save what he really was. Fire! The gold and red beauty of it, the heat of it, the deadly power of it. Man had always yearned for it. The gods had always possessed it. Prometheus stole it and gave it to the humans and had his liver pecked out daily by the birds as punishment. But he was fire. Fire was him. He flared with joy and he made a column of fire, ten miles high.

He saw above him the galaxy of stars. The other Fire Arks would see his signal and the nuclear fires would be unleashed across the world, cleansing the world. Rending the Sacred Veil. Breaching the barrier between universes. Soon smoke would veil the planet, screening out the stars. When the smoke finally died, in months to come, those stars would belong to him. Everything would belong to him.

Chapter Sixty Seven

∞ Veil of Fog ∞

THE HEAT STILL RAGED across the dark desert after Jehannem had gone back underground. When the flames had raged before them, Finn and Georgie had shielded their eyes from the harsh brilliance that would have scalded their retinas, shrivelled their flesh. But for one thing; an encircling fog, so thick and damp it felt to Finn like liquid air. It rose from the sand of the desert, about one hundred feet back from the inferno, high into the earth's atmosphere, higher than the fire. It looked like a deepening of the dark of the night. Jehannem in his fire lust, had not seen it.

Finn and Georgie sat in its outer tendrils, cooled by it, refreshed by it, protected by it.

'Triton did it!' Finn yelled at Georgie. 'He veiled Jehannem's signal.'

Georgie smiled. 'He did. But, d'you think the fog went high enough?'

'Has to have done,' replied Finn, praying that he was right, wondering at the world beyond the fog, across the sands, across the waters of the Arabian Gulf. Were nuclear bombs being detonated as they spoke? Was the inferno building even as they sat there, chatting?

Finn almost felt like holding his breath.

Now that the fire had gone, the fog dissipated. In seconds, it had gone.

'Right,' said Finn. 'We have to go back into the Fire Ark, rescue Fred and all the kids from the Excellence Academy.'

'And anyone else who's been kidnapped and burned,' added Georgie.

Triton, thought Finn. I'm here, by the thorn bush. I ne-

He stopped as a falcon arrowed down through the air and landed on the sand before him.

'Triton?' asked Finn in amazement, staring at the bird's brilliant green eyes.

'It is I,' answered the bird.

'You veiled the fire signal,' said Finn in wonder. 'You did it!'

The bird gave a slight nod.

'And we aborted the nuclear bomb sequence,' said Finn, his words tumbling out in a rush, 'thanks to Georgie. But the Djinn has booby trapped the Fire Ark. It'll blow up in less than twenty minutes and he's sealed the entrance with a slab of metal.'

'There must be another way in and out,' said Triton.

'There is,' said Finn, 'through the Djinn's Fire Chamber.'

'But that's a thousand feet high,' shouted Georgie, desperation in her voice. 'We can't climb it, and you can't travel out with everyone one by one.'

'I have an idea,' said Triton. 'This is what you need to do.' The Falcon spoke in a high, reedy voice. Finn and Georgie listened, nodding gravely.

'You think you can do this?' asked Triton.

'Yep, I reckon so,' answered Finn. 'Don't you George?'

Georgie gave a fierce nod.

Finn studied the frail-looking bird beside him. He could see the falcon's chest heaving. He checked his watch. Triton had been away from the sea for a long time. Manifesting as fog would have drained Triton massively. The Sea Djinn's powers would be waning by the second. They were running out of time.

CHAPTER SIXTY EIGHT

∽ Into the Dark ∽

FINN GRIPPED GEORGIE'S HAND. 'Are you sure you want to go back down?'

'Of course I'm flippin' sure,' snapped Georgie. 'Let's get on with it.'

Finn sucked in a deep breath, blew it out slowly, and fixed his mind on the stationery cupboard. His thoughts seemed to wobble and it was hard to keep the image. His body began to tremble with the effort. He felt waves of tiredness clouding him. He wondered for a moment if he could do this, then, angrily he pushed the thought away. You will do it, he said to himself, fixing his mind again on the stationery cupboard, seeing it, believing....

He and Georgie landed with a thud. Quickly they jumped to their feet. Finn paused before he opened the door.

'We don't know what tricks he can pull,' he whispered. 'Be careful.'

Georgie nodded. 'You too.'

Finn swallowed. He knew the Djinn would try and kill them as soon as he saw them and this time, for Triton's plan to work, they would be unable to travel to escape him.

The corridor was eerily empty. The siren screamed on in the background as if it were declaiming the end of the world. Finn and Georgie hurried along until they were just outside the Control Room. There was no sign of Jehannem. There was no sign of Fred either, but they could see Vlad, pacing agitatedly back and forth.

They ducked down out of sight.

"Where d'you think they've got the guys from school?' asked Finn.

'Let's start down there,' said Georgie, pointing down the corridor. 'We should be able to hear them if we get close enough.'

Finn set off at a run. It was hard to hear anything save the infernal screaming of the siren. There was no sign of the children in the first corridor so Finn ran on, stopping to listen outside each closed door. The corridor forked repeatedly and Finn took more turns, almost heedless of where he was going, just desperate to find his school mates as the minutes ticked by.

Finally, as he paused outside one of the doors, he heard something. A soft sobbing was coming from inside.

He gestured to Georgie. 'This is it.'

'Slavel will be with them,' said Georgie.

'Burned or bad?' asked Finn.

'Burned,' said Georgie. 'I saw it. He's not bad by nature, but he's the Djinn's creature now. We'll have to overpower him,' she added. 'And he may have guards with him too.'

Finn glanced down the corridor. He ran twenty yards and ripped a fire extinguisher from the wall.

'Nice one,' said Georgie.

Finn grinned then rapped ferociously on the door.

Slavel opened it, forehead creased with worry.

'What's going on? Finn Kennedy, what are you doing?'

'There's a fire,' yelled Finn.

'Where?' asked Slavel.

'Right here,' answered Finn, whacking Slavel's knees with the fire extinguisher. Slavel fell to the ground with a curse and a thud.

Two guards rushed up towards Finn and Georgie. Finn set off the fire extinguisher and a jet of foam hit both guards full in the face. Finn then kicked their feet away from them and they fell, screaming to the floor.

'Run' Georgie shouted to the children. 'Follow me. Quick!'

The children ran, jumping over and round the bodies of the guards. Finn waited until all the children had got out, then sprayed the guards again, whacking them on the head for good measure. He saw Slavel, lying on the floor, eyes vacant. Then he had an image of him at school, eyes bright, striding across the Astroturf in his Panama hat. Finn hurried across to him, taking off his pendant as he went. He reached down, gripped Slavel's wrist and sank the pendant into the burn. Slavel screamed, he rolled over Finn. He thumped Finn's arm. Finn flinched with pain, but he summoned all his powers and managed, just, to keep the pendant in place. Slavel started to shake. Smoke poured from his wrist. Then he stopped screaming. Next he stopped fighting. Finn kept the pendant in place for another thirty seconds, then he pushed Slavel aside and glanced into his eyes. They were wracked with pain. And horror.

'Vat have I done? Dose children…'

'You can help save them now,' shouted Finn. 'This place is going to blow up and we need to get them out of here. Follow me.'

Slavel pushed himself to his feet, knocked the guards, struggling to get up, into each other so that they fell over again, then he ran after Finn.

Finn sped down the corridors, back towards the Fire Chamber, with Slavel loping along beside him, huge strides devouring the ground. Finn skidded round the corners, eyes searching for Georgie. At last he came round a corner and spotted her auburn pony tail bobbing wildly, then everything went dark.

He screeched to a halt, bumping into bodies ahead of him. He fell with them in a great tumble to the floor. Whimpers cut through the darkness, the fluttering murmurs of fear. Finn could hear the edge of hysteria in the faltering cries. Careful not to tread on anyone, he got to his feet.

He fought down his own rising panic, trying to calm his rapid breathing.

He knew if he didn't do something pretty amazing, he and all the rest of them would die here.

'Stay calm,' he said. 'We will get out of here. I promise. Georgie, are you all right?'

'I'm fine,' he heard her say. 'Just dandy.'

Finn could hear the fear she was attempting to bury. Use your powers, he told himself. He remembered Triton telling him that in the Cave of Light. He smiled suddenly in the darkness.

'Get out your sea glass pendant Georgie,' he called. His fingers found his own. He gripped it hard. It felt warm to his touch, almost alive. It glowed pale aquamarine in the darkness. This is just like the Cave of Light, Finn told himself. There is goodness here, there is Light. He saw it in his head. He filled his mind with it so that the shrill screaming of the siren sounded suddenly remote.

There were mutterings on the floor around him. He glanced down. He could see faces gazing up at him in amazement.

'You're light, Finn,' said Harry Ibbots, the school chess champion. 'You're glowing.'

Finn laughed. He looked past the mass of bodies, getting to their feet. He could see Georgie easily. She was glowing too. They caught each other's eyes, their teeth flashed white as they shared a smile. The light grew and now they could see their way.

'Come on,' said Georgie. 'Not far now.'

CHAPTER SIXTY NINE

∽ Light Fire ∽

IN THE CRYO CHAMBER, a sound like a gunshot rent the air. Fred's body, slumped against the ice, slipped down to the floor as the ice cracked in two and splintered like forked lightning. Chunks of ice plummeted to the floor where they shattered and glittered like enormous diamonds. One hit Fred's head, smashed and showered his blanched face with freezing shards.

His pulse jumped in shock, but it was still so slow. Slowly, slowly, ebbing away into a frozen waste where nothing lived. Warmth, oh to have warmth. His dulled brain grasped at the dream. A roaring log fire in a cosy hearth in a little cottage in the mountains. FIRE! Something in his mind screamed. Fire. No! Too much fire! His chest heaved and he sucked in a breath. His hand moved groggily to his face. His fingers swept away the ice flakes. He heard a crash. He opened his bleary eyes.

There were chunks of ice littering the floor. Water was pooling all around him. The ice column was melting. It was just a thin statue of ice now that glowed a brilliant blue-green. Fred somehow found the strength to push himself to his feet. His teeth were chattering and his body felt numb, but he was standing.

The remaining ice melted away in a stream of water and something dazzling stood before Fred. A sinuous column of colour, radiant blue and green with the tiniest hints of yellow, flickering as if moved by an invisible breeze. It was fire, but nothing like fire that Fred had ever seen. It was beautiful, utterly, mesmerisingly beautiful. Fred wanted to walk into it, to bathe in it. He stared harder as he saw a face; golden eyes ancient and rich with power, lips, curved into a smile.

'You came. You found me,' said the Voice. That same voice that had haunted him, Finn and Georgie. The same voice that had brought them into this hell. But it was stronger now, not a haunted whisper. It was deep, determined, blazing with cold rage. A hand snaked out from the column of colour.

'I am Vulcan.'

Fred tentatively took the hand. It felt hot but it didn't burn. Instead it sent the most amazing warmth surging through him. Fred started laughing, shaking and laughing.

'You're the Fire Djinn of the Light,' he said through teeth that still chattered, but not as much.

The column nodded.

'I'm er, I'm Fred,' said Fred with a smile. The hand still gripped his. The warmth still flooded his body and with it a strange new power. Fred's teeth stopped chattering. His skin, white as snow, began to turn pink.

'We need your help. We don't have much time,' said Fred, glancing at his watch. Eight minutes past ten. Perhaps time had already run out.

Chapter Seventy

∞ The Sacrifice ∞

EORGIE AND FINN POURED with sweat. The air conditioning system had broken down, and the air filtration. The great mechanical bellows sound had ceased. The Fire Ark had stopped breathing. Now the air grew hotter, thicker, almost unbreathable.

Georgie felt as though the walls were pressing in on her. The ceiling bearing down on her. Claustrophobia roiled around her like a kind of insanity. Fighting it took more energy until Georgie felt as if she were drowning in sweat.

She elbowed the sweat off her face.

'Not far now,' she said, praying it were true. She turned to give a smile of encouragement and froze. Finn saw her face and wheeled round.

Standing at the end of the line was Jehannem. He was in human form, but he too was glowing. His body was edged in red, bright and deep as embers. His eyes were demented. In the red pall of his light, Georgie's and Finn's flickered and faded.

Jehannem stalked up to Finn.

'So, you've re-appeared, Prince of Atlantis, to save the little sprats. How noble.' He laughed and Finn saw flames shoot from his mouth where breath should have been.

'How fortuitous,' Jehannem continued. 'Now I have you all together, I shall kill you all together. I won't be deprived of this moment a second time.'

Finn stood his ground. There was no travelling away to safety now. He would not leave the children, most of whom stood quietly weeping, eyes filled with horror and hopelessness.

Jehannem raised his fingers, flames shot from them. He traced a pattern through the air, eyes on Finn.

Ropes of fire wound round and round Finn, burning about a foot from his body. The children jumped back.

'Let him go!' screamed Georgie. 'Get that fire off him.'

'So that he can de-materialise again?' hissed Jehannem. 'I don't think so. I won't be robbed of him a second time.'

The Dark Fire Djinn laughed. 'Not so much a Prince now, are you, now that you're looking death in the face? More just a lowly Fish Boy.'

'You'll die too, won't you?' said Finn. 'Down here.'

The Djinn screamed with laughter.

'I won't die. I can live with the nuclear fires. I can live above ground. Watching the planet burn, destroying man. So you have achieved nothing, save to torture yourself further. There's no escape for you this time.'

Jehannem elbowed children out of his way, closing the gap Finn had opened up between himself and the Dark Djinn.

'Are you ready to die, Fish Boy?' hissed the Djinn. He slowly raised his fingers, pointed them at Finn.

'No!' screamed Georgie.

'Wait,' said Finn, green eyes fixed on Jehannem. 'Think of my powers. What if I joined you? What if you burned me, on my wrist…I could help you. I could live above ground too. You would have all the powers of a Prince of Atlantis to help you fight the Light Djinns.'

Jehannem paused. Finn could see the visions swimming in his eyes. Then he smiled, reached through the flames and grasped Finn's wrist. Finn stifled his screams as his flesh burnt. He felt the awful contagion as everything good began to be polluted by the Djinn's evil. Jehannem smiled as he burnt him. Hatred flooded Finn's veins. And love for what he was losing. Hang on to that, he told himself, hang on to yourself. It was hard, so hard. He felt himself ebbing away as the pain rose to a crescendo. He ground his teeth. Hang on, he told himself. Hang on. The pain began to wane. The Djinn released Finn's wrist.

With a sickening whomp, a huge explosion boomed through the corridors, followed by the sound of crashing masonry. The ground trembled beneath their feet .

'What's that?' cried Rania.

'Explosions,' said Jehannem. 'The booby trap. The Fire Ark is beginning to fall.'

He turned to Finn. 'There is something I must do,' he said. 'Come with me. Quickly.'

He raised his arm, pointed towards Georgie and the other children. The flames licked obscenely from his finger tips.

Finn laughed. 'Leave them. Where will they go in the darkness? They'll soon be covered in a mountain of rubble.'

The Djinn's hand dropped.

'True. Let them die a slow death. Come with me.' He strode off down the corridor. Finn turned to Georgie.

'Go!' he mouthed. 'Get out. Now!'

She nodded, tears in her eyes. She waited until Finn had followed the Djinn round the corner of the corridor and out of sight. With the Djinn and his flickering red light gone, darkness closed around them.

Another explosion rocked the floor, closer this time.

Georgie held her pendant tightly, she summoned all her strength. The light flowed from her once again.

'Come on,' she called. 'Follow me. Stay close.'

CHAPTER SEVENTY ONE

∞ Vulcan ∞

F RED OPENED THE DOOR and Vulcan shimmered
out into the corridor. A distant boom thudded
through the darkness. Fred's eyes opened wide.

A nuclear bomb? Please no. He had to get back to the
Control Room, to Finn and Georgie.

'Unak told me about you,' he said, setting off at a run.
'He feared you were dead.'

'Unak?' intoned Vulcan. 'My Commander. Where did
you meet him? Did you pass through into my Kingdom?'

'Not yours,' replied Fred. 'Jehannem's. Unak and about
fifteen other of your Fire Rukhs are Jehannem's captives.
There was a battle apparently. They lost. Jehannem stole
their fire and made them slaves.'

Vulcan hissed in a breath of fire. 'I must go and rescue
them. Immediately. How did you get through into the
Kingdom of Dark Fire?'

'Through Jehannem's Fire Chamber. I'll show you
where it is,' said Fred. They twisted and turned their way
through the Fire Ark, their way illuminated by Vulcan's
shimmering green-blue light.

Suddenly, Fred stopped. 'Wait! Can you hear something? Voices shouting, calling for help.'

Another explosion ripped through the corridors. Fred fell to his knees. He pushed himself up and glanced down a side corridor.

'Voices. Down there. I'm sure.'

Vulcan shimmered towards the voices, Fred running after him. They stopped before a glass window looking into a large conference room. The tea lady, Hilda, stood on the other side of the glass, banging it and shouting:

'Let us out of here. The door's locked. We're trapped.'

'She's a LightFighter,' said Fred. 'She pushed her tea trolley at Jehannem.'

'Stand back,' said Vulcan.

The shimmering light seemed to solidify. It turned a darker blue, shot through with orange. Vulcan pointed his fingers at the door. There was a loud hissing sound, then the metal began to melt. Vulcan pushed at the door and it swung open.

The tea lady bowed at Vulcan, grinned at Fred.

'Phwoar. Thanks for that,' she said with an enormous grin. 'These here are good people, the rubbish collectors, the cooks, the cleaners. All held against their will. I got together as many as I could.'

The humans flinched as another explosion rocked the corridor.

'He's booby trapped the place,' said the tea lady. 'I overheard him in a meeting. Said if anything ever went wrong, this whole place would just crumble into the sand. Said he'd laced the place with explosives.'

'Hurry,' said Fred, heart racing. 'Follow me.' He headed back towards the main corridor. 'We've got to find Finn and Georgie.'

CHAPTER SEVENTY TWO

Bombs
and Bombshells

FINN FOLLOWED JEHANNEM. HE reached under his shirt, pulled out his sea glass pendant and held it to his burn. Georgie had said how much it hurt, but nothing could have prepared him for the agony that ripped through his body. He clenched shut his mouth to stop from crying out. His whole body rocked. His blood felt like it would explode from his veins. He wanted to fall to the ground and writhe in agony, but he forced himself on. Suddenly the ground shook and another explosion ripped through the corridors. Finn did fall to the floor and he lay there for precious seconds, ramming the pendant into his skin, feeling the agony flood him.

'Get up,' hissed the Djinn.

'Yes, Sir,' answered Finn, hunching over so that Jehannem could not see his hands.

'You're not impressing me, Prince of Atlantis. I might just have to kill you now.'

'Just winded myself when I fell. Getting up now, sir,' said Finn.

Jehannem turned his contemptuous gaze from Finn and hurried on.

Finn pushed himself to his feet. He could feel himself

returning, all the good things that he was. The pain was beginning to abate. The screaming madness in his blood was quietening. He froze suddenly. He could have sworn he heard Fred's voice, just off to his right in a side corridor. He hesitated.

Jehannem wheeled round and screamed at him.

'Mooove.'

Finn moved. He felt sure it was Fred's voice he had heard. Oh Fred, he said silently. Hurry. Get to the Fire Chamber. Hurry.

The Djinn snaked through the corridors, right and left, right and left. Finn tried to record the route in his mind.

Another huge explosion rocked the corridor, nearer this time, and Finn heard the thunder of falling rock.

They passed a large, glass-fronted room, heaving with hysterical people. The Chosen Ones. Finn saw a face, pressed at the window, mouthing wildly. The words were drowned by the siren, but Finn could read his lips.

Help me. Get me out. Save me. Finn knew that face. He had seen it in the papers. Genocide, he thought. War criminal. Justice at last. He smiled and moved on.

'We are here,' said Jehannem, pausing before a huge steel door and tapping in commands on a panel on the wall. There was a click. Jehannem swung open the door. And screamed.

Chapter Seventy Three

∞ One Good Turn ∞

EORGIE MADE HER WAY through the darkness. She was nearly at the Fire Chamber now. She was sure of it. The heat was infernal. The air thick with dust. It was getting hard to breathe. Her legs were so heavy, like running in treacle.

Another explosion rocked the corridors, followed by the sound of crashing rocks.

'We're going to be trapped in here,' wailed a voice.

'No we won't,' replied Georgie fiercely. 'We're going to get out,' she said, but the same thought blurred her own vision. The rocks falling, barring their way...

She heard a sudden cry off down a corridor to the left. She paused, strained to listen above the screaming siren. There it was again: someone crying. A child crying. Fred! She thought.

'Quick! Follow me,' she said, running towards the cries.

She turned the corner. The corridor before her was blocked by fallen rubble. The Fire Ark was beginning to crumble. Lying on the floor in front of her, beside the pile of rocks, was a body, but it wasn't Fred. It was Vlad. Georgie wanted to turn and run, leave him to his fate.

'Daddy. Help me!' Vlad called out. 'Daddy! Where are you? I can't see. My eyes…'

Blood was pouring from his face. Georgie hurried up to him, crouched down beside him. She looked at him for a second, curled up on the floor. He had denounced her as a traitor. He would have seen her killed by his father. But that was after he had been burned by him. That was not his nature.

She reached out and took his wrist, turned the burn towards her and plunged her sea glass pendant into it.

Vlad screamed. He kicked and writhed. With inhuman strength, Georgie held him down. Second after second after second. Time they did not have. Another explosion thudded through the corridor. Vlad flinched, then slowly, he stopped struggling.

Georgie removed her pendant, yanked him to his feet. She dragged her sleeve across his face, wiping the blood from his eyes. He looked back at her, terrified.

'Follow me, Vlad. Do exactly as I say and I will save you.'

CHAPTER SEVENTY FOUR

ᴤ Fire Rukhs ᴥ

ERE'S THE FIRE CHAMBER,' said Fred, 'but how will you get through to the Dark Kingdom?'

'Djinn Lords can pass at will through the veil between worlds,' replied Vulcan. 'But it's quicker to use a known Portal.'

Fred nodded. 'Good luck!'

Vulcan smiled, raised a fiery arm in farewell. He glided into the centre of the circle. His whole being shimmered and shrank. His blue-green colour became bright as a gem, radiating a light so strong Fred had to look away.

There was a rush of air, and Vulcan was gone.

Fred stood alone, in darkness. The black surrounded him like a hostile force. The infernal siren still rang. Explosions boomed out. Where was the door? Panic rose in Fred's chest. Stay calm, he told himself, breathe, deeply. But he couldn't. There wasn't enough air.

There was a hiss and a sucking feeling in the air. Fred whirled round. The door had opened. A pale light glowed through. Someone stood silhouetted in the doorway; five foot, wildly curling hair.

'Georgie?' whispered Fred.

The light moved into the Fire Chamber. 'Fred! Oh

Fred. Thank God,' Georgie rushed towards Fred.

Fred gaped in amazement. 'Georgie. You're radio active. You're glowing,' he said in horror.

Georgie laughed. 'It's the Light of the LightFighter, Fred. You can summon it too.'

'Wow! I- You've got them!' he shouted, seeing the faces of the JAM children.

Georgie nodded. 'All of them. And Mr Slavel. Finn cured him,' she said quickly when Fred glared at Slavel. 'He'd been burned too.'

'Where is Finn?' asked Fred, eyes searching.

Georgie's face turned grim. Quickly she told Fred. 'He ordered us to go, Fred. We have to get out of here. He'll follow, somehow.'

'Will he? Can he?' asked Fred, eyes desperate.

'We have to believe he can,' answered Georgie.

A huge explosion thundered out and rubble flew down the corridor outside the Fire Chamber.

'We have to summon Triton now,' said Georgie. 'This whole place is going to blow.'

'What's Triton going to do?' asked Fred.

'Turn into a whirlwind. Fly us all up and out of here.'

The air seemed suddenly to thicken and bend like a pane of glass in a hurricane the moment before it shatters. Then something did seem to shatter, for there, before them, in a screaming, snorting, fire-breathing winged mass, were fifteen Fire Rukhs.

The children of the Excellence Academy as one began to scream. Mr Slavel screamed. Georgie gaped. From the midst of flapping flock of giant birds, shimmered the blue green light. The light made some sounds, like wind through trees and the Rukhs fell silent.

'What the....?' exclaimed Georgie, eyes wide. The shimmering moved towards her and Fred. Only then did she see the mouth, the golden eyes, the lips, moving, forming words.

Her school mates stopped screaming. Now they gasped, trembling as the apparition shimmered past them.

'You freed the Rukhs,' said Fred with an enormous smile.

'Thanks to you,' said the shimmering column. It turned to Georgie, its eyes taking in the light flooding from her.

It bowed. 'Hail LightFighter. I am Vulcan.'

Georgie smiled. 'The Voice,' she whispered in amazement. 'The Fire Djinn of the Light!' She could see goodness in the eyes, the power and wisdom. She could see the same fleck of rich humanity that lit Triton's eyes.

'I am Georgie,' she said with a bow. 'Look, sorry to rush this, but we have to get out. We need to call down Triton.'

'Triton is here? Away from his sea?' asked Vulcan. 'But he can't survive out of his domain. Not for long.'

'He can and he will, if we hurry,' answered Georgie.

I'm here, Triton, she called, summoning him. I'm with Fred and the children. And with Vulcan. Come down, please. Help us, please.

She heard a whisper and then a roar. The air pulsated in the Chamber. Her hair blew back from her face until it was streaming horizontally. Some of the children started screaming again.

'Quiet!' yelled Georgie. 'This wind will save you. Trust me.'

The roar of the wind increased until Georgie felt it

would rip her arms from her body. She gathered everyone together in a tight circle in the middle of the Chamber.

'Everyone hold on to each other. Hold tight and whatever you do, don't let go,' she screamed.

The wind seemed to gather itself. Round and round it swirled. Vulcan seemed to be helping, becoming part of the wind for Georgie saw the sinuous blue-green flame whirling around them. It didn't burn though. She felt it's power, but it was warm, not hot. Georgie's clothes plastered themselves to her and wound round her as if trying to strangle her. She grabbed hold of Fred and Rania and held them tight. Then her feet left the ground. Everyone's feet left the ground.

The whirlwind gripped them as it barrelled up through the Chamber, one hundred feet, two hundred feet. Below them another huge explosion breached the walls of the Fire Chamber. Where they had been standing just moments ago, rubble and shards of copper sliced through the air.

The children screamed as they rose. Georgie looked up. She saw the copper dome, gleaming, barring their way, then, suddenly, a huge flap shot open. The whirlwind carried them up and through, into the night.

CHAPTER SEVENTY FIVE

The Trap

THE DJINN'S SCREAM RICOCHETED through the Cryo Room.

'What's wrong my Lord?' Finn asked.

The Djinn wheeled round to him.

'He's gone. Melted.'

'Who, my Lord?'

Jehannem turned to Finn.

'Vulcan,' he hissed, 'The Fire Djinn of the Light.'

Jehannem rushed into the room, gazing round wildly. 'He was here. I froze him. I kept him imprisoned in ice and now he has gone.'

There was nothing save a pool of water, with something floating in it. Finn bent down and picked it up. Fred's handkerchief. He pocketed it, trying to veil his enormous smile. Result Fred!

Jehannem hurried over to the controls and glared at them. He paced round the perimeter of the room as if he might find some answers there. Finn walked up to the controls.

Rapid Freeze. The button glowed blue. Finn looked from it to the huge metal funnel that stood sixty feet up in the centre of the room. His pulse raced as an idea leapt into his head.

'My Lord, in the funnel. I can see something at the top,' called Finn, pointing.

The Djinn gave a muted roar and hurried onto the platform, into the centre, below the huge funnel. He gazed up into it.

Finn said a silent prayer, and pushed the blue button.

CHAPTER SEVENTY SIX

Riding
the Whirlwind

GEORGIE AND FRED RODE the whirlwind. Buffeted and battered by the wind they found the best way to ride it was spread-eagled like a star fish. The air around them spun, but it moved forward faster. Inside the whirlwind, they didn't spin, they were just propelled along. The children from JAM, Vlad, tears coursing from his eyes, Mr Slavel, the tea lady, the other adults rescued with her gazed round and down at the desert speeding past underneath them.

Georgie saw Fereed Abbas, his eyes glazed and dead. She saw the burn on his arm, livid in the darkness. She hauled on Fred so that she could get closer to Fereed. He hardly seemed to notice her. With a great effort, Georgie managed to pull her sea glass pendant over her head, grab onto Fereed's arm, and plunge the sea glass into his burn. He lurched and tried to throw her off, but Georgie gripped on with all her strength. The wind caught Fereed's screams of pain and hurled them away. Georgie saw the agony in Fereed's eyes, but then that gradually abated, and she saw life return. When she was sure he had been healed, she withdrew the pendant, gripping onto it as hard as she could, and looped it back over her head, tucking the sea glass safely under her shirt. Fereed smiled at her and turned to gaze about him, eyes wide with wonder.

They must have been a thousand feet up, rocketing through the air with nothing between them and the ground save wind, save Triton and his power. Georgie saw the streaks of blue-green that told her that Vulcan was mixing his energies with Triton's, that his power too was keeping them aloft. Around them, like a phalanx of terrifying guards, flew the freed Fire Rukhs. Every so often, one of them, seemingly for the pure ecstasy of it, would fly straight up towards the heavens, unleashing a torrent of flames as it did so.

But that was the only fire that Georgie could see. Her eyes hunted through the darkness. There were no nuclear fires lighting up the sky. Just the soft light of a quarter moon and the stars and the celebration of the Fire Rukhs.

They had foiled Jehannem and his mad, murderous plot. But the Djinn was still alive, holding Finn captive, so Georgie could not rejoice. She saw again Finn's face as he told the Djinn to burn him, as he told Georgie to go. Hope had still flickered in his eyes, but could he really escape from Jehannem, fight the battle he had fought three months ago and win again? Georgie said a silent prayer.

Suddenly, the whirlwind lurched and dropped, like a plane hitting turbulence. The air around them was shuddering. Children screamed. Georgie glanced grimly at her watch. Triton had been out of the sea too long. The air shuddered again and they dropped another hundred feet, but they still kept going. Triton was running out of time, running out of life.

'Leave us here, in the desert, get back to the sea,' Georgie yelled.

The air lurched again and the word 'NO' boomed through the roaring wind.

Georgie could sense his desperation. 'You can make it', she yelled. 'Triton, you will make it.' The blue light burned brighter and she knew Vulcan was helping Triton, she just prayed that he was strong enough after being frozen.

They sped on through the night. Georgie's arms and legs began to throb. How much further? she wondered. How fast were they going?

As if in answer, she saw the lights of Dubai. They were just a distant glow at first, then as they drew closer, she saw the glittering pinnacle of Burj Dubai, knifing the sky in the distance.

The wind gave another great lurch and shudder and Georgie felt as if her stomach had jolted into her mouth. The wind was juddering like an engine breaking down. Now there were not above the yielding sand of the desert, but above buildings, concrete and glass, marble. They were losing altitude.

'Come on Triton, you can do it,' yelled Georgie. They were losing height fast. They were now just above the buildings. The palm fronds on the trees below them danced madly in the tumult. The whirlwind began to spin dizzily, and the children spun round the vortex.

We're falling, thought Georgie. He's dying. We're not going to make it. Her body was suddenly grasped by a huge talon.

'Hold on,' shouted a voice.

'Unak!' yelled Georgie. With his other talon, Unak grabbed Fred. The great bird flapped his enormous wings and they rose up, away from the buildings. Around her, Georgie saw other Fire Rukhs grabbing falling children, some birds, like Unak, holding a child in each talon.

Screams rent the air. The adults were falling, so near to the ground now, so near, and still going so fast. Triton's whirlwind was plummeting. He's dying, thought Georgie. He's not going to make it.

Then she smelled the tang of the ocean, glimpsed the foaming waves.

As Unak flew down gently to land, Georgie saw the whirlwind and the adults falling falling, falling, spinning into the ground. With a tangle of arms and legs and screams, they crashed onto the sand.

CHAPTER SEVENTY SEVEN

∽ Entombed ∞

FINN STARED AT THE vision before him in stunned amazement. The air had simply solidified into ice the moment he pushed the button. Jehannem was trapped in the column of ice! The only sign of his presence was the faint hue of red.

Finn shivered. The cold was like a physical force, sticking his eyelids to his eyes, his tongue to his mouth. He could hardly breathe the frigid air. But he had trapped the Djinn!

He started to smile, then he was thrown to the floor as an explosion ripped through the room. The force punched the air from his body. Behind him, rocks crashed down. He lay still, trying desperately to gasp in air. Awkwardly he turned to look towards the door. A pile of rubble blocked it.

He tried to push himself to his feet, but collapsed back to the ground, head spinning. He sucked in a thin steam of the filthy air and tried again to stand. This time he made it. He rubbed his arms. The ice blast had chilled him to the bone. He began to shake violently. He cast his mind to Shell Beach. See it. Feel it. Jump. Nothing happened. Finn tried again. And again. He was shivering uncontrollably now, with cold, with fatigue, with terror. He couldn't Travel. He didn't have the power anymore. He was too weak, and each attempt weakened him further. There was no way out. He would die here, entombed with the Djinn.

CHAPTER SEVENTY EIGHT

Dying on Shell Beach

GEORGIE GAZED AROUND HER. Bodies were strewn on the sand, groaning and trying to get up. Some lay prone. Delicately Unak unfurled his talons and Georgie and Fred climbed away.

'Thank you,' said Georgie. 'You have saved my life twice now.'

'Mine too,' said Fred.

Unak's eyes smiled. 'It is obviously my destiny.' He glanced around him, suddenly uneasy.

'We must go now, to our own Kingdom. We have a long journey ahead, and it is better that no more humans catch sight of us.'

Unak made a couple of short screeches, then, in a radiant mass, having unloaded the children, the fifteen Fire Rukhs took to the skies.

Georgie turned to Fred.

'Where's Triton?' Her eyes raked through the darkness. She saw something down the beach, a movement. She and Fred sprinted off towards it.

'Triton!' she yelled. The dolphin man was dragging himself down the sand towards the sea. His great eyes were dull and his face was contorted with pain.

Georgie and Fred grabbed his hands and pulled. He was so heavy. God he was heavy.

They pulled with all their might but Triton was moving just inch by inch and she could see he was dying before her eyes.

No, she cried silently to herself as the tears spilled down her cheeks. You will live. You will live. She heard stumbling footsteps and suddenly Vlad was there, and Rania and Fereed, Henry and Francesca and a load of the kids from JAM. Mr Slavel and Hilda too.

'Pull him,' she cried. 'Get him into the sea.'

The children gasped as they took in the form lying on the sand, but then everyone grabbed Triton, arms, body and massive tail and they pulled and pushed and this time they all got him moving, foot by foot.

The sea gleamed just thirty feet away.

'Keep going,' urged Georgie, her breath rasping with her effort.

Foot by foot by foot. Second by second. They hauled and pushed and pulled. Georgie saw Triton's eyes flicker and close.

'Come on!' she screamed. 'Nearly there. Ten feet.'

With a superhuman effort she pulled. She felt herself staggering back into the water. They got Triton's body into it, and then his huge tail.

'Deeper,' urged Georgie, 'so his whole body's covered.'

Triton moved easily in the water now, but his eyes remained closed. The children let go of him, all save Georgie and Fred.

'Wake up, Triton,' pleaded Georgie, stroking his noble head. She pulled off her sea glass and held it to his closed eyelids. Fred did the same with his.

'Wake up, Triton. Please wake up.'

The body of the great Djinn just hung in the water, swaying gently with the currents of the sea.

CHAPTER SEVENTY NINE

The Desert Collapses

FINN LAY ON THE floor, his freezing body juddering with cold. He thought of Georgie. He hoped she and the kidnapped children had made it with Triton to Shell Beach. He imagined them there, safe, alive. What of Fred? he wondered. Had he got out too or was he trapped in this prison, dying slowly underground from lack of air before the explosions covered him?

No, Finn would think of him on the beach, with Georgie. Good friends, such good friends. It had been so good to know them.

He thought of his parents and his sister Bess with a pang. Now he would never see them again. But at least they would be alive, not incinerated with the planet in a nuclear inferno.

It was cold, so cold it almost felt hot. If only he could feel the sea, one more time, feel it on his limbs, move through it like a fish. Just one more time. See. Believe. Jump. There was a massive explosion. Rocks rained down, crashing into the ice column, filling the room. Sand poured down on the rocks. The desert collapsed. Trillions of tons of sand fell into the giant hole where the Fire Ark had been.

CHAPTER EIGHTY

Surviving on Shell Beach

TRITON'S EYES SUDDENLY FLICKED open and he gave an almighty sigh. He looked from Georgie to Fred, enormous eyes blinking at them as if re-born.

'You made it,' said Georgie, struggling to keep her tears at bay. 'You're alive!'

Trion gave a small nod. 'Finn?' he asked.

Fred shook his head. 'We don't know where he is.'

'He went with Jehannem,' answered Georgie, tears now streaming down her face. 'He allowed himself to be burned and he offered his powers to the Fire Djinn so that we could escape.'

She turned away from Triton and screamed into the night.

'Finn. Finn. Where are you? Finn. Come to us. Come to Shell Beach. Finn. Come back.'

She screamed her longing into the night and soon Fred's voice joined hers. 'Finn. Come to Shell Beach. Come back to us.'

Vlad and the children from JAM joined in until thirty voices were calling into the darkness.

Triton submerged himself in the water, veiling his own

tears. Weakly he moved his tail, swimming away, heading for the Cave of Light. If he did not get there soon he would die before the night was out.

Georgie and Fred staggered out of the water, calling still, and headed up the beach. They could see a small fire, burning on the sand with no kindling.

'Vulcan,' said Fred, seeing the pale eyes in the fire. The flames hardly moved. Vulcan too had used up nearly all his powers in flying them back to the beach.

Georgie wheeled round suddenly at a sound in the darkness.

'What was that?' she asked.

The sound came again. A sort of wheezing. She and Fred ran towards it.

There, on the sand, trembling violently, blood pouring from his head, was Finn.

Chapter Eighty One

∾ Healing Fire ∾

EORGIE AND FRED CRIED out with relief and joy. They fell to the sand by Finn's side.

'Cccccold,' stuttered Finn, his eyes rolling back in his head and his teeth chattering. 'So cccccold.'

Georgie and Finn picked him up and carried him to the where Vulcan was burning softly.

Vulcan turned his eyes upon Finn.

'Get stones,' he rasped, 'from the sea shallows. Put them in my fire.'

Mr Slavel, Francesca and Rania and a gang of other JAM children ran to the sea, scrabbling up stones. Fred took off his shirt and staunched the bleeding cut at the top of Finn's head. He wrapped the shirt round Finn's head and tied it in place.

Mr Slavel and the children rushed back with handfuls of stones. They gently placed about thirty stones in Vulcan's flames.

There was a great hiss and steam rose from the fire. With a roar the flames grew. Everyone jumped back as the heat scorched out from the fire. Vulcan's face grimaced and Georgie could only guess at the effort this cost him.

After about a minute he spoke.

'Cover him with the stones,' he rasped. His fingers emerged from the flames with handfuls of stones which he laid on the sand.

'Won't they burn him?' asked Georgie.

'No. Feel them yourself. They are charged with healing, not burning.'

Georgie tentatively reached out and touched the stones. They glowed with warmth, but they did not burn.

She and Fred laid the stones all over Finn's body. Finn gave a great sigh. After five minutes, he stopped shaking. He lay on the beach, the stones warming his body to the core, with Fred's school shirt wrapped round his head, with his best friends by his side. He gazed up at the stars, glittering in the heavens, and he smiled.

CHAPTER EIGHTY TWO

Reunion

A POLICE CRUISER TURNED OFF Beach Road and curved through the side streets and headed onto the beach. The driver and his fellow policeman scanned the darkness, not expecting to see anything much at this time of night, save sand. It was their first week as qualified policemen and they were enjoying the quiet of the night.

The driver squinted sharply though his windscreen.

'What on earth is going on over there?' he asked his colleague, pointing through the darkness.

Mr Slavel, the tea lady, Hilda, and the other adults with her, seeing that the children would now be safe, melted away into the darkness.

The police car accelerated over the sand, then slowed and parked and the two policeman jumped out.

'Children?' the driver gasped in astonishment.

'It's two a.m. Are you having a party?' he asked, eyeing the small fire that flickered listlessly. Then he saw Finn, lying shivering beside the fire, covered in blood.

'Dear God. What has happened here?'

Georgie rose from tending to Finn.

'We were all kidnapped,' she said, 'by a man called Ivan Czarovich.'

'We got away,' said Fred.

'We want to go home now,' said Georgie. 'Please take us home.'

Phone calls were made. An ambulance came to take Finn to the American Hospital. Finn refused to go in it. He insisted he was fine, said it was just a flesh wound, caused by a falling rock which had dealt him a glancing blow. Georgie's parents arrived, said they would tend to Finn. The police got more details from Fred and Georgie. Vlad stepped forward and explained that his father had gone mad, had kidnapped the children, held them some-where, none of them knew where as they had been blind-folded. Then people helped them escape. Drove them to the beach and left them there, then disappeared. The other children all said the same. No-one wanted to speak of the Fire Ark, of the horrors they had seen there. That belonged to a different world and they did not have the words to describe it.

Vlad's mother arrived. She was beautiful, with long, tawny hair and haunted eyes. She scooped Vlad into her arms and held him as if she would never let him go. Vlad turned to Georgie.

'Thank you,' he said, his voice hoarse. She nodded and smiled.

Fred's parents came, white faced. They sandwiched their son in a hug and took him home.

Georgie's parents drove her and Finn home. Gradually other parents came, gathered up their children, and went. The police should have taken names and numbers, they knew that, but as they stood by the small fire, inhaling the smoke that spiralled up from it, they felt a strange lassitude steal over them.

After the last child had been collected by his parents, the policemen sat on the quiet beach for a while by the small fire, idly staring into the night. After half an hour, they dreamily got back into their car and drove off.

The next morning they wondered at the strange dreams they had both had.

CHAPTER EIGHTY THREE

Fire Stones
and Farewells

F INN AWOKE TO THE smell of pancakes frying. He lay in his bed, the duvet warm and cosy about him. He stretched luxuriously. His fingers and toes bumped into strange, hard, warm objects. He grabbed hold of them and pulled out a load of dark, smooth stones. He held several in his palms. They still glowed with warmth. He slipped three into his pyjama pocket, then slid out of bed, following the smell of pancakes.

Aunt C smiled when she saw him, pulled him into a fierce bear hug and proceeded to cook him five pancakes. He sat with Georgie, Uncle Johnny and the twins and he ate.

He looked amazed, thought Georgie, as if the mere act of sitting with them and eating pancakes was a miracle. He hadn't told her how close he had come to death, but the haunted look that still flickered in his eyes revealed it better than words.

That evening, with the blessing of Aunt C and Uncle Johnny, Finn and Georgie headed to Shell Beach where they met Fred.

There was no sign of Vulcan. The little fire burned no more.

'Let's go to the breakwater,' said Finn. 'And wait there.'

All three of them sat in the darkness, legs hugged to them.

Triton, they called. Where are you? We want to see you, see that you're OK.

Vulcan, called Fred. Where are you? Can you come to us too, somehow. Please come. Please be alive. We're here on Shell Beach.

They waited, the three of them, staring into the velvet night.

A police cruiser drove down the beach, some way away. Inside sat two bemused policemen, eyes scanning the sand, discussing their weird dreams of the night before. Dreams that felt disturbingly like reality, but, in the absence of any evidence, could not have been.

'Come on,' said the passenger. 'There's nothing here. Let's go and drive up and down Sheikh Zayed. Catch some speed freaks.'

'All right,' said the driver, brightening at the prospect of a bumper crop of arrests.

Finn and Georgie and Fred watched the police car turn onto the tarmacked road and drive away. They looked at each other and smiled.

'Our friends from last night?' asked Georgie.

'Maybe,' answered Fred. 'Night shift, same beach.' He reached out his arms and gave a huge stretch.

'Aaah!' he exclaimed suddenly.

'What?' asked Georgie and Finn sharply.

'That!' answered Fred, pointing to a streak of light that was heading their way. Blue-greenish light.

It looked like a laser, arrowing straight towards them. It hit the rocks beside them, then coalesced into a flame.

'Vulcan!' cried Fred. 'It's you!'

A face formed in the blue-green flames. The lips and eyes smiled broadly.

'It is me,' answered the voice, a low, deep, quiet rumble that would have been a great roar if louder.

'Where've you been?' asked Fred. 'You sound better. Stronger.'

'In the Gulf, on the oil rigs, feeding from the flame-offs.'

'Right,' nodded Fred, 'great.'

'Have you seen the Sea Djinn?' asked Vulcan.

Finn shook his head. 'We're calling him, but he hasn't come yet.'

Suddenly Finn stiffened. 'Triton,' he called. 'Is that you?' he gazed at a patch of sea. The moon flickered on the surface, silvering the water, silvering the face of the Sea Djinn who rose majestically from the waves.

Finn flung himself into the water and swam to Triton. He hurled his arms around the Sea Djinn's neck and held on tight.

'You made it,' said Finn, eyes bright with unshed tears.

'So did you,' answered Triton, his own eyes shimmering.

Together they swam up to the rocks.

Triton and Vulcan bowed to each other.

'You've recovered,' said Georgie, slipping into the water to grab hold of Triton. Fred followed suit and the three children hugged him. He smiled.

'I've been in the Cave of Light. I'm fine now. Go on, climb out. Warm up.'

Finn, Georgie and Fred climbed out and sat by Vulcan, revelling in his warmth. It seemed to fill them, to flow over them, to fortify their bodies and minds. One by one, they told their tales.

'Will Jehannem have survived, do you think?' Finn asked, after he'd explained how the rocks had come raining down, just as he managed to Travel to Shell Beach. 'He would have been completely covered in rocks and the ice would have been smashed up,' Finn added.

'You lured him into the perfect trap, Finn,' replied Triton. 'Fire needs oxygen, and there isn't much to be found under a billion tons of sand. If Jehannem is alive, he should lie impotent. No threat to anyone.'

'Should, but might not?' queried Fred.

It was Vulcan who answered. 'Jehannem has shown himself to be remarkably durable. He should have died many times already. He is strong that one. Unfortunately.'

Georgie shivered.

'If Jehannem really is dead, then the new Fire Djinn of the Night probably won't feel too friendly towards us either, will he?' asked Fred.

Vulcan turned to Finn. 'You have the fire stones I warmed you with?'

Finn nodded. 'I've kept them all. Most of them are back at the house, but I've got three here in my pocket.' He drew them out. 'I like carrying them around.'

'May I?' asked Vulcan, reaching out his hand.

Finn passed them over, gingerly. As his fingers touched Vulcan's he felt a pulse of power, not a burn.

Vulcan took the stones and breathed on them. Then he turned to Fred, Georgie and Finn in turn.

He handed each of them a stone.

'This is to say Thank You, for heeding my message, for coming to free me. The others in your world have a debt towards you that is unpayable. As is my own debt to you, but I will do all in my power to help you, when and if you need me. Until then, keep these with you. They will offer you some protection. They will warm you if you are cold, cool you if you are hot. If Jehannem, or a new Djinn of Dark Fire comes near, they will burn you as a warning.'

'Do you think they might?' asked Finn.

Vulcan and Triton exchanged a glance.

'The worlds are stirring, becoming more troubled,' replied Vulcan. 'Peace never seems to last for long.'

Triton turned to them with a gentle smile. 'Treasure the peace that you have won. Live for the day, each of you. All I know for sure is that the five of us will meet again.'

THE END

GRAMMATICAL AND HISTORICAL NOTE

Scholars will know that djinn is the plural and djinni the singular. I have invoked artistic license to spell both the same as I think it sounds better. There are alternate spellings - jinn (plural) and jinni (singular) and of course, the English but sometimes cliched-sounding genie.

Djinn are alluded to in both Christianity and Islam. The Holy Qur'an describes how Allah created two parallel species of creature; man and djinn, the one from clay, the other from fire. According to the Holy Qur'an, djinn are supernatural spirits below the level of angels (who were created from light) and demons.

Djinn can be good or evil. They can be visible or invisible and can shape shift, assuming human, animal and inanimate forms.

According to the Arabian Nights, Solomon was reputed to have mastered djinn, imprisoning them in sealed jars and throwing them into the sea.

Early Islamic belief suggested that shooting stars were darts thrown at djinn by angels, on whom they were attempting to eavesdrop.

Djinn are altogether rather wondrous creatures. Look out for them! Cunning humans who know the right charms, like Solomon, are said to be able to control them.

Acknowledgements

I have many thank yous to say:

My husband, Rupert Wise, and our three children, Hugh, Tom and Lara have again played a huge role in this novel by inspiring me with their perceptions of life and all its multiverses, and by their practical input. They combine support with brilliant, incisive criticism; a rare and dangerous balance. Rupert patiently and engagingly reads countless drafts round a variety of firesides. He is critic, foil and stimulant and much, much more. Hugh relentlessly picks up any gaps or flaws in my logic. He and Tom dream up brilliant ideas. Lara shines her light. She and my boys make me fill the unforgiving minute. To you four, my love and thanks.

Isobel Abulhoul and Jane Hodges have been wonderfully supportive of my writing and have given valuable and much appreciated editorial input and time. As always, they have been great fun and inspiring to work with. Thanks also to Jane for pulling all her wonderful tricks (party) out of the hat.

Noel has been a constant source of creativity, producing beautiful images seemingly effortlessly. Gina and Tensingh and Haithem and the rest of the Jerboa team have also been wonderful.

Jeremy Brinton and the Magrudy's team, including Haithem and Mia and April and team have tirelessly sold and beautifully displayed Sea Djinn.

I have visited many schools to talk about Sea Djinn and the process of writing. I thank the teachers for organising my visits, and the pupils for listening, buying, and inspiring!

I also thank my girlfriends who have helped me out when I was off gallivanting talking about writing; Philippa, Mia, Pia, Fatima, Mary, Sarah and Dodi. Special thanks to Philippa and Glenda for all their support.

To Mark and Becky, Shokran.

And many thanks and huge appreciation to the ever helpful and smiling Doris and Jenie.

Photo by Stu Williamson

Linda Davies read Politics, Philosophy and Economics at Oxford University and then worked for seven years as an investment banker in New York and London. She escaped banking to write bestselling novels. Her novels have been translated into more than thirty languages and have sold over two million copies. She lived for three years in Peru before returning to London. For the past four years she has lived in Dubai with her husband and three children. Her first novel for children, Sea Djinn, the first in the Djinns of Dubai quartet, was published in 2007 to widespread critical acclaim.